I CAN'T TELL YOU WHY

Elaine Robertson North

For Mum

1

"Well this is a first." Dani sat down in front of the glass of wine that was waiting for her. "Since when did you start arriving early?"

Alex smiled at her. "So I've been late a few times." He shrugged, unable to see why this was worthy of comment.

"So come on then, how did it go?" she asked.

"Oh who knows? It's a great part, there's no doubt about that. We'll just have to wait and see."

Dani watched Alex for a moment, the conversation having prematurely dried up. His brow was furrowed, his hand rubbing it roughly as if trying to iron out the creases. She decided he looked nervous. "Alex?" There was a slight delay before he looked up. "What's on your mind?" Dani continued to scrutinise him, keen to know where this was heading.

Alex took a large gulp of his drink and then looked at her for a moment. "How would you feel about getting involved with me?"

"I am involved with you."

"No, more involved." He hesitated, a growing awkwardness inhibiting his normal eloquence. "I mean properly involved. A relationship."

"No thanks."

Alex looked a bit taken aback at the speed of her answer. "Don't you even want to think about it?"

"No."

"Well pretend then, if for no other reason than to protect my fragile ego."

Dani smiled. "It's a ridiculous idea as you well know."

Alex shifted uncomfortably in his seat. "The way I feel about you doesn't seem ridiculous."

Dani took a deep breath. For a moment, she had wondered if he was playing with her, thinking that maybe he was rehearsing a script, trying out a particularly important line on her but the look in his eyes told her he had never been more serious. "You're married, you have three children and I can't make a relationship work when it actually stands a chance, never mind starting one that's doomed from the start. And I'm your agent. Sounding pretty ridiculous so far." Alex lowered his head leaving Dani wondering if she might have been a little brutal. "Maybe you just can't see it but it seems to me like you have it pretty good."

He looked up at her again, his eyes heavy. "Maybe I don't."

Dani laughed. "Oh save me from the 'my wife doesn't understand me' line!"

"I wasn't going to say that at all. I love my wife and I'd never leave her."

Dani looked confused. "If you mean that, what was in this for me?" Alex looked at her but as he went to answer she stopped him. "No, don't answer that."

So he wanted to keep his neat little family life and use her for sex. No involvement, no prospect of a future, just an occasional shag. Not the most attractive offer she'd ever had. Dani decided the conversation had gone quite far enough. "Go home Alex. I'll see you tomorrow."

The next morning, Dani emerged from Leicester Square tube station with her normal unconscious sigh of relief at the very welcome sight of daylight. The literal light at the end of the tunnel. There was something both comforting and tedious about the repetitive nature of how each working day started. As always, she headed north, thinking as she often did how London was like some kind of bizarre adult theme park, its areas neatly segmented and labelled accordingly as she crossed through Theatreland and on up towards Soho, or Sexland, as she called it. Although, with the influx of media companies, perhaps Luvvieland was more appropriate or perhaps Debauchery Canyon. That one had all bases covered. Here was where the worlds of TV and film merged with the capital's equally colourful, if not slightly diminishing, sex industry or so it appeared to the untrained eye. The result was a unique and intoxicating atmosphere fuelled by a constant search for satisfaction.

The pavements she walked on were undergoing their daily wash-down, the events of the previous night being swilled into the gutter. She stepped carefully over puddles with a quick nod and a smile to the poor chap whose job it was to administer said pavement cleansing and moved on to negotiate her way through the daily construction of market stalls. The banter between the larger-than-life stall holders swept over her, a mix of inaudible words and waves of laughter, with more nods and smiles for those who caught her eye, feeling in some way like she knew them, without actually knowing them at all. Despite that, they were firmly part of her morning gang, along with its other resident members like Fabric Shop Man, opening shutters and meticulously sweeping his doorstep every morning like clockwork; and Newsagent Man, on his way back into his shop with a bacon butty from the café next door, the daily reward for having been open and busy for a couple of hours already. Then there were the transient members like Delivery Man, today humping large boxes into one of the many fashion retailers under the watchful and slightly bleary eye of a young shop assistant, whose penance for inexperience was clearly the task of coming in early to supervise the arrival of new stock. She even knew the names of some of them. There was Marco from the dry cleaners whose services she employed on a regular basis and Carl from her favourite coffee shop, who had a skinny cappuccino ready for her every day at 8.45 without fail, so that she needed to do no more than sweep by, pick it up with a wave and a thank you, always stopping for a brief chat and to pay her bill on a Friday.

There was something ridiculously monotonous about taking the same walk every morning but Dani always felt just a little buoyed by this unique twenty minutes of her daily routine where familiarity and anonymity sat so comfortably side by side.

Her feet now firmly in Luvvieland and with coffee in hand, Dani pushed open the heavy doors to the offices of Stacey Walker, a company responsible for guiding the careers of a host of top actors, comedians and presenters. The corridor that led her away from the reception was over-hung with pictures of the artists the company represented, opening out to reveal banks of desks all typically stacked with scripts, proposals and photographs. Dani wound her way between them until she reached her own special corner of the office where her faithful team, Sammy and Toby, were both already on the phone. Nothing if not dedicated, she thought, as she watched the two twenty-somethings, relaxed and confident and in mid-flow.

Dani took off her jacket and unwrapped the large, vibrant scarf from around her neck, providing the only splash of colour to her usual office attire of jeans, boots and a white shirt. Her shoulder-length brown hair was loose and straight, a long fringe framing her face and sitting just above deep brown eyes with her make-up minimal. Her eyes were alive with ambition and determination but her smile was warm and inviting. Hers was an understated, unassuming beauty.

She slumped into her chair. Behind her was a large window spilling precious daylight into their many hours spent cooped up inside, the hectic sound of the bustling street she'd left only moments before barely audible above the constant chatter of the office, the cacophony of ringtones and permanent tapping of keyboards.

Straightening herself up, Dani began sorting through the mountain of stuff on her desk, starting with a large brown envelope. She pulled out two sets of publicity postcards for two of their artists that would be sent out autographed to adoring fans. She wandered over to Toby's desk just as he was hanging up. "So who do you want to be today?" she asked. "Polly or Damien?"

Toby rubbed his hands together in delight. "Ooh, Damien Cane please!" Dani put the pile of Damien's postcards on Toby's desk and, grabbing a thick black pen he immediately started signing, 'Best wishes, Damien', with great gusto. No one would ever know.

As Sammy finished her call, Dani had already moved to stand over her, waiting for the full explanation of what had obviously been an interesting conversation. "That was Dave on the phone. He got caught in a fight last night over a girl and the police were called. Apparently she was being threatened by an angry boyfriend and he stepped in to try to help and then it all turned ugly. Despite the heroic attempt to rescue a damsel in distress, he got kept in a cell overnight but was released without charge this morning. Do you want me to do anything?"

Sitting back down at her desk, Dani thought for a moment. Nothing much was happening for Dave at the moment which was a constant frustration. "Was he hurt?"

"Black eye, bruising."

"Great, call the Daily Mirror."

Without hesitation, Sammy picked up the phone and started dialling. "And Alex has called you a million times already this morning," she said as she tapped in the number. "He wants to know what time he's meeting you at the press launch today. And that new casting agent called to say Alex got the part."

Well thank God, thought Dani, immediately and somewhat selfishly relieved that Alex would be leaving for Scotland within weeks and staying there for three months. Some good Scottish air was just what he needed to clear his confused head. She pulled out his file from her desk drawer and was immediately looking at his latest publicity shot. Warm, dark blue eyes. A relaxed, infectious smile. A slim face framed with loose waves of blond hair, sitting on broad, square shoulders. All of which came together with an air of casual friendliness. She felt her chest tighten. 'Bloody idiot,' she muttered under her breath, as much to herself as to Alex.

She had been representing him for almost four years now and after a series of parts in established TV series, everything was about to change. Having been cast as the lead in a major new drama, he was about to become a household name and today was when the first episode would be shown to the press. For the first time he would be featured in newspapers and magazines, would start the rounds of daytime shows and chat shows and play his part in fuelling the insatiable twenty-four hour online and social media machines. Anonymity would soon become a distant memory. She would do her best as always to prepare him for what would be a monumental change to his life and again, as always, he would insist he was ready. That's what they all said.

A few hours later, Dani tried not to look anxious as she waited for that air of casual friendliness to appear in person in the foyer of a large, fashionable London hotel. The reception staff looked like Armani models and the artefacts and decoration were so on trend it was possible to feel a tad intimidated if you let your guard down for even a second.

Dani had arranged to meet Alex for a coffee before the press launch and it seemed his temporary bout of punctuality had indeed been just that – temporary. He was traditionally now twenty minutes late. Just as she began to wonder if he would ever turn up, the revolving doors in front of her began to turn and he emerged, looking calm and relaxed, dressed in black jeans and a fitted black shirt, a brown leather bag hanging casually across his body. He smiled as his eyes found her.

"I'm late. I'm sorry." He kissed her on the cheek and taking her arm, started to walk her towards the lounge. They found a table and, moments later, sat in silence with coffees in front of them. Alex watched Dani nervously play with several uneven lumps of sugar, wondering if she was aware that all he wanted to do was whisk her away to a bedroom and spend the day having wild, passionate sex with her, and that at least three of those sugar lumps were now slowly dissolving in her coffee. Eventually she looked up.

"You're staring at me."

"Does it bother you?"

"Yes. Stop it."

Alex smiled at her. "So will you be around while I do my interviews this afternoon?"

"Yes I'll be around."

"So we can have a drink and a chat later to go over everything?"

"Yeah, sure."

Alex looked at her, his eyes narrow. There was no denying she was being terribly subdued. Not rude or abrupt but she was obviously trying to be completely devoid of emotion, terrified she might give out the wrong signal. He was kicking himself now for his ineptitude, unsure why he had chosen to ask her how she felt about changing the boundaries of their relationship instead of just making a move. He wondered, as he had again and again ever since, if she would have so quickly rebuffed lips over verbal clumsiness. His heart subsequently made a perfect leap to his mouth and back again at the thought things might have turned out differently, leaving him momentarily breathless.

Dani was aware he was losing himself to thoughts of who knew what and immediately felt the need to distract him. "By the way, when this is all done, you need to pack your thermals. You're off to Scotland for a while."

Alex slumped back in his chair in disbelief. "You're kidding?"

"The part's yours. I need to sort the contract but it's a done deal. Congratulations."

"Fuck!" Alex felt a nervous excitement start to overtake the sense of shock but, before they could discuss it further, a sleek and highly polished woman approached them in confident strides. She was dressed all in black with a perfect and equally black bob framing her face. Her professional, red-lipped smile and matching manicured hand, targeted Alex first.

"Hi Alex, I'm Wendy, I'm co-ordinating today's fun and games. It's great to meet you at last."

Alex stood up and took her hand. "Hi Wendy. This is my agent, Dani."

Wendy turned to Dani with the same immaculate smile. "Hi Dani. We spoke on the phone."

Dani smiled and shook her hand. "You'll be staying here for the interviews will you?"

"Yes that's right. We'll be screening the first episode and then we've got a suite booked upstairs for the interviews or we can just come back in here. The suite's booked for the night if you wanted to stay in town tonight Alex. Be our guest."

"That's very kind, I might just do that."

"Right then, if you're ready, I'd like to take you through."

Dani watched them go and then slipped into the back of the room to watch Alex in action. She was not surprised the first episode of this six part TV epic was excellent but she hadn't expected to be quite so blown away by Alex. She knew beyond doubt this was his turning point. Her phone would be red hot as soon as the first previews were published and all those who'd met him or screen-tested him would come flooding forward, their interest confirmed now that someone else had had the fortitude to give him a break.

Dani maintained her chosen role of voyeur as Wendy led everyone out of the screening room for nibbles and drinks and then expertly led Alex from one group to another, ensuring he had at least said a brief 'hello' to anyone important, as other press officers did the same with his co-stars. She watched Alex too as he looked people directly in the eye as he was introduced, oozing confidence rather than arrogance, taking each warmly by the hand. Charismatic, that's what he is, she thought.

As people started to leave, Alex and Wendy approached her, Alex clearly desperate to know what she thought, his eyes even brighter than usual. "It was great Alex. You were great." They looked at each other for a moment, their eyes held by a thread of mutual respect and a great fat rope of sexual tension. Oblivious, Wendy cracked on.

"Right, Alex. Your first interview is scheduled to start in five minutes so we best get on. Are you coming with us Dani? I thought we would just go into the cocktail lounge as there's hardly anyone around."

"No, I think you can manage perfectly well without me. And I have a meeting to go to."

"You are coming back aren't you?" For the first time all morning, Alex suddenly looked anxious.

"I'll be back before you finish. Thanks for everything Wendy. I'm sure we'll speak again soon. See you later Alex."

Dani made a dash for the café opposite her office where Steve Preston, a tabloid journalist, was already waiting. He was dressed in a dark blue suit and a white shirt - one of three identical suits he owned and seven identical shirts - with his hair cropped as short as possible without making him look too threatening. This was a chap who had far too much to think about to waste time styling his hair or choosing what to wear every morning. His brown eyes were full of ice and sparkle in equal measure.

Steve and Dani enjoyed a classic love-hate relationship. They were sparring partners and, while each was capable of making the other one's life an absolute misery, they enjoyed every moment of the game they played together. Despite that, today the pleasantries were quickly out of the way.

"So are you going to give me an interview with Damien or what?"

"How badly do you want it?" Dani smiled her most flirtatious smile. It was a look Steve recognised and he visibly shivered.

"Oh God, what do you want?"

"I want you to leave Jake alone." Jake was a young actor destined for great things but he was wild and just didn't get that he was a tabloid dream for all the wrong reasons. His recklessness could easily ruin him before he'd barely got started and Dani was prepared to try anything to stop him blowing it. Easier said than done.

"You know he's been seen a million times taking drugs?"

Dani laughed. "Oooh, hold the front page!"

Steve wasn't going to be put off. "Well I think it's in the public interest to…"

"Don't give me that 'public interest' bollocks! Leave Jake alone and the interview with Damien is yours – exclusively."

Steve shook his head and thought for a moment. It never did to give in too easily but, as actors go, while Jake was definitely a huge pull, he wasn't in the same league as the mighty Damien Cane. Every newspaper and magazine wanted him and now he was his.

"Oh come on, I've got work to do. Deal or no deal?"

Steve sighed and then holding on to what he hoped was a dramatic pause for as long as he dared, he finally spoke. "Deal."

Back in the safety of the office, Dani sat down at her desk, a smiling image of Alex firmly and annoyingly lodged in her brain. As Sammy approached her, she swept the latest pile of scripts to one side to make way for the steaming cup of tea that was heading her way and, with massive inward effort, she dismissed the annoying and distracting picture from her mind.

"There you go. A lovely cup of tea and a jammy dodger."

Dani smiled. "Perfect, thank you." She slowly dunked the sweet treat and felt herself relax as she sucked on the soggy biscuit. The day was quickly flying by in the usual chaotic fashion and she really didn't need Alex dominating her thoughts. As she took a moment to drink her tea, she was suddenly thinking about her twenty-first birthday, a moment in time that she now saw as a significant turning point. It was a fantastic party. Everyone talked about it for months afterwards, some because they simply couldn't remember such a great evening; others because they had witnessed Dani's boyfriend, Nick, dumping her just as she was about to enjoy a slice of the modern sculpture that was her birthday cake. Childhood sweethearts, they had been together since they were fifteen so, needless to say, it kind of took the edge off the evening for her. She never did taste the cake although was reliably informed afterwards that it was indeed delicious.

And a significant moment for the simple reason that it was to mark the start of a rather tragic pattern that had now been in play for the best part of fifteen years. This had been Dani's first serious relationship and, like every one that had come after it, it had failed and always for a different reason. Over the years she had heard it all – 'it's not you, it's me', 'it's just my life is so complicated at the moment' and of course, 'I'm just not ready for commitment'. She had always prided herself on wiping the slate clean each time, never burdening any new start with the wounds of failures past but each time she was left with the same heap of questions.

What had she done wrong? What could she have done differently? Why did she keep making the same mistakes?

Dani jumped as the phone on her desk started to ring loudly, its piercing trill shattering the self-indulgent bubble she'd been happily wallowing in. "That's Max for you," Sammy shouted over to her. "Sounds like he's ready to finalise Alex's contract."

Dani immediately grabbed for the handset.

2

When Dani arrived back in the hotel's cocktail lounge, she sat herself at the bar and ordered a drink, ensuring she stayed well out of Alex's eye-line while still able to watch what was going on. He looked very relaxed and the interviewer, a woman, was smiling and laughing as he talked. Finally, she watched the woman pick up her phone to stop recording the interview and then, after a few moments of casual chat, they all stood up, shook hands and Wendy led her away. Spotting Dani at the bar, Alex picked up his bag and wandered over, dragging a stool with him so he could sit down next to her. "How was it?"

Alex edged his stool a little closer. "Everything was fine but I don't want to talk about that."

"What did they ask? Anything too personal?"

"I want to talk about us."

Dani suddenly found it difficult to hold her nerve, so intense was his stare. "I did tell Wendy I wanted her to watch the personal stuff."

"Dani! You're not listening to me!"

Dani felt herself redden. "No. I'm not."

"I've taken the room for the night. Stay with me." Alex went to take her hand but Dani snatched it away.

"No. It's the middle of the afternoon and I have to go back to the office."

"Come back later then?"

Dani looked at him. She couldn't explain it but there was something about him, something about the way he looked at her that saw her ability to think clearly and rationally discarded like a piece of clothing. Not the best analogy under the circumstances. This was an alien feeling for her. She was a strong, grounded woman, not some flighty teenager. Get a grip woman! she silently shouted at herself. She stiffened. "No Alex."

"Well at least call me later then. Just in case…"

Before he could finish, Wendy returned. "All journalists are now safely off the premises! Well done Alex that was great. Now, can I get you a drink, something to eat? Some of the cast have gathered in the other bar if you want to join them?"

Alex hesitated so Dani saw her opportunity and jumped in. "That sounds like the perfect way to unwind." She slipped off her stool and picked up her bag. "Have fun Alex and thanks again Wendy." At which point, she turned and left them to it.

After a few minutes back at her desk, Dani was desperately trying to get her brain back on the job as Sammy and Toby watched her, waiting for her to say something. "Okay, run me through it again."

Sammy took a deep breath. "Jake spent the night with a lap dancer. He paid her to keep her mouth shut but she's told Steve Preston he paid her for sex. She's told him Jake took her to see a film and she gave him a blow-job in the cinema, that they went to a late-night bar and took cocaine, shagged in the loos and then finished the night off in a hotel with more sucking, snorting and shagging."

"Has Sadie given birth yet?"

"Steve called her for a quote and she went into labour. Speeded things up that's for sure. She popped the little mite out in a couple of hours."

"So they want an interview or they'll just go with the lap dancer's side of the story?"

"That's about it, yes."

Dani sat back in her chair, her eyes suddenly raised to the heavens. "How come we ended up with all the reprobates? It wouldn't be so bad if I hadn't just done a deal with Steve to leave Jake alone." And then she was sitting bolt upright. "Looks like I got in just in time doesn't it?" she said, reaching for her phone. "Steve, it's Dani. I thought we had a deal?"

"Oh come on, I can't just ignore this! It's a great story as well you know."

"Well it would be if it wasn't all lies."

"Prove it."

"She'll be calling you back within the hour to retract."

"And I'll print it anyway and say she was put under pressure to lie, the poor victimised girl!"

There was a determined steeliness in Dani's eyes as she continued. "Okay, first and only pictures of the baby and the proud parents as long as you drop the lap dancer."

There was a pause. "Can we do it at home?"

"Yes at home. Which will be another first."

"Well I don't know Dani. It's not going to be easy to persuade my editor to drop this one."

"I take it you still want the interview with Damien?"

"You promised him to me!" Steve was still basking in the unfamiliar praise from his editor for securing such a coup. There was no way he could go back and tell her the interview had now gone elsewhere.

"Well as deal breaking seems to be the theme of the day, I might have to reconsider." Dani waited, aware that Steve was struggling with the new dilemma he now faced. Eventually, he answered.

"Okay, you win. But you owe me big time and you better promise me I won't read her story somewhere else. I'm gonna get such a beating….."

Dani rolled her eyes. "Yeah, heart bleeding and all that. Bye," and she hung up, bowing her head with a smile as Sammy and Toby applauded.

"But what about the lap dancer?" said Toby.

"Get hold of her. Find out how much it'll take to really shut her up. Threaten her, frighten her, kidnap her, I don't care. Then get legal to lock her into a contract that'll see her beheaded if she breaks it." Toby picked up his phone as Dani continued. "And get Jake off social media. You can tell him from me that if he so much as hints about all this on Twitter I'll hunt him down and castrate him myself."

Toby grinned. "Hashtag newballsplease!" he shouted to no-one in particular, as he hurriedly started to make his first call.

The day almost over, Dani was just putting the finishing touches to Alex's forthcoming publicity itinerary when Amanda arrived. Dani looked at her watch incredulously. "Is that the time already?"

Amanda smiled. "Bad day at the office dear?"

Amanda and Dani had been friends for as long as both could remember. They had joined hands somewhere around the age of seven and had never looked back, Dani attracted by this colourful, mischievous character who seemed afraid of nothing and prepared to try anything; Amanda equally attracted to the comparatively quiet but determined Dani, happy to be led into trouble knowing she had the verbal dexterity to talk them both straight back out again.

"You look stunning Amanda. One of your own I assume?" Sammy asked, stopping on her way back to her desk to admire Amanda's dress.

"You're too kind, thank you. And yes, it's one of my new collection. You should stop by the shop. I've got loads of great new stock with the odd wild piece of my own thrown in. And there's always a substantial discount for my favourite people."

"I will, thanks."

Toby stood up to put his coat on. "Watch her tonight Mand, she's on fire!"

Dani said her goodbyes to Sammy and Toby and then turned back to Amanda. "Ignore him. It's just been one of those days. Right, I'm almost done. I just have to catch someone before they go and then change quickly."

When Dani returned with her daytime attire swapped for a simple black, knee-length dress and elegant black high heels, Amanda was sitting at her desk looking at her diary. "So you're off with Alex next week?"

"Yes, that's right." Amanda raised her eyebrows, waiting for some elaboration. "One of his TV series is about to start so we're off doing interviews. It's what I do, Amanda." Dani did her best to sound convincing, forgetting momentarily this was her best friend she was talking to.

"You're tempted aren't you?" Dani ignored the question and practically tipped Amanda out of her chair so she could tidy her desk and get out of the office. Amanda watched and waited as Dani busied herself, moving things from one side of her desk to the other and then back again, her inner torment obvious. Finally Dani stopped what she was doing and turned to look at her friend.

"It would be kind of comforting though, wouldn't it? Knowing from the start that it was destined to fail? Take out all the angst about whether or not this one might be 'the one'?"

"Do you have any idea how ridiculous and pathetic that sounds?" Dani's head fell, her own quiet way of admitting that of course she did. Amanda shrugged, deciding this was neither the time nor the place for a discussion on affairs of the heart. "Come on, we'll save that particular chat for another time. Put your best showbiz smile on and let's go. The film starts in less than an hour and you know the kissy mingly stuff at the beginning is one of my favourite bits."

Dani took a deep breath. "I just need to make one last call. You go on. I'll see you across the road in two minutes."

Dani waited until Amanda was safely out of earshot and then picked up the phone and dialled. "Oh hi, could you put me through to Alex Cambridge's room please?" Dani waited, aware of tiny beads of sweat on her upper lip, suddenly wondering what on earth she was doing and perhaps more importantly, what the hell she was going to say. "Yes hello? Oh right, thank you." She replaced the handset with a wry smile. So he had checked out. She had turned him down and he'd gone straight home to his wife. What had she expected? That he would sit alone in a hotel room just in case she changed her mind? Well maybe she had, only now he would never know. Dani picked up her jacket, her bag and the tickets to the première and went in search of Amanda and a very large glass of wine.

After a brief drink, Dani and Amanda headed for the cinema and the intimidating walk through the crowds of people crushed against barriers, all desperate for a glimpse of their favourite celebrity. For Dani, film premières were work and important for networking which took the edge off the fun part; for Amanda, it was fun all the way. Clustered around the door was a huge collection of paparazzi, flashing indiscriminately at people walking in. Amanda giggled, enjoying every surreal moment.

The film was two hours of hair-raising adventure and then it was on to the party. As they picked up their first drink, Dani recognised a few faces and smiled a few 'hellos'. She had passed on invitations to a number of her clients and knew she could have offered one to Alex. For tonight at least, she just wanted to relax and have some fun which would definitely not be possible if Alex's eyes were following her around the room.

"Hey guys, it's my own little Rottweiler!" Dani turned around to see Jake with a couple of friends and was unable to hide her horror.

"What on earth are you doing here?"

"Wetting the baby's head of course! It's a boy!"

Jake disappeared with his friends in tow leaving Dani dumbstruck. "God help me", she muttered to herself, "and it's really not nice to refer to someone as a breed of dog you know, even if it is meant as a compliment." Dani drained her glass. As she lowered it from her mouth, she was startled by a blinding series of flashes, leaving a delightful constellation of stars before her eyes. They faded to reveal Sean MacDonald, one of the favoured paparazzi guys who always seemed to have an exclusive invite to events while his disgruntled colleagues were left snapping at the door. He had expertly schmoozed all the right people and had developed a reputation for being quite considerate, a rare quality in his trade. Or so she had heard. Despite seeing him at endless functions, they had never formally met.

"Sean," he said with a warm smile. Dani instinctively took hold of his outstretched hand. "It's Dani isn't it?"

"Yes that's right."

"I was just taking a picture of Dave over there and he told me if I misused it, I'd have you to deal with, so I thought I'd better come and see what I was up against."

"And what do you think?"

He looked her up and down. "Oh you don't look too scary to me."

She laughed. "That's because I specialise in the art of deception."

"Well I'd better watch my step then, hadn't I? See you later."

"Who was that?" Amanda returned to her side in time to see Sean leave. They watched together as his tall frame quickly melted into the crowd, his short dark hair and black suit making him immediately indistinguishable.

"He's a photographer."

"No shit Sherlock! He's gorgeous. And I didn't miss the way you were looking at each other."

"Oh don't be fooled. He was just doing his job."

"Did you get the chance to ask if he was married?"

Dani glared at her. "Oh…just…", she stuttered, struggling for a suitably poignant response. "Oh just fuck off Amanda."

That would do.

3

When Dani arrived at the breakfast TV studio less than a week later, Alex was already sitting on a sofa in the plush Green Room, the holding bay for the show's guests, drinking coffee and with a plate of enormous pastries in front of him. She wandered over and sat down next to him. "Do I look as bad as I feel?" he said, his voice edged with an adrenaline-fuelled angst.

Dani looked closely at him. "You'll look fine once they put some make-up on you."

"I've already been in make-up!" he replied with more than a little concern.

Dani smiled. "I know. It was a joke."

Alex frowned, the joke seemingly lost on him. "Remind me again of today's schedule?"

"Well, we do this and then on to some press interviews, one of which is over lunch. A photo shoot and then a train ready for another breakfast show tomorrow."

"Jesus. Perhaps we could take a detour and I'll find the FBI's most wanted while I'm at it."

Dani smiled but, before she had time to respond, a young woman in her early twenties appeared in front of them, wearing jeans, a t-shirt with 'Barbie's younger sister' printed on it and a pair of headphones buried in her blonde curly hair. "You ready honeybun?"

Alex looked at her, his eyes wide. "I guess so."

As Alex and 'Barbie's younger sister' disappeared, Dani settled herself in front of a monitor where she could watch the show, with a cup of coffee and one of Alex's untouched, delicious-looking over-sized pastries. As she sunk her teeth into it, she watched the female presenter, poised and ready for the interview. "Time for a break now but coming up next I'll be joined by the latest heartthrob to hit our TV screens, Alex Cambridge."

An hour later Dani and Alex were sitting in a quiet corner of a café with a female journalist, Alex having barely had time to recover from his first live television appearance which had left his nerves jangling and his mouth desert dry. He was subsequently downing his fourth glass of water as the journalist switched on her recorder. "So Alex, you're married?"

"Yes I am."

"And you have how many children?"

"Three."

She paused, obviously knowing the answers already but hoping this would be enough of a prompt for a lively conversation about family life. She waited with a fixed smile for Alex to continue. He didn't. "And how do you manage to juggle your work and home lives?"

"Like any other working father. It's always a challenge but you find a way."

Another pause and then, reluctantly, the journalist started talking about the TV show, forced to accept that

Alex was not going to help her fill pages with insight into his personal life.

And so the pattern was set for the rest of the day. Interview two and another female journalist.

"So what does your wife think of you becoming a sex symbol Alex?"

Alex smiled. "She thinks it's hilarious."

"What does she think of your on-screen romance?"

"She thinks it's just that – an on-screen romance."

"How did you find the sex scenes?"

Dani frowned and then slowly relaxed as Alex expertly changed the direction of the conversation. "They were an important part of the character's make-up but there are so many more powerful ways he was shaped." And he was off, talking eloquently and intelligently, the journalist having no choice but to just move on with him. Dani smiled. She had been about to butt in, which she genuinely hated doing in interviews knowing it both annoyed the interviewer and made the interviewee look somewhat impotent. It was immensely satisfying to know Alex had been listening when she told him it was absolutely possible to stay in control.

Interview three and this time with a young, male journalist. "It's a great series Alex."

"Thank you. I knew as soon as I read the script it was a great drama. I've been very lucky."

"Having sex with Tori Harper! Yeah, lucky just about covers that!"

Alex looked at the journalist with a friendly smile. "You are familiar with the term 'acting'?"

The busy morning set the pace for the rest of the day and it wasn't until they were finally on a train that Dani and Alex had the chance to relax. Sitting comfortably in first class, a lovely lady with a well-stocked trolley provided some welcome drinks and for a moment they sat in contented silence. Alex downed a few healthy glugs of cold beer and then, taking in a deep breath, he slowly exhaled, letting the pressure of the day go along with the breath. "What a ride! Live television is a nightmare. I've never been so nervous in my entire life."

"It was great. That was a fantastic clip they showed and there were lots of plugs for the drama which is what it's all about."

"Wendy said to me a million times, 'Don't forget to say when it's on!' and I was concentrating so hard on getting that in I didn't even hear the first question!" Alex was animated by adrenaline but then he frowned. "I'm not sure the journalists liked me much though. I just don't feel comfortable talking to complete strangers about my personal life."

Dani smiled. "You did fine, really. You shouldn't feel you have to lay yourself bare and you have to start the way you mean to go on. Trust me."

He smiled back. "I do trust you. I just hate the idea of being seen as difficult or stroppy."

"No one will have thought that. They have to ask, you don't have to answer." She shrugged. "It's all just part of the game."

When they arrived at their designated hotel, they agreed on half an hour to freshen up and then a drink in the bar but Dani had barely been in her room for ten minutes when there was a knock at the door. She opened it to find Alex armed with a bottle of champagne and two glasses. Her shocked expression caused him to hesitate slightly, his smile immediately at odds with the anxious look in his eyes. "Aren't you going to invite me in?"

Alex held his breath until finally Dani stood to one side. He headed for a table and opened the champagne, quickly pouring two glasses and handing one over, relieved that Dani was now smiling as she raised her glass. "Here's to a very successful day and a flourishing ca…."

Before she could finish, Alex had taken her glass back and slid his arms around her waist. Immediately, Dani was unable to speak having completely lost her train of thought. And then he kissed her. The most gentle of kisses barely touching her lips but the impact was immense. She knew this was wrong but it was hard to fight it when the attraction and sexual tension between them was so intense. He kissed her again and then suddenly, the most primal passion took over. They started to quickly remove each other's clothes as Alex moved her towards the bed. Pillows were thrown out of the way, one catching a lamp which rocked precariously but neither noticed. The sex that followed was equally intense, as if time was limited and they could be found out at any moment.

As the noise of the evening traffic slowly faded outside, Alex took her in his arms and held her tightly for several minutes, too frightened to let her go for fear of never experiencing such intimacy with her again. Eventually it was Dani who pulled away and they smiled at each other, their eyes exchanging an acceptance that they were now firmly locked together in their own secret, forbidden world. "This is madness, you know that don't you?" she eventually said.

Alex looked at her, his eyes serious. "You have to remember that a short time ago, my life was very different. Small town, same group of friends since school, working locally and still with the girl I'd met at eighteen. Everyone was the same. The year I got married I went to seven other weddings and then the following year, I went to as many christenings. No one believed I was serious about becoming an actor and now here I am. Maybe if I'd waited, hadn't been in such a hurry to be the same as everyone else, things might have turned out differently."

"But you must have loved your wife?"

"And I still do. We have three beautiful children but they're what pull me home. Breaking Victoria's heart would be one thing but breaking theirs is just inconceivable."

Dani smiled. "So much to lose and yet you're still in my bed."

Alex looked at her, his heart heavy. Some things were just impossible to explain. He had looked at women before and imagined what it would be like to have sex with them but he had never felt compelled to make a move. With Dani it had been different. He had known the first time he met her that he could never accept her as just a colleague or even as a friend. It was therefore equally inexplicable why he had waited so long to act on his feelings. Most likely it was because he knew he had no right to pursue her. He meant it when he said he would never leave his wife although, if he pushed himself, he wasn't quite sure whether that was because he never wanted to be without her or because he felt duty bound to make his marriage work. He allowed himself a wry smile. Having an affair hardly seemed a productive way to secure its survival.

When the alarm went off the next morning, Dani felt completely flat. She turned it off and gently shook Alex awake. He smiled as he opened his eyes and saw her beside him, pulling her into his arms and gently kissing her forehead. "Come on Alex, you've got to get back to your room and get ready."

"Do I have to? Can't we just stay here for the day?"

"No, we can't. Come on, get up."

Alex struggled to open his eyes completely and then forced himself to his feet. He pulled on his clothes and then returned for one final kiss before slipping out into the corridor. Dani lay exactly where she was, the sense of time passing lost, the room still and eerily calm. In those quiet few moments, it was almost possible to believe he had never been there at all.

The day passed without a hitch and, by the middle of the afternoon, they were once again back in London.

Alex had his final television appearance that night and one more day of interviews before it was all over. Dani had agreed with Wendy that she would take over for the second leg and, although Alex would be staying in London overnight, he wouldn't be back in the hotel until after midnight and Wendy would be with him from early the next morning. Dani had therefore felt she should stay away. For the time being, their relationship was back to one of business. Business as unusual, you might say.

The next morning, Dani sat at her desk almost completely obscured by the biggest bunch of flowers she thought she had ever seen. And they were beautiful. Not your usual bouquet of carnations or roses but the most exotic collection of flowers Dani couldn't even begin to name. The message in contrast was simple. "Looking forward to the next time. Alex." The next time. Presumptuous bastard, she thought but Dani couldn't stop herself remembering the first time and she smiled. There was no denying it had been amazing. On the one hand, the pressure was well and truly off. It was a completely nonsensical argument but the anxiety she would happily accept as normal at the start of any relationship simply wasn't there. She had no expectations to live up to, no plans to make, no concern at all about making this one work. She would just enjoy it while it lasted. But of course the other hand was weighed down with guilt, with her total dislike of Alex's deceitful behaviour and, more importantly, a complete and utter disgust of her own. And when it all came to an end, which at some point it would have to, what would happen to their working relationship? She sighed. If you were going to have a complicated relationship, you might as well do it properly, she thought.

"Someone's birthday?"

Dani jumped as Bernie appeared beside her. Bernie Walker made up one half of the Stacey Walker partnership and he was considered one of the best in his field. Not that you'd know it to look at him. Dressed in jeans and a polo shirt, his greying hair short and neat, his face gently lined with the creases of a life well-lived, he looked more like an off-duty tennis coach than the shrewd businessman the entertainment world knew him to be. "Oh they're from Alex." Bernie raised his eyebrows. "The screening was very well received and his interviews went well. I think he's momentarily lost touch with reality."

Bernie smiled. "Well you obviously impressed him. I love it when you go that extra mile," he said as he turned and walked away, leaving Dani wondering if he'd noticed she had turned a gentle shade of pink.

Dani dragged her attention back to her work. She had so much to do she didn't really know where to start. Looking at the stack of papers and messages in front of her, not to mention the overloaded inbox that glared at her from the large screen on her desk, she decided she would just start at the top of the pile and not stop until her desk was clear and every email had been dealt with. If nothing else, it would stop her wondering if Alex was going to call her or if, in this game they were now playing, she was expected to call him. Then she looked at the flowers again and her heart sank. Of course she now had to call to say thank you. Before she had time to change her mind, she picked up the phone, convinced she could successfully put him out of her mind for the rest of the day if she spoke to him now and got those first difficult words out of the way.

"Hello?"

Dani was immediately thrown. Struggling to understand how on earth Alex's wife could have answered she looked at her phone to see the word 'home' under Alex's name. Why the hell had she called him at home? She could only assume his last call to her was from this number. All pretty immaterial in the moment. What she needed to do was pull herself together and say something. "Hello Mrs. Cambridge, it's Dani from Stacey Walker. Is Alex there?"

"No sorry Dani, he's not back from London until later. Can I get him to call you?" Dani was once again struggling for words. Of course he wasn't there! "Dani?"

"I'm sorry, I was just thinking. I wonder if you could pass on a message? Could you just say thank you for the flowers. It was very kind and unexpected. I would of course have done exactly the same for any of my clients."

"Of course, I'll let him know."

"Thank you." Dani slumped over her desk, her head in her hands. It was a terrible moment to have made such an error, forcing her to hear the last voice on earth she was ready for. What a vile and despicable person you are, she thought. She was losing her grip and knew that, however painful, some serious straight-talking was her only hope.

"You complete and utter slut."

Dani looked at Amanda across the café table, her shoulders curled in defeat. "I know, I know. What was I thinking?"

"I think that's the point, you clearly weren't. But something must be wrong if he's coming after you?"

"He has no plans to leave his wife. I'd be the traditional bit on the side."

"Mmm. Not the most attractive offer you've ever had."

"True but an offer none the less."

Amanda gasped. "Oh stop with the victim routine! You're not the only person in the world whose ever had their heart broken you know."

"Not many could equal my record."

"And dating a married man will help change that how exactly?"

Dani looked at her friend, her eyes narrowed. "Oh shut up. And can I just remind you that you're supposed to be making me feel better?"

"Actually, no. I'm supposed to be telling you the truth. And as you well know, the truth always hurts."

Dani looked at her trusted friend and couldn't help but smile. "And so the clichés start. I really must be in trouble."

"Are you?"

Dani looked confused. "Am I what?"

"In trouble?" Any sense of fun disappeared as Amanda waited. Dani's head lowered, a raw nerve clearly exposed. "You know I'm really not one to judge but I'd be a liar if I didn't say this feels a little....out of character."

Dani played with her fringe for a moment. She reminded herself that the reason she had wanted to see Amanda was for exactly this reason - that she would say what Dani was thinking but was too terrified to say out loud. But having thought she wanted to talk about it, she now just wanted to shut this down. She sighed and then in a decisive move, she sat up straight and forced a smile. "You're right. It was a mistake. Best forgotten."

Amanda watched Dani for a moment as she suddenly busied herself rummaging in her large handbag for nothing in particular and she smiled, a very sad, knowing smile. The shutters that were all too familiar had been well and truly pulled down.

Later that night, Alex was finding it difficult to settle. He watched Victoria sleeping peacefully beside him and knew that he did love her. So how could he explain his attraction to Dani? An attraction he had felt compelled to turn into something real. Something he could actually touch and taste and completely lose himself in. If he concentrated, he could still smell her, still imagine her hands on his body. He shook his head violently in

an attempt to dislodge the memory. The sudden move-
ment caused Victoria to stir and he froze. He didn't
want her to wake up. He would be forced to talk to her,
to explain why he was still awake. Maybe she would
want to have sex and he knew he couldn't do that. His
head would be full of images of Dani and that wouldn't
be fair. Fair! He smiled a desperate smile. In the
scheme of things, it was hardly an appropriate word.

He wondered how Dani was feeling. Did she regret
what had happened? Maybe it would be better if she
did but he knew that whatever feelings of guilt he was
battling, he definitely wanted to see her again. So she
would have done the same for any of her clients would
she? He tried to imagine how it must have felt to hear
his wife's voice on the end of the phone, knowing it
would have been a shock for Dani to speak to his wife
the morning after they had had sex. He turned to look at
Victoria. No more shocking than it was for him to lie
next to her as if nothing had changed between them
when it was clear, to him at least, that nothing would
ever be quite the same again.

4

Dani and her team were on a recruitment drive for new clients. Keeping half an eye out for up and coming talent was all part of the job and that meant regularly going to see low-key plays and comedy shows in pubs and small theatres. It was, however, all too easy to let day-to-day life take over and, before you knew it, the roving eye would go temporarily blind. So, every month or so, Dani insisted on a concentrated week where new talent was the focus, designed to reignite their interest in finding the next big thing, in whatever shape or form that might take. The process hadn't proved itself to be a winning formula just yet though and they had seen some truly awful stuff but Dani remained convinced it could work. This, she had told her team on many an occasion, was their equivalent of kissing frogs.

"Come on, let's get this week finalised." It was Monday morning and Dani was keen to make sure they had a full itinerary planned. "Let's ease the pain with a coffee." Sammy and Toby dutifully followed her to the office kitchen and its accompanying area of sofas, designed to provide the occasional break from the monotony of sitting in the same place all day. Armed with fresh coffees and a plate of biscuits to further soften the blow, the trio sat down. "Right, so it's our favourite pub theatre tonight," Dani kicked off.

"Where we're yet to see anyone even vaguely representable."

"Thank you Sammy." Dani refused to be put off. She was well aware these full-on weeks could either be loads of fun, often for all the wrong reasons, or the longest five days of your life. "So, tomorrow?"

Toby leapt into action with mock enthusiasm. "Tomorrow is drama student night. Yay!" And then he laughed. He loved the thrill of potentially discovering someone promising and, despite his playfulness, actually took it all very seriously. "It's not the end of term all-singing all-dancing stuff, just a mid-term production but I think it's worth including."

"Great. Anyone in the slush pile?" Dani turned to Sammy who pulled out a wedge of CVs and accompanying head-shots of wannabe actors. Sammy looked decidedly nonplussed.

"On any other day I'd say no but as it's recruitment week, I've selected two." Sammy passed them each the relevant CVs and pictures as she spoke. "The first one, Dan Ebworth is in tonight's pub theatre spectacular."

"That didn't have anything to do with why you chose him did it?"

Sammy smiled. "I don't know what you mean." She chose not to rise to Toby's over-stated mouthing of the word 'cheat' and continued. "The second, Maisy Moore, is in a regional theatre production that we'll see on Thursday. And that really good West End youth theatre we've seen before has a cool new production that we could see on Wednesday."

"And we've already agreed the late-night comedy sketch show for Friday which means we have a full house." Dani closed her note book with a satisfactory slap. "Sorted."

Within a matter of hours, they were taking their seats in the back room of a north London pub that had been lovingly converted into a miniature theatre. Of course, on a Monday night it wasn't exactly a priority ticket and a very quick head count was all that was needed to confirm there was every chance there would be more people on the stage than in the audience. Dani sighed with more than a little dread. As the lights dimmed, she chose to remind herself it was a place not too dissimilar to this that she'd found Damien and look where his career was now! She sat up straight, determined to be positive.

The feeling lasted for all of seven minutes. Maybe eight. She didn't want to be unnecessarily harsh. She was aware of Sammy fidgeting beside her while Toby constantly checked his watch, his frustration quickly turning into pure disbelief at how painfully slowly the time was passing. The play would run for eighty minutes with no interval. There would be no half-time escape here and there was no way on earth they would be able to slip out unnoticed. She might as well accept they were temporarily incarcerated.

Tuesday night's entertainment wasn't much better, forcing Dani to wonder if these recruitment drives really were nothing more than the waste of time Sammy and Toby already believed them to be. Wednesday was marginally better and then they hit a new low on Thursday. The production was so appallingly bad that Toby had had an uncontrollable fit of giggles, much to the annoyance of their fellow audience members who had to be the friends and family of those on stage. Impossible to work out why else they would be there. The only saving grace was the very welcome interval. A quick nod from Dani and her partners in crime swiftly donned their jackets and happily headed for the door.

Dani was at her desk early on Friday morning, enjoying the rare stillness in the office. She had wanted to make sure all the final points raised on Alex's next contract had now been included and the only way to guarantee the time needed to really focus on something important was to be the first through the door. Happy that everything was now as she wanted it, she hit the send button that would take her final approval to the company's legal department. It was time to sign on the dotted line.

With a large mug of coffee, she then sat back and flicked through the tabloids, stopping suddenly with a finely tuned sinking feeling as she saw a picture of her favourite client, Polly. She had been snapped on her way into the theatre she was currently appearing in, wearing a simple figure-hugging dress and she looked stunning. Dani was forced to look closer as she took in the headline and copy which posed the question of whether or not she was pregnant. Dani scrutinised Polly's tummy. If that was a bump, Dani concluded she must surely be obese by comparison. This was the third or fourth time this had happened. If she wore loose clothes then she was pregnant. If she wore tight clothes and revealed anything more than a millimetre of tummy then she was pregnant. Dani knew better than most about the insatiable hunger for the minutiae of celebrity lives but bloody hell, even she couldn't remember the moment when banal, gossipy speculation metamorphosed into something worthy of column inches. She rolled her eyes and tossed the paper aside, hoping as she did so that Polly wouldn't see it and then Sammy appeared, looking remarkably buoyed considering the week they'd had. "Have you seen that crap on Polly?"

"Indeed I have. I'm ignoring it."

Sammy took off her jacket and started preparing herself for the day ahead. She switched on her computer, pulled her note book from her desk drawer which was packed with neatly written to-do lists and other vital information and then selected a black pen from a pot full of identical implements that sat beside her phone. She was nothing if not supremely organised. "Did you catch the byline?"

Dani stretched down to retrieve the paper from the floor where she'd dropped it and took another look. "Dylan Kent. I might have known. I'll try to see him next week."

"Isn't it better to ignore him?"

Dani smiled. "You know what they say. Keep your friends close and your enemies in a permanent head lock. Or something like that."

Sammy's attention was distracted by an email she was now reading. "That bloke Dan from Monday's play's been in touch. He heard I was in the audience and wondered if I fancied a coffee sometime."

The ensuing silence set off a gentle alarm bell and Dani looked up. "Oh no, you're weakening! Have I taught you nothing?" It was obvious to Dani that the owner of the theatre would of course have tipped off the actors they would be there the minute they'd booked tickets. Her only surprise was that just one of them had had the nous to get in touch.

Sammy felt herself blush slightly. "I'm just saying. I know he wasn't right for us."

"Talentless is the word you're looking for."

Toby's voice could be heard long before he reached them as he crashed in in his usual unsubtle way. "Morning ladies! What have I missed?" Without waiting for a response beyond the expected 'hellos', Toby was quickly scanning emails, easy to do as he hadn't bothered to switch his computer off the night before. His desk was exactly as he'd left it. It was as if he'd just stood up and walked away, which of course he had, allowing him to simply sit down every morning and literally pick up where he'd left off. "Ooh that Dan chap's been in touch. Wants to buy me coffee. How sweet." His delight was obvious.

Dani smiled. "Well, you have to give the guy marks for trying," she said as she looked over at Sammy who was suddenly very busy with her head down.

"Should I get him in?"

"No!" Toby jumped at the ferocity of the word, shouted in perfect unison.

He looked from Dani to Sammy and shrugged. "Yeah, he was pretty shit wasn't he?"

Several hours passed in a flash and suddenly it was time for the final leg of their marathon scouting expedition. Dani stood up. "Right then, come on gang. I have a good feeling about tonight!" Sammy and Toby looked at each other and laughed. Dani was about to reprimand them for their lack of optimism and then, deciding it was a fair cop, thought better of it.

After a few rounds of Dutch courage in a nearby bar, they headed for the comedy club and were relieved to find it packed. It had a good reputation and a lively atmosphere would definitely help things along.

Tonight's entertainment was a sketch show version of an open mic night where comic actors and writers had a rare opportunity to see if their talents were anywhere near good enough to hold a crowd; a crowd who would have bellies full of beer and have parted with hard earned cash for the privilege of seeing them perform. No pressure then.

Sammy and Toby were already seated when Dani joined them. She had been caught by the club's owner, someone she had known for many years now, who had often tipped her off when someone new and exciting took to his stage.

"What did Pete have to say about the show?"

Much to Dani's relief, Toby was immediately distracted by the lights dimming. He would know the answer soon enough.

A very slow forty minutes later, the lights came back up again. Toby pushed his cheeks upwards. "Maybe I've had a stroke and that's why I'm finding it impossible to crack a smile?"

Sammy put her head in her hands. "Oh dear God. That was awful! I think I might actually cry."

Dani immediately stood up. "I'll get some drinks."

As she waited for her turn at the bar, Dani was suddenly aware of someone beside her. She looked up to see the photographer, Sean McDonald, smiling back at her. "Hi Dani."

Dani felt her cheeks flush. "Sean! What are you doing here?"

"Well it's been a busy week so I was hoping to unwind with some comedy." His face suggested that wasn't about to happen anytime soon.

Dani smiled. "Not exactly a belly laugh is it?"

"So what brings you here?"

"We're scouting for new talent."

They looked at each other and then burst into fits of laughter. "There we go," said Sean, wiping the tears from his eyes. "I feel better already!"

"What can I get you?" They were interrupted by the barman and Sean gestured to Dani for her to order.

Armed with refills there was then an awkward moment, neither sure what to do next. Dani chose to nod towards her colleagues. "I'm here with the team. Better get back."

"Of course. Good to see you."

Dani returned to the table and sat down. "Who's the hottie?" Toby nodded towards the bar. "A hottie who, by the way, can't take his eyes off you. Why does he look so familiar?"

"He's a pap," Dani replied in the most nonchalant way she could manage.

Toby groaned. "Shame."

With contract negotiations concluded, it was time for Alex to start packing. He was of course thrilled to have landed the role but it would be another stint away from his children, his longest yet, and that would be hard. He wandered into his bedroom to find Victoria surrounded by neat piles of clothes and an open holdall. "I did say I was happy to do this."

"It's fine," she said, looking up briefly. "I like packing. And you don't pack, you stuff. You know I hate that." Alex found a small, empty space on the bed and gingerly sat down. He didn't want to upset the incredibly well-organised operation taking place in front of him. "Are the kids settled?"

"Eva's still asking why she can't come with me." Alex looked slightly traumatised as he spoke. "Is there room in there for her?" He gestured towards the bag with a smile but Victoria remained focused on the job in hand

and for a moment he was forced to accept the silence and simply watch her systematically pick items up, neatly fold or roll them and then place them carefully in the next available gap. Her hair was pulled back into a ponytail and he found himself studying her eyes. Whatever she was thinking, they were giving nothing away. He was always struck by how blue they were, all the more striking because each of his children had inherited them making it impossible to look at her and not see them too. He felt his heart constrict, his mind immediately flooded with an image of his wife and kids as delicate china figures bound tightly together. He shivered, reminded that breaking one would leave them all damaged. He dragged his eyes away from hers and wondered for a moment if she'd lost weight. Not that she needed to. She'd always been slender and running around after three children was more than enough exercise for any human being as far as he was concerned. He narrowed his eyes. The familiar loose sweatshirt that she often wore suddenly seemed to drown her, making her seem small and vulnerable.

"Do you think you'll need another jumper?"

Alex shook his head, relieved to be distracted from his thoughts. "I'll be in costume most of the time so I really don't need much."

Alex continued to watch her and, as the silence grew, his mind wandered again. He wanted to know what she was holding back. In life before sex with Dani, he would have accepted without question that she was simply trying to be brave, wanting to make him feel it was okay to go away again when really, she wanted him at home with his family where he belonged. She was incredibly proud of how his acting career had taken off but had never really stopped to think of the long-term implications and, in particular, the fact he would inevitably spend large chunks of time away. With two children already in school, dropping everything and going with him clearly wasn't an option. But this wasn't life before sex with Dani. This was the newly complicated, full of deception, heart-wrenching life after sex with Dani. Not for the first time now, Alex looked at Victoria with a degree of unease. He looked at the ever-so-slightly watery eyes, the pinched lips, the keep-busy-and-focused approach to everything and his instinct as to what was going on in her mind was immediately overtaken by the fear of wondering if she knew something already. That she had somehow sensed something different about him that even he wasn't yet aware of.

His attention was brought quickly back to the room by the sound of a large zip, gathering speed until its job was done and the bag was duly closed. Victoria stood for a moment, horribly aware of the significance of the act. They were another step closer to the bit she hated most. Saying goodbye. Her slightly blurred gaze was distracted by Alex checking his watch.

"How long till the car gets here?" Alex was booked on an early flight to Edinburgh the next morning and he had decided it made sense to spend the night in a hotel close to the airport. Taking hold of Victoria's hand, he pulled her down next to him and took her in his arms.

"Ten minutes or so." He hugged her tightly. "It'll be alright Vics. You've got a copy of my schedule so we can FaceTime every day. It's only a few weeks till half term when you'll all be coming up and then we'll be nearly half way already! And I'll come home any chance I get." He did his best to sound light and reassuring.

"I know. I'm just being silly." Alex wiped away the few tears that had broken rank and spilled onto her cheeks and his heart took an expected lurch. Partly because he would genuinely miss her and partly due to the now inevitable guilt. With one last hug and a lingering kiss, Alex stood up. "Come on. Best wait downstairs." Picking up his bag, he waited for a moment for Victoria to make a move and then followed her out the door.

Fifteen minutes later, Alex was pulling away from the house. He closed his eyes for a moment and let all the competing emotions spinning around in his head have their mad, crazy moment, completely giving in to the dodgems in his mind. And then, with a deep sigh, he finally felt a well-needed calm slowly take hold.

Sitting forward, his eyes now wide open, he took out his phone and typed a text, '60 minutes and counting', and sent it to Dani.

5

As soon as Alex had left her, Dani had felt immediately flat and twitchy, if it were possible to feel both things at the same time. Due to his early departure, she had been in the office at the crack of dawn but had been unable to concentrate on anything useful. Once the clock had hit nine, her phone had let out its first piercing shrill and hadn't stopped ringing since which had forced her into action whether she liked it or not.

She finished a particularly difficult call and had just enough time to rub her tired eyes before it rang again. "Hello?" The supposed greeting came out far more aggressively than she had intended.

"Have I caught you at a bad moment?"

"No, of course not!" She attempted to sound decidedly friendlier than she felt as she frantically tried to put a name to the voice.

"That is Dani?"

"Yes, speaking." She winced, aware that her efforts had been wasted. She still sounded curt and irritated.

"Dani, it's Sean. Sean MacDonald." There was a pause. "Photographer. Although I suppose some might prefer to call me a general pain in the arse."

Dani laughed with both relief and embarrassment. "I know who you are! The phone hasn't stopped and it's been one problem after another. I'm sorry, I'm not normally so abrupt."

"I'm very glad to hear it." There was another pause as Dani waited to hear the reason for his call. As the silence verged on becoming awkward, she decided just to ask. "So what can I do for you?"

"I was just wondering if you're allowed out for lunch?"

She smiled. "I think that could be arranged for a good enough reason."

"Would meeting me count?"

Her smile widened. "Oh I think it could stretch to that!"

"Great. Well I'm in town today, so how about I meet you at one? You pick where."

Dani was momentarily thrown. She frantically checked her diary to make sure she was actually free then quickly scanned what she was wearing before grabbing a mirror from her bag to check exactly how big the bags under her eyes were. She hadn't imagined for one minute he would suggest today.

"Dani? Any suggestions?"

"Oh, uh, what about the White Room?"

"Yeah, great. I think they let me in there if I leave my camera at the door. I'll book a table for one o'clock and see you there."

A meeting, half an hour of emails, another meeting, a quick team chat followed by a few phone calls and the morning was done. After ten minutes spent brushing her hair and applying what she hoped was just the right amount of make-up, Dani left for the restaurant, determined to arrive just a teeny bit late. She couldn't ignore that she was feeling slightly anxious. He was an attractive man and, while she could try to dismiss this as just work, the preparation she had felt necessary to ensure she looked her best suggested she was thinking of it as anything but.

Dani was relieved that Sean was already there when she arrived and immediately tried to look more relaxed than she felt as she made her way towards him. "Dani!" She was suddenly stopped in her tracks by a hand reaching out from a table to block her way. It was the publicist, Wendy.

"Hi Wendy. How are you?" she said disingenuously, her forced smile and overall lack of sincerity totally lost on Wendy who was far too busy looking over her shoulder to see where Dani was headed.

"Lunch with Mr Pap eh? Lucky you!" She waved over at Sean with a perfect white-toothed, red-lipped smile. Sean had no choice but to wave back in as low key a fashion as he could manage. "Business or pleasure?"

Dani raised her eyebrows. It was a more polite response than what she was actually thinking - that it was none of her fucking business. "Enjoy your lunch Wendy," she said as casually as she could manage and quickly moved on.

Sean stood up as Dani finally reached him. He was wearing jeans and a black jumper that made his hair and eyes look even darker than Dani remembered. "Hi Dani. Really glad you could make it." She smiled in response as they sat down, unsure for a moment how to answer. "What about a drink?" he asked.

"Yes thank you, a glass of white wine would be great."

Sean ordered drinks and then relaxed back in his chair. As he did, Dani's shoulders suddenly slumped over the table as if by lowering her body, she would somehow become invisible. "Oh no! Lucien Wooden." Sean glanced over his shoulder. "No don't look!" Dani pleaded in a frantic whisper.

Sean smiled, his eyes immediately alive. "I think you mean Lucien Waden!"

"What's that saying about looks and instant death?"

"Don't worry. The daggers will all be for me."

"Not this time. He thought a part was all his and then I made Damien available. And if gazumping him wasn't bad enough, he's with Lucy Martin who plagued me to represent her. I think I was polite in my decline the first few times and then I may have been a little...." Dani thought carefully about what words to use. "Unnecessarily honest."

Sean laughed loudly. "Bloody hell, you're even more unpopular than me!" he said as he watched a very pained Dani nod uncomfortably with an apologetic smile in the direction of what he could only imagine was a now very disgruntled looking couple.

His delight was hugely infectious and Dani felt herself relax, immediately recognising a common bond with her fellow partner in celebrity crime. And then, as if

57

suddenly remembering something, he started to root around in his bag. "I have something for you."

Dani looked amazed as he handed her a photograph. It was the one he had taken of her at the première party and she had to admit it was stunning. He had caught her completely unaware and although at the time she had felt like a startled rabbit, in the picture she looked totally expressionless but composed, her eyes wide and clear. She smiled. "Wow!"

Sean smiled at her reaction. "Not bad is it? Perhaps I have a future in this game after all!"

"Can I keep it?"

"Of course, I've already blown it up to the size of my living room wall so I have no need for it!"

She looked at him, a heat slowly permeating up from her feet, making her knees tingle. "Thank you."

Sean picked up the menu. "Right, food. What do you fancy?"

Slightly flustered, Dani quickly scanned the menu. "Oh just something light or I'll be asleep at my desk this afternoon. The salmon, I think."

He looked around for a waiter and with their order made, they settled into an easy conversation. Sean was fascinating and Dani bombarded him with questions about the people he'd photographed and the places he'd been. He was an accepted face in the very best places and was known by everyone from Liam Neeson to Liam Payne. He was invited to every significant function in the showbiz calendar and to private events too. Basically, if there was a picture to be had, he was there and always ahead of everyone else. "You must have one hell of a contacts book to make sure you always know where to be?"

Sean shrugged. "It's a different game now. Thanks to smartphones, everyone's a pap these days so yes, it's all about contacts I guess. Assuming the celeb doesn't simply invite you along themselves. I've just had to learn who to get to know, who to charm."

Dani looked at him, her eyes suddenly more serious. "Is that what you're doing now?"

"What?"

"Charming me in case I might be useful some time?"

Sean looked surprised. "Is that what you think?" Dani raised her eyebrows. "Okay. Well, at the risk of embarrassing myself, the reason I invited you for lunch is because I'm attracted to you. Simple as that. Not for any ulterior motive. Not because I might be able to use you in the future or because I need a favour."

"Oh, I see." Dani smiled nervously, liking but slightly thrown by his directness. "That's okay then."

"Is it?"

"Yes, it's fine," she said quietly, her eyes flitting up and down, unable to hold his stare.

"Good. So shut up and eat your lunch then!"

Despite her polite protestations, Sean insisted on paying for lunch and then walked her back to the office which was only minutes away. As they reached the door, she turned to look at him. "Thanks, I had a really good time."

"Does that mean you'll come out with me again?"

She smiled. "Maybe."

"I'll call you then." He kissed her on the cheek and with a brief wave, turned and walked away. For a moment she stood and watched him go with a smile but, as he faded into the crowd, so did her expression, slowly transforming into something altogether more anguished. What was she doing? She was at the very least already ankle deep in an affair with Alex. It was only a matter of hours since she'd been in bed with him! And yet here she was embarking on what exactly? She could wage her own debate on whether or not lunch was indeed a date but there could be no doubt about the label on a follow-up.

Dani looked at her watch and groaned. She was late for a meeting, the inner conflict immediately forgotten as she raced back to the safety of her desk to do what she did best - deftly untangle someone else's problems.

When Dani finally got home that night she was exhausted. She shut the door of her flat behind her and felt the tension of the day slowly dissolve. She had bought the flat five years ago and it had quickly become her sanctuary. She had taken her time to find the right place and had known immediately this was it; a two-bedroomed north London maisonette, spread over three floors and bursting with wow factor. With each staircase, the wow just got bigger with the loudest released right at the top with a door onto a roof terrace, where the whole of London was laid out in the most stunning visual feast for the eyes. She had spent many an hour sitting out there at the end of a long, arduous day, a glass of wine in one hand, secateurs in the other, occasionally standing up to lop the head off a plant housed in one of a small selection of terracotta pots. She had taken her time furnishing the place and the finished look was charmingly eclectic. Old sat alongside new with splashes of colour from carefully chosen pictures, cushions and lamps. It was beautifully stylish and had Dani written all over it.

Dani stopped in the kitchen to pour herself a glass of wine and grab a large bag of assorted nuts before heading for the lounge and her favourite old chair that folded around her in a warm hug. The sofa to her left was over-sized and ridiculously comfortable. She'd subsequently spent many a night unintentionally sleeping on it after a typically exhausting week. A beautifully restored fireplace took pride of place opposite her, flanked by two bookcases housing a mix of books, family photographs and the television, with a low wooden coffee table filling the space in between, perfectly positioned so it was close enough to rest her feet on.

As she dined on nuts, she was forced to accept that her eating habits were definitely on a slippery slope towards totally unhealthy but she could never be bothered to cook for herself. A small glimmer of redemption came as she reminded herself that at least she'd had a proper lunch. She smiled, immediately thinking about her time with Sean. She was incredibly attracted to him and, by his own admission, he was attracted to her. Facts that suddenly made her feel horribly anxious, made her feel weighted down by feelings of expectation, fear and hope; all the unavoidable emotions synonymous for her with meeting someone new. Emotions that she had been able to totally avoid when she got together with Alex, accepting that their relationship simply had nowhere to go. Which of course meant she was now thinking about Alex. She wondered for a moment exactly what he expected of her. Was he imagining there would be no one else in her life? That her brief and sporadic liaisons with him would be enough? She took a large sip of wine and then threw a handful of nuts into her mouth which she crunched on with great purpose. Then with another large swig she stiffened, suddenly finding the silence of the room almost stifling. Why did it even matter what Alex expected? Surely she should be thinking about what she wanted and what was enough for her? One thing felt crystal clear. She had no idea what would happen with Sean but she knew she wanted to find out. Reaching out to the table in front of her, Dani grabbed a remote control and with the press of a button she was hit by the sound of raucous laughter from a panel show's studio audience and was immediately engaged in the banter. A few more hearty mouthfuls of wine and she felt the tension in her neck and shoulders begin to subside. She slowly turned up the volume until the banal chat finally drowned out the last troubled thoughts whirring in her head, her attention now entirely focused on the television.

By the time Dani reached her desk the next morning, her phone was already ringing. "Hello?"

"I thought it was best to get in early before anyone upset you."

She smiled. "Hi Sean."

"So about that second date you almost agreed to? What are you doing tomorrow night?"

"Nothing."

"Good. So what about dinner? Or a film? Or both?"

"You choose."

"Oh no, the pressure of getting it right!" He hesitated. "I need time to think about it so why don't I meet you in that bar opposite your office around seven and we'll take it from there?"

Sean decided on a light supper in a restaurant he had carefully selected for its total lack of celebrities and media types. He wanted to be able to get to know Dani better and felt that would only be possible if they were both able to relax with nothing but good food and wine for company. The conversation had flowed along with the Pinot Noir and Dani didn't think she had ever laughed so much in a single evening. Here were two people armed with more than their fair share of anecdotes, inhabiting a world where there were endless great stories to tell, where the subjects were rightly or wrongly treated as fair game. The point they chose to ignore, or perhaps were simply oblivious to, was that they inhabited this bizarre and colourful world too and actively played their part in it.

Sean was really enjoying the evening too, loving the fact that the conversation was so easy and so interesting. As their main courses were cleared away, he sat back for a moment and then decided to probe a little deeper. "So would it be a terrible cliché to ask why you're single?"

Dani smiled. Just what she needed. Someone else in her life with a cliché for every occasion. She shrugged. "Probably because I rarely get the chance to meet normal people."

"What does that make me?"

"Anything but."

Sean held her eye, unsure for a moment how to respond and wondering if his question had been even vaguely answered. A different tack maybe. "So what do you look for?"

Dani felt her guard rising and immediately did her best to suppress it. She wanted to give this a chance didn't she? And that meant being open and honest. "My only rule is not to have any. Clean slate, no 'type', no expectations and just see what happens. How does that sound?"

"Sounds good."

"So what's your excuse?" It seemed only fair to ask the same question of him.

Sean thought for a moment. "Work tends to dominate. You know the score." Indeed she did.

The waiter arrived with dessert menus which they both immediately dismissed. They finished their wine and then, despite neither feeling ready to call it a night, it was time to go home. "Which way are you going?" Sean asked as they stepped outside on to a bustling pavement.

"North."

"Typical." Sean looked disappointed. "I'm going south but I'd be only too happy to see you home."

Dani smiled in response to the mischief in his eyes. "Don't be silly. I'll be fine."

"That's not why I offered." And then he kissed her, the waves of people heading for tube stations and bus stops instinctively parting to avoid them.

"Come for dinner on Saturday," she found herself saying.

"Great. I'll call you tomorrow and you can give me the address. Look, there's a cab." He called it over and gave her one final kiss before waving her off.

Dani managed to wait until the cab had pulled away before allowing the first tear to escape. She quickly brushed it away with an air of irritation. She just felt so angry with herself. It was like being sucked into the eye of a terrible storm. Although that would mean she had no control over the situation which of course she did. Suddenly she was properly crying, which she immediately saw as a shameless display of weakness. It was as if she'd just accepted she was heading into a completely untenable situation without offering up even the slightest resistance. As the tears continued to fall, she swiped viciously at each one, as if the speed of removing them somehow made them less significant. Then she pinched herself in an attempt to ram home the

65

metaphorical need to get a grip. She'd had sex with Alex twice and two dates with Sean. It was hardly the crime of the century. In fact, there would be no crime at all if she never had sex with Alex again and just concentrated on seeing how things worked out with Sean but, however simple that sounded, however clear and straightforward, Dani was only aware of a volcanic anxiety, barely able to keep the growing rumbling under control. As she stared out of the cab window, she knew that both of them had started to burrow beneath the surface, worming their way into her thoughts and igniting feelings and physical reactions that couldn't just be dismissed with a simple objectiveness or a smart one-liner. She was emotionally awake for the first time in a very long time and it was terrifying.

6

Sean had been walking for a while when he arrived at his favourite café in the heart of town and took up his usual position by the window. There had been no real need to head out at all but he liked to be around people. That, along with force of habit, had propelled him to his usual haunt. His eyes were immediately hypnotised by the constant traffic of people on the pavement outside. Everyone seemed in such a terrible hurry to be somewhere. It was a beautiful spring day. The kind that reminded you that winter was indeed only temporary and in a way that lifted your heart. At least that was how it made Sean feel, so convinced was he that no one else had even noticed. He watched another stream of lifeless faces race by, saw people checking their watches and wondered where on earth they needed to be in such a dreadful rush. That kind of mundane pressure was something he happily lived without.

His ears tuned into the conversations around him. You never knew where your next tip-off might come from after all, although with this particular mid-morning clientele, it was unlikely he would pick up anything more startling than what video game was currently causing the most parental angst, or which marriage was the latest to fall foul of an affair or simply buckle under the weight of middle-aged boredom. Scandalous to those involved, but of absolutely no interest to Sean.

After a while, he not surprisingly found himself bored by the tedious conversation next to him and, as his mind drifted off, he found himself thinking about Dani. Most of his relationships had been built on mutual need and over time, the line between a leg up and a leg over had become blurred. But there was immediately something very different about Dani. She was so confident, so together and yet there was a childlike quality to her, a hint of innocence, of vulnerability that drew him to her in a way that excited and terrified him in equal measure. He smiled, his third cup of coffee now in front of him and stretched out his long legs with a contented sigh. Roll on Saturday, he thought.

Dani was looking forward to Saturday night too but she still had Friday to get through. She looked over at Toby's empty desk and wondered for a moment how he was getting on. Today was the photo shoot and interview with Jake, Sadie and Beau. She had sent Steve Preston an email wishing him well with it all and reminding him that the detail of his interview with Damien would be confirmed once she was confident all had gone well with Jake, a final nod that if he broke their agreement and threw in even the vaguest reference to the lap dancer, she would give Damien to someone else. It may or may not work but it was important to at least attempt to appear in control. Sammy was on the phone so Dani waited till she'd finished then jumped in. "Right, let's have a newbie push. First to get one on to the active board wins a prize." Sammy stood up with an air of smugness.

"That was Geoff on the phone," she said as she casually walked over to the board that gave them an instant overview of who was currently doing what and where. She picked up a marker pen. "Gabriel did a fab job at his second audition and, fanfare please," she said as she unpinned his picture from the newbie board and ceremoniously stuck it alongside the usual suspects who were all currently active, "the part is well and truly his." She added the production title and filming dates and then turned around with a big smile. "Prize please!"

Dani put on her best sympathetic smile. "Oh sorry, you misunderstood. I meant starting right now. Sadly that means Gabriel doesn't count." Sammy raced back to her desk and frantically started making calls, resisting her immediate desire to scream foul play. After an hour, Dani found herself flinching every time Sammy hung up as the ferocity of the action increased along with her growing frustration. With a deep breath, she scanned through her pristine notes for the umpteenth time and then with eyebrows raised in anticipation, she dialled a number and waited.

"Susie, hi, it's Sammy at Stacey Walker returning your call........You did? That's great.....Yes, that would work.......Brilliant. I'll let him know and be in touch." Sammy slowly stood up and with the air of a champion headed back to the boards, unpinned the shot of Sonny and placed it slowly and carefully alongside Gabriel on the active board. She looked over at Dani. "In your face oh great leader of mine. Now cough up!"

Dani laughed. "Okay, you win! Lunch is on me."

They'd had a really good run on breakthrough moments over the last couple of months and there were now five new faces showing as active. It was always a great boost to the team when they moved someone over and there was a healthy competitiveness to getting someone their first break. A free lunch was one thing but a score of 3-2 to Sammy was the real prize.

Dani's mobile rang and there was a spontaneous sharp intake of breath as she saw Toby's name. "Just to warn you this phone is only accepting good news today," was her opening gambit.

"Bye then!" Dani froze as he went horribly quiet. "Only joking. All very good here and going swimmingly."

"You little shit. I almost had a heart attack." Dani quickly reminded herself it was this spirit and character that made her love him so, as she smiled at the sound of Toby's giggling.

"Sorry, I'm just so relieved the interview's done and Steve's gone. It's made me mildly hysterical. Just the pics to do now then I'll be back."

Dani treated Sammy to a lovely lunch and, as they walked back into the office, Toby appeared behind them with a loud, "Boo!" Neither flinched.

"If you want to sneak up on people you need to learn to be a little less heavy-footed." Dani smiled at him as he produced bag after bag of sweets from his over-loaded pockets.

"Friday treats. Sugar rush here we come!"

Dani then rolled her eyes as he raced past them. He would be bouncing off the walls in minutes. And then he stopped in his tracks, his eyes fixed on the active board. "No way!" He turned to look at a very smug Sammy. "Game on bitch," he said with playful determination as he grabbed for his phone, scanning his notebook to see who he could chase first.

Dani enjoyed planning dinner. Armed with a very comprehensive list, she set off for the shops on Saturday morning but didn't think about buying food until she had found herself something new to wear; a pair of jeans to go with the twenty she had already and a fitted black shirt that covered her up and revealed everything all at the same time. Next was a visit to see the lovely Gary who trimmed her hair and dried it in a way only a hairdresser ever can and then she finally headed for the supermarket. Her list suitably checked and laden with bags, she then struggled back towards home. She had chosen a menu with as little room for error as possible and something she had made before to avoid any last minute panics. An accomplished cook she most definitely was not, relying totally on the advice of the accomplished Mr Oliver to guide her through the process.

Before long the main course was bubbling away nicely and dessert was setting in the fridge. For someone who barely cooked, Dani had an impressive kitchen.

The worktops housed beautiful jars of pasta and spices, an array of cooking oils sat in wait beside the cooker while a retro-looking food processor took pride of place in the corner. Pans and various utensils hung above the cooker and the drawers and cupboards revealed a collection of hand-picked crockery from a range of individual shops and markets, alongside the best of what John Lewis had to offer in the shape of dishes and baking accessories. It all looked suitably inspiring and basically reflected the cook she would like to be rather than the one she was. The majority of the equipment therefore remained virtually untouched by human hand.

When Sean arrived, he was overloaded with a huge bouquet of beautiful flowers and a couple of bottles of wine. He followed her into the kitchen and put everything down on the wooden table, set stylishly for two and then looked at her properly for the first time. He took hold of her and a bolt of something incredibly sensuous sent one message shooting to his brain and another screaming to his groin. He kissed her. "How long until dinner's ready?"

"Why, are you hungry?"

"I was just wondering how long we had?"

She smiled at him, his arms still firmly wrapped around her. "Five minutes."

He loosened his grip on her and smiled. "Later then."

Dani turned away and picked up a bottle of wine, trying not to appear flustered as she clumsily grappled with a bottle opener until the cork was finally freed. "Here you go," she said, offering him a glass. "Take your jacket off and sit down. I'm just going to put these in water and then everything should be ready."

Dinner was a strange experience. The food was surprisingly edible and Sean was obviously enjoying it but both knew the sooner the meal was out of the way, the sooner the evening could develop. Conversation was therefore limited as, without wanting to appear as if they were hurrying, they set about demolishing three courses at an extremely healthy pace.

Dani swiftly cleared away the plates and they moved to the living room with some coffee. She sat down next to Sean on the sofa and looked down at her stomach, convinced that her waistline had expanded horribly. No doubt something to do with the gallons of air she had swallowed in her frantic attempt to dispense with her dinner. And then Sean's arm was around her and he was kissing her. As buttons were slowly undone between a series of soft, gentle kisses, Sean took a moment to hold Dani close, breathing in the smell of her. Without feeling the need to say anything, she stood up as his arms loosened around her and took him to her bedroom.

When Dani woke the next morning she smiled as she watched Sean sleeping. She felt completely wanted and desired and it was a feeling that she never wanted to end. Suddenly one of his eyes opened, the other staying firmly shut. "Are you staring at me?"

Hadn't she said that to Alex once? Dani dismissed the thought immediately and smiled. "Maybe just a little."

He shut his eye again and smiled as she kissed him and then he opened his eyes fully as if it was now acceptable to be awake. "So what do you want to do today?"

He thought for a moment. "How about I buy you breakfast somewhere?"

"That would be nice. There's no hurry though is there?"

Sean smiled as she snuggled up to him. No, there was no hurry and certainly time to have sex again in the lazy, relaxed way that is privilege to Sunday mornings.

It was almost two hours later when they finally made it out and choosing to stay close to home, they set off on foot. Within a few moments they turned a corner and the quiet street that housed Dani's flat was replaced by a bustling Sunday market, full of bric-a-brac and strange items that at any other time would almost certainly be of no interest at all. But on a Sunday, when time lost all importance, there was no shortage of people who seemed happy to spend hours picking their way through the piles of random stuff, convinced that hidden amongst the rubbish would be something of great value.

Dani and Sean ambled their way through the crowds and headed for a café where their hunger was quickly satisfied by eggs, bacon and muffins and huge mugs of tea. When the plates had been cleared away, they sat for a moment, happy to just gaze at each other in contented silence. Sean felt as if he wanted to say something but could think of nothing but words that would sound horribly inadequate compared to the way he was feeling. He felt as if he had known Dani forever, as if he could tell her anything, as if he already knew that he never wanted to be parted from her. And yet despite all that, a simple, "Do you want anything else?" was all he could muster.

Dani smiled. "No thank you."

"Fancy a walk?"

Dani stood up and they wandered outside, squinting at the brightness of the afternoon. The streets were even busier now, the noise of chatter and laughter an assault on their ears after the relative calm of the café. Immediately taking control, Sean took hold of her hand and carefully led Dani back through the market towards home.

When Dani left for work the next morning, Sean was forced to leave with her, still half asleep and hoping to stay that way so he could go back to sleep the minute he reached his own flat. He was working that night and would no doubt be out late so would be glad of any extra sleep he could get. Dani kissed him as she got off the train, confident that he would be unconscious in minutes and finish up at the end of the line, miles away from anywhere. She smiled as she left him, unable to think of a better way to start the week than after such a magical weekend.

Feeling ready for anything, she breezed into the office and sailed through the morning. The first event on the agenda was a coffee with Dylan Kent, the journalist of

'Polly Potter's pregnant' fame. They were meeting in a café and he was late which Dani would normally have found really irritating but not today. At least when he arrived, he had the good grace to look like he'd been rushing to get to her. "Sorry Dani. Bloody Piccadilly Line."

"No problem. I'm sure an hour of your company will be well worth the wait." He smiled at her, immediately remembering why he so loved dealing with her as he ordered himself a well-needed extra-strong coffee. He was about to relax when Dani leaned forward with her most terrifying smile, one that Dylan knew only too well. He braced himself. "Let me ask you a question," she said. "When you were on the tube this morning, if a woman of Polly's size and shape had been standing in front of you, would you have offered her your seat?"

Dylan beamed. "Yes!"

"She's not pregnant!" Dani shouted at him.

Dylan's smile widened. "Says you."

"Because it's true, you completely annoying bastard!"

"You're forgetting you and I don't deal in truth."

"Speak for yourself! And I'm sure it would warm your editor's heart to hear you say that." Dylan shrugged. It was probably the most honest thing he'd ever said. Dani looked at him. "Why don't you go back to writing about the colour of her jumper every day? That was really gripping."

"It's been a slow couple of weeks, what can I tell you?" There was a momentary pause as Dylan waited.

"This is where you change all that by giving me something amazing to write about."

Dani looked away for a moment as if deciding whether or not to help him out. As always, it was very convincing. "How about I talk to Polly about a proper sit-down interview?" It had of course already been discussed and agreed with her. "Off the record for the moment, she's moving on to a lead role in a low-budget British film. Your eyes would water if I told you what we've turned down but she's not interested in cashing in. She wants to be challenged, wants the best scripts and that means sometimes saying no to the more obvious, commercial stuff. If we time it right, I could talk to the film people about announcing that as your hook." The reality was Polly was contractually obliged to do an interview so, rather than just give it away, Dani had seized on the opportunity to try to get Dylan off her back at the same time.

"Can we do a photo shoot?"

"I don't see why not." She had already warned Polly this would be an expected part of the deal.

"And this would be exclusive?"

"Yes. And you know this will be the first interview she's done in a very long while. And now there's a really great story to tell. Just don't expect her to talk about Harry."

"I'd have to ask."

"Ask what you like. I'm just telling you she won't talk about him. And, at the risk of telling you how to do

77

your job, perhaps you could slip in the fact that she's not actually pregnant!"

Dylan smiled. This was so much more than he had expected. "Well great, if you think you can sort it?"

"For you, Dylan, anything." Dani sat back, her eyes alive and sparkling.

"Cos you really screwed me over Jake and Damien. How could you give them both to Preston?" Dani raised her eyebrows. "No, don't answer that. All water under the bridge now," Dylan said quickly, shifting uncomfortably in his seat. He was horribly aware how quickly Dani might just snatch it all back.

Dani shook her head. "You're like overgrown school boys, the lot of you. Now sod off!"

By lunchtime, Dani was beginning to wonder why Sean hadn't called her. She had been so cool about everything, enjoying the way he had pursued her, the way he paid her so much attention, the way he had spent so much time trying to please her but, despite how close she already felt to him, she had to admit she didn't really know him. Everything had moved really fast and now they had slept together, the 'I can take it or leave it' attitude had been replaced with a strange feeling of nerves and a bizarre sense of paranoia. What if he never called again? What if sex was all he had wanted? Dani felt horribly deflated. A substitution had taken place. Off with the afterglow and on with a black cloud that shadowed her for the rest of the afternoon.

When she got home, Dani found it impossible to concentrate on anything and instead, opted for a hot, soothing bath and an early night. When her phone rang at half past ten, she was already in bed. "Hello?"

"Hi, it's me."

Dani smiled at the sound of his voice. "Where are you?"

"In town but I've finished earlier than I thought. What are you doing?"

"I'm in bed."

"Excellent. Stay right there and I'll be with you in half an hour."

Dani smiled, the afterglow already back off the substitute bench and warming up on the sidelines.

7

When Dani arrived at work a few blissful weeks later, there were already several cards and presents on her desk. She smiled, unable to stop the excitement that didn't seem to have faded with the passing years, as she set about ripping them open. Before she thought about doing any work, she picked up her phone to call Sean. He answered horribly out of breath and obviously running. "What on earth are you doing?"

"I just got a rare tip-off but I've got to get there quick." The words were gasped out amidst a great deal of huffing and puffing which made Dani smile.

"I was only returning your call. Try me again when you've done what you have to do." There was a pause as the grunting came to an abrupt end. "Sean?"

"Oh bollocks!" he yelled. "Bloody, sodding, bollocks!"

Dani laughed. "I take it they got away? So what was so urgent?"

Sean took a moment to catch his breath and then burst into a rather tuneless version of 'Happy Birthday to You'. Try as she might to stop him, he was not going to be interrupted until the final word had been sung. Dani only hoped no one else could hear him. She smiled. "Thank you. That was very moving."

"So how shall we celebrate?"

"Oh I don't know. What about dinner tonight?"

"You really know how to party don't you? Leave it to me. I'll pick you up at home at seven so make sure you leave on time. And wear something stunning that I can still easily get off you after several bottles of champagne."

Dani smiled. "See you later then."

The day just seemed to be getting better and better and it was still only nine thirty. Dani had spoken to Amanda and they made plans to go out the following night but the best news of all came from a message from Billy. He was finally moving down to London.

Billy was a friend from Dani's college days. It was one of those rare boy-girl friendships that had never been confused by sex. Neither was sure why, although it probably had a lot to do with Nick. Dani had been with Nick for the majority of her time at university and, when they split, Billy had been her crutch, her ear, her shoulder and the friend who slowly coaxed her out of the black hole she had subsequently dug herself into. The timing or opportunity had therefore never presented itself and the result was the most amazing and enviable relationship.

If there was one common theme professionally between Dani and Billy, it was their immense ability to negotiate but, while Dani's chosen commodity was people, Billy had built his equally revered reputation as a buyer with a major supermarket, negotiating the best deals on everything from tea to leafy salads and every other dietary necessity in between. He was charming

81

and fair but tough too and his colleagues respected him hugely. His rise through the ranks had subsequently been speedy and his latest reward was a new role as director of trading which would finally bring him to the Big Smoke. Dani had absolutely no idea what the job title meant but was suitably impressed nonetheless. Of far more interest to her was that he would once again be a physical presence in her life and not just a voice at the end of the phone. Dani dialled his number and waited.

"Billy that's fantastic news!"

"The move had to happen eventually and it's a great job, I never thought I'd get it for a minute. And now there's loads to do. First off, I've got to find a flat."

"Leave that one to me. I'll get some viewings set up and then I can make sure you end up living near me."

"Thanks, that would be a great help."

"So when do you start?"

"It's all been rushed through so two weeks and counting. You'd better get your skates on."

Dani replaced the handset slightly in shock. She couldn't think of anything better than having Billy close by but she hadn't even had the chance to tell him about Sean and that, more than anything, showed her how little time she'd had with her friends recently. No time to dwell on that now. "Come on gang, let's talk." Sammy and Toby immediately wheeled themselves across the office in their chairs until they were sitting opposite Dani across her desk, pads and pens at the ready.

"Me first!"

"Come on then Toby, make it a good one to get us started."

"Melody Bell's been in touch". Two blank faces looked back at him. "You know, the foxy one from one of those pretend reality shows." Still nothing. To be fair, his brief description did little to narrow it down. "Anyway, she wants to be an actress and wants us to represent her."

Dani grimaced. "We're good Toby, but not that good."

"My turn." As Sammy raised up her pad, Toby scribbled on his - 'roster full, couldn't give her the attention she deserves, WLE,' their shorthand for 'wish luck elsewhere'.

"The publicity people on Damien's film want a meeting. There's not much time in his diary between jobs so we'll need to be selective. And the team on Jake's project want to talk too."

"Okay, I'll cover Jake. We'll need to be really careful about what he does. Maybe just TV and radio and possibly a broadsheet if the PR team can pull it off, with a damage-limiting wide berth given to the tabloids. And definitely no live online chats. I'm not making that mistake again. But you do the Damien stuff." Sammy smiled, thrilled to be given the chance to go it alone.

Back to Toby. "As you've mentioned Jake, he's been asking about memberships to pretty much every club in London. What do I tell him?"

"If only it were possible to say no." Dani thought for a moment. "Pick the ones we know are discreet and convince him they're the only memberships worth having.

83

Then check his diary and book him a holiday with his family and book Miles to go with them. He can get some of those, 'ooh look, I've stumbled across Jake Peterson and he really is a family man after all' type pictures and we can enjoy looking at those for a change. How's Sienna getting on?"

Toby's face fell slightly. "Trouble brewing I'm afraid. It's the usual problem. Booked for her huge audience and natural, off-the-cuff, tell-it-how-it-is approach to make-up and now they're trying to script her. Standoff looming."

It had been Dani's idea that they should start representing social media stars. It had been a steep learning curve for them all but hugely rewarding financially. They were a feisty bunch, bringing with them a whole different set of challenges or problems, depending which way you looked at it.

"Okay. Get the number of the marketing client and I'll give them my 'how to get the best out of working with an influencer' speech." Back to Sammy. "What about Polly?"

"Harry's packing his bags as we speak and she's in pieces. We haven't had any calls about the state of their relationship for a few weeks but it would be naive to think the vultures aren't circling. Her play's still got a week to run so she can't hide away. How can we help her?"

Dani's distress was immediately obvious. "I can't bear it. We've said it a million times before but I'll never be comfortable with people like Polly having to have their personal tragedies serialised in the bloody Daily Mail. Let's just be grateful we got Dylan's piece done and out before this happened." She thought for a moment. "So do we take a pre-emptive strike and make an announcement or hope no one notices, even just for a while, to give her some time?"

Sammy hesitated for a moment. "You could ask Sean if he's heard anything? Chances are even if it's not the type of picture he would go for, he'll know if someone else is lurking?"

Dani's face hardened. "Yes, I could ask. Leave it with me. Okay, are we done?"

A cloud of tension hovered uncomfortably and, without a word, Sammy and Toby retreated to their respective desks, Sammy wondering if she'd just committed a faux pas of epic proportion. Dani started moving stuff around on her desk but she wasn't actually looking at anything. She wasn't sure yet if she was really angry or if she wanted to cry, with neither emotion currently making any sense. Her head was buzzing but the only clear thought was a question - how the hell was she going to keep her relationship with Sean and her work separate? She had no right to ask him for favours. She had no right to stop him taking pictures of someone just because it might give her another fire to fight but what about other agents in the office? They would be delighted if a harmless picture made the papers and furious if a picture of his exposed a wrong doing or caused embarrassment. Would they all now be thinking Sean was controllable? Would Dani's reputation be damaged when they realised he wasn't? It was a horrible situation to find herself in and Dani had no idea what to do about it. Actually, yes she did. She would enjoy her birthday and worry about it tomorrow.

When Sean arrived promptly at seven o'clock, Dani was waiting for him, wearing an incredibly simple dark red dress that skimmed her figure and flowed down to just below her knees. She opened the door to find him in his traditional black and her stomach did a perfect somersault. She smiled at him. "You look gorgeous!"

"Aren't I supposed to say that to you?" He kissed her instead and immediately woke up the now resident butterflies in her stomach.

"Are you ready then?"

"I'll just get my coat."

"Did I tell you to pack a bag?"

Dani swung round, her mouth open. "No you didn't!"

"Oops! Well you don't need much - certainly no PJs, just something to wear to work tomorrow."

"Are you serious?"

"Yes I am! You didn't really think I wouldn't plan something a little bit special did you? Especially as I couldn't be with you this morning." Dani remained glued to the spot. "Well hurry up or we'll be late!"

Sean drove them an hour or so out of town and Dani watched as the endless rows of houses were finally replaced by wider, open spaces. The seemingly endless high-rise buildings gave way to lush green fields and trees that were weighted down with thick, pink blossom. She watched the sun begin its descent beyond the horizon, its heat already surrendered to the cool, spring evening while a voice on the radio chatted away in the background, the words and intermittent music washing over her in a blissful blur.

Just as she was beginning to wonder where on earth Sean was taking her, he turned off the main road and ten minutes later, was pulling up in front of a beautiful old hotel. Completely spellbound, she followed him into the reception area and then on into the most fabulous bedroom, dominated by a huge bed. Pushing open two doors, she then found herself on a balcony and out in the cool night air. She smiled at the sight of the hotel lights reflected in the river below, just feet away from where she stood. Suddenly Sean was beside her and taking her hand, he led her back inside. "Tempting as I know it is to just stay in here all evening, there's a table waiting for us. But I have something for you first."

Dani watched as Sean pulled a beautifully wrapped square shaped present out of his pocket and handed it to her. She removed the paper to reveal a small presentation box, inside which was the most stunning pair of diamond earrings, as simple as they were elegant.

"They're beautiful," she gasped. "Thank you!"

"You really like them?"

"Of course!" Dani was already in front of a mirror, putting them into her ears and then she stood back to fully admire them, Sean now beside her. "They're perfect," she said as she reached up to kiss him.

"Come on, let's eat," he said as he encouraged her away, relieved that his gift had been so well received.

They headed downstairs where champagne and the most amazing meal waited. In their usual fashion they chatted and laughed their way through three delightful courses, completely oblivious to those around them - a room full of people who looked on in envy at this striking couple, so in tune with one another, so happy and so charged with sexual energy.

When they got back to their room, Sean turned to look at Dani. "So, was my wish granted I wonder?" He watched as Dani stepped out of her shoes and then slipped the straps of her dress off her shoulders. It slithered to the floor and he smiled as he slipped his arm around her waist. The heat of his hand on her bare skin sent a shiver rippling through her body, the warmth creeping up around her neck, making her breathing quicken. She was unable to speak, choosing instead to simply surrender to the intoxicating desire that was about to completely overwhelm her.

As Dani and Sean drove back into London the next morning, the last twenty-four hours felt like a dream. They sat in a wonderfully contented silence, both bursting with a potent mixture of love, lust, excitement and genuine happiness, all coated with the glorious fuzziness of just a little too much champagne. It was a bubble worth preserving but Dani knew she had to talk about work, a reluctant verbal pin at the ready. "Harry's finally leaving Polly." Dani held her breath as she watched for a reaction but, with his eyes firmly on the road ahead, it was hard to gauge what Sean was thinking.

"She's better off without him. He's a shit." Couldn't really argue with that. He wasn't exactly a model boyfriend. Dani waited. She had hoped he would volunteer something more but nothing was forthcoming. She would just have to take the direct route.

"Do potential conflicts of interest between us worry you?"

"It's not something I've really thought about."

"What if you'd heard about Harry moving out? What if you'd got pictures of him leaving their home with suitcases and boxes? Would you tell me or just let me see your name credited alongside the published pictures?"

Sean looked genuinely unsure as he processed the questions. He had meant it when he said it wasn't something he'd given even the briefest consideration. "I really don't know. It's not really me to go chasing that kind of picture. You know most of my stuff is done through agents and publicists with just the odd little surprise snap when no one's looking!"

Those were exactly the ones she was terrified of. "But if it was, what would you do?"

"What would you expect me to do?"

Dani sighed. "I don't know. I wish we didn't even have to talk about it but I think we do. Honestly, I'd expect you to do whatever you would have done before we got together. Doesn't mean I wouldn't be seriously pissed off though."

Sean smiled. "But you'll also know about stuff that I'd definitely want to snap and won't tell me either so it works both ways doesn't it?"

"That's obviously different."

"Obviously!" he laughed.

So it looked like there couldn't be any boundaries and they simply had to carry on regardless but Dani wasn't quite done. "So, with Polly, is it okay for me to ask if you know Harry leaving is likely to be snapped? And if I asked and you didn't know so I end up telling you and it was a picture you wanted, would you then go and take it yourself?"

"Bloody hell Dani!"

Dani's expression perfectly captured her agonising frustration. "I know, I'm sorry but this is really important to me. Word's getting out we're together and I need to be confident about what it means at work."

Sean exhaled loudly as he tried to work through the moral dilemma presented to him. "No, I hadn't heard Harry was moving out and if you inadvertently told me about something of course I wouldn't then stitch you up. I kind of hoped you would know that already." Dani winced as he continued. "And you can ask me whatever you like and if I can help I will. How's that?" She smiled and squeezed his leg.

"Perfect, thank you."

"And great to know I can therefore ask you about your people and know you'll share too."

"Not a chance."

Sean laughed, expecting nothing less and loving the steely determination in Dani's eyes as he glanced over at her but, as he turned his attention back to the rush hour traffic ahead, he missed her shift uncomfortably in her seat. There was a sadness hidden in her eyes that he couldn't possible have seen. She had got what she wanted but she still felt uncomfortable. She had wanted openness and honesty and was quietly devastated that it felt like anything but. It was openness but through a filter and, while it was the best she could have hoped for, that didn't make it feel any less sullied.

When an hour later Dani was comfortably back at her desk, she was delighted that her loved-up, champagne-infused bubble was still intact. Without exception, everyone who passed her desk, stopped to comment on Dani's appearance. Had she changed her hair? Was that a new jacket? No one could quite put their finger on it but, despite that, a significant change had clearly happened. Dani smiled to herself, aware that she had the answer. She was absolutely and totally in love and it felt fantastic.

Deciding she might as well put her unexpected effervescence to good use, she threw herself into her work and the morning flew past in the usual flurry of meetings, frantic phone calls and email writing. She had a quick lunch with a magazine journalist just to keep in touch, which was a far less stressful relationship than she enjoyed with her tabloid pack, and was back in time for a meeting with a producer about plans for a major new television drama. He only had eyes for Damien and had wanted to meet face to face to make sure his desire to bag him was unmistakably clear.

"So what did Damien think of the script?" Rob Baker was one of the good guys. Full of talent and integrity, his list of TV and film credits read like a permanent nomination list for the BAFTAs.

Dani smiled. "He thought it was great. As always, it will no doubt come down to timing."

"We can be flexible to a degree." There was a pause and then Rob smiled. He'd been round the block enough times to know if he wanted the best, he was going to have to at least audition a lesser known actor for one of the smaller parts. "Come on then, who else should I be looking at?"

Dani immediately opened her large notebook and pulled out a CV and photo of Dave.

"Well as you've asked, I thought Dave would be great for the part of Seymour. Worth your casting team meeting him, don't you think?" Dani was confident Dave would be great and he both needed and deserved his break. She simply wouldn't be doing her job if she didn't take advantage of Damien's current prominence. Dave would do the same for him if roles were reversed. He might not know it, but he definitely would.

"Sure, why not?" Rob wasn't one for unnecessary game playing and he trusted Dani not to waste his time. If Dave turned out to be right for the role then great, if not, he had really lost nothing. "And Damien?"

"I'm sure we can work it out. He's really keen to work with you and provided his current project doesn't run over, we should be okay with your preferred dates. I'll make sure you know as early as possible if that changes."

Rob stood up. "Thanks Dani. I'm delighted."

Dani took his hand. "Thanks for coming in. And for being so accommodating." She was of course talking about Dave.

Dani headed back to her desk thinking what a really pleasant change it was to have such a civilised meeting. It was surprisingly reassuring to know that it was indeed possible. With Damien sorted, she turned her attention to Polly. A decision needed to be made within the next hour or so on whether they would leak the split so it was out there, or just keep quiet. She called Sammy over and asked for an update.

"Harry left last night as discreetly as possible. Although I'm not sure how achievable that was ever going to be when you're clearly exiting a building carrying your worldly possessions."

Dani thought for a moment. "I don't think anyone knows." Sammy decided not to ask how as Dani continued. "So I think we leave it. Hopefully it'll be a few weeks before Harry's spotted out on the town on his own by which point we'll have a chance of passing it off as old news. Dylan's piece has already run and I just don't think we should risk drawing attention to her. It'll just give journos the perfect excuse to rake up all the old reports of affairs while it's still so raw. Once her play's finished, perhaps she should take a holiday? If we then feel we have to say something, at least she'll be out of the country. What do you think?"

"Sounds like a plan to me. I'll go speak to her."

Working on overdrive and with more energy than she had had for months, Dani was on a high. She had barely looked at her watch all day and was only aware that it was time to call it a night when Amanda arrived.

"Come on you bloody workaholic, I need to eat!"

Dani looked at her desk and then hesitated for just a second before she picked up her jacket and quickly walked away. It would all still be there in the morning.

They set off for a nearby Italian restaurant where the food was fast and delicious and the atmosphere lively without making conversation impossible. As soon as they were seated, Amanda reached into her bag and produced a beautifully wrapped present.

"Here you go," she said as she handed it over. "Happy birthday!" Dani beamed as she took the parcel, quickly opening it to reveal a beautiful evening bag. "It's vintage. I hope you like it."

"Like it? I love it! Your presents are always the best."

"So come on then, I want all the details on Sean." She waited while Dani thought for a moment.

"He's amazing. He's attentive, he's kind, he's funny. Gorgeous looking, obviously. And he buys expensive gifts." She pulled back her hair to reveal her newly acquired diamonds.

"For fuck's sake."

"Well you asked!"

"Yeah maybe but now I wish I hadn't."

Amanda had never been short of admirers and over the years had had a series of dalliances. They never lasted long enough to qualify as a relationship which was always her choice. She enjoyed having someone around for a while but as soon as it started to feel like something that required real investment, her interest inevitably waned. It was never a big deal. Amanda remained convinced that she simply hadn't met the right person for her and, when she did, which she believed she would at some point, everything would be different.

"It's got to be my turn soon," she said. "Maybe he's here tonight?" Amanda looked around the busy restaurant and shrugged. "I guess not. So what about Alex? You won't be hooking up with him again, right?"

"No, things are different now." Amanda watched Dani closely, aware that not for the first time recently, Dani was suddenly unable to look her in the eye. She waited, allowing an agonising silence to infest their conversation, determined that the next words spoken would be from Dani. "It is, it's different, honestly." Unconvincing didn't come close.

"Well in that case I'll spare you the pigs might fly routine but only 'cos you're my best friend."

"Alex, hi it's Dani. I have good news. You got the part."

"Yes!"

Dani couldn't help but smile at his obvious excitement but her feelings were mixed. She and Sean had hardly been apart since that first lunch which was over two months ago now and she had never been happier. It had been more than enough time for her to completely fall in love with him and for Alex to finish his latest project and be back in her life, relying on her to find something else to take up his time. She was in no doubt about the strength of her feelings for Sean and yet, despite that, there was something so potent about this man's voice, so hypnotic almost, that she couldn't prevent a seed of excitement growing inside her at the thought of seeing him again.

"They want to have a read through almost straight away so you'll need to come to London for a couple of days."

"Fine by me. You'll let me know where I'm staying?"

"Yes of course." There was a pause.

"That's it then is it?"

"For now."

Despite the obvious brush off and a certain coolness to the exchange, neither seemed able to hang up. It was Alex who finally decided to take the plunge. "So, how are you?"

"I'm really well thank you. What about you?" The formality was bordering on the ridiculous. There was another pause and then Alex decided he couldn't stand it any longer.

"Look, I know this is a difficult situation for lots of reasons but I've missed you and I can't think of a reason not to tell you as much."

Dani hesitated. "I can think of several."

"Too late. I said it already."

Dani swivelled around in her chair to face the window, aware that she was in an open office with a permanent gentle breeze from all the flapping ears. She lowered her voice. "What are we supposed to do? I'm your agent and I have to be able to think rationally about decisions I make on your behalf. You're married and say you want to keep it that way…"

"Oh stop, you're depressing me."

"I'm only telling you what we both already know."

"Yes but you're choosing to leave out one vital element. You know there's something there, something between us that we may try to pretend doesn't exist but it does. And no amount of practical talking is going to change that."

Dani thought for a moment. She felt trapped on a roundabout that was spinning out of control. The question was, did she have the courage to risk injury and jump off? "This is getting us nowhere. I'll see you next week and we'll talk about it then."

"Have dinner with me on Monday night when I arrive?"

"Fine. I'll call you later in the week when I've booked a hotel for you."

Dani replaced the handset with a sigh. How ironic, she thought, that Alex and Billy would arrive in town within a matter of days of each other. Which reminded her. She had a flat to find.

By the time the weekend and Billy arrived, Dani had details on six flats all within walking distance of her own. Naturally Billy was happy to take the first one he saw but Dani insisted on seeing them all, just to be on the safe side. Several hours and much grumbling later, he hadn't changed his mind. A call to the appropriate agent and a flurry of emails and online transactions and everything was arranged. With some necessary and effective sweet-talking, Billy would move in the following Saturday.

At six o'clock, they finally sat down for a drink in a small bar a stroll away from Billy's new front door and only a short walk from her own.

"So this will be my local? Not bad I suppose." He yawned loudly. "I'm knackered. Think of the time we'd have saved if you'd just let me go with my instinct."

"Stop complaining. At least now you know you made the right decision. Otherwise, you might always have wondered."

"Believe me, I wouldn't have."

Dani smiled. "You are such a miserable bastard! But it's still great to have you here. I've missed not having you around."

"At least I can keep an eye on you now. Make sure you don't get yourself into any unsavoury situations. Assuming you're aren't already in one?"

"I'm in a wonderful situation thank you. I met my perfect man. You should come over for dinner next weekend once you're here to stay and meet him. I'll ask Amanda as well."

He sat back in his chair. "How quickly things change. And here was me thinking you'd be totally wrapped up in Alex and in need of a serious talking to. I prefer it this way."

Dani looked at him. "Yeah, so do I. You'll really like Sean."

"I'd like another drink more!" Dani shook her head at him in mock despair as she accepted her cue and went in search of refills.

Two days later, Dani sat in a hotel foyer in a carefully chosen spot so she would see Alex before he saw her. She was working on the assumption that her immediate reaction on seeing him would determine exactly how much trouble she was in and in her current position she would be able to recover, if necessary, before walking over to greet him.

Oh dear God am I in trouble, she thought, her heart going into a monumental spin as she watched Alex step out of the revolving doors. And he was on time. It was getting worse by the minute. Get a grip, she urged herself, for God's sake get a grip! A thin film of sweat broke out on her palms and she felt physically sick. Meanwhile, valuable seconds were ticking by. As Dani stood up, Alex immediately headed towards her, his smile growing with every step until he was standing in front of her. "Hello stranger."

"Hi," was all she could manage as they stood there, eyes locked. For a moment, neither said a word until Alex decided it was up to him to take control. "I'll just go and check in and then….."

"Then we can have dinner," Dani shot in. "I booked us a table in the restaurant. I hope that was okay?"

Alex smiled at her. "Sure. I'll be back in a minute."

Dani was relieved they were given a quiet table away from the masses where conversation would be easier. It was hard to explain but as she watched him browse the menu, nothing else, indeed nobody else, seemed to exist. How does he do that? she wondered. How does he just walk in and take such control?

"Dani?" She hadn't realised Alex was talking to her. "Is everything all right?" She had been staring somewhere in space, a slightly pained and anxious look on her face.

"Yes, of course." She did her best to produce a relaxed, nonchalant smile. "I'm just deciding what to have."

Alex continued to watch her and felt his stomach tighten. She looked uneasy but was trying so hard to looked poised and in control. Her obvious vulnerabilities just heightened the attraction, a side to her that he knew many never saw. She was undoubtedly a tough negotiator, a claim firmly substantiated by his latest contract but looking at her now, he found it almost impossible to imagine her around a table, taking command of proceedings, striking deals and making demands until she got what she wanted. As the familiar smell of her perfume slowly drifted across the table, he felt his breathing quicken. He had been so busy but she had never been far from his thoughts. He had missed her in a way he had never expected to.

The waiter arrived to take their order and then they were alone again. "So, are you ready for tomorrow?" Dani decided it was her turn to get the polite conversation rolling.

"I guess so. I've read the script anyway. That's always a good start!"

"I'm sure you'll be fine."

Alex watched her look nervously around the room. "Dani, this is ridiculous!" She looked at him, her cheeks lightly dusted with an obvious glow of embarrassment. "Are we just going to chat politely all night, like strangers?" She said nothing. "I mean, it wasn't all that long ago that we were in bed together! If it was a mistake then at least let's talk about it. Anything but this bizarre civility."

"Is that what it was? A mistake?"

"You know I don't think that!" There was a rawness in Alex's eyes and the intensity of his stare held Dani with such a fierceness, she felt momentarily suspended in time. "I just don't feel in a position to apply any pressure. You know if I had my way we'd be upstairs now."

"So it's all up to me is it? I have to decide where we go from here? That hardly seems fair."

Alex looked at her, aware that with every word spoken he was getting closer to his imaginary thin line. A line he had drawn up as some kind of naive protection that signified the difference between a degree of safety and that slippery slope to emotional involvement. "None of this is fair! We just have to talk about it and see whether or not we can find a way of doing this that works for you. Like I said, I'm not really in a position to make demands."

Dani thought for a moment. If they were baring their souls then she might as well be completely honest. "Something's changed." She fidgeted slightly. "I'm seeing someone."

Alex was distracted momentarily by a noise and quickly realised it was his heart hitting the floor. No, this wasn't supposed to happen! He wasn't supposed to feel anything! She'd pushed him over the line! Oh no! He sat back in his chair, an air of resignation suddenly surrounding him. I've fallen in love with her, he thought. Fuck. "I see."

Dani watched him carefully. "You see? That's it?"

Alex's slick exterior started to show its first crack. "Jesus, what do you want me to say? How dare you? How dare you see another man when you've been sleeping with me? I have a wife for Christ's sake! I can hardly demand exclusivity can I?" Alex had raised his voice a little louder than he had meant to. A fact he assumed as he watched Dani squirm in her seat, her eyes frantically flitting around to see if anyone was watching them. Meanwhile, her mind was a mass of static, the sparks flying. She had never wanted to believe that lust was his only driving force and now she knew. Alex really cared. He couldn't demand exclusivity but she knew he wanted to.

"It's serious. I may never have another chance like this and you've always made it clear you're not available. What was I supposed to do?"

Alex rubbed his forehead. "I know, I know. I can't have my cake and eat it and have seconds and then still expect more." He looked up and they attempted to smile at each other for the first time in a while, cheeks pushing against an overwhelming feeling of sadness.

Dinner arrived and brought with it a forced reprise. For some reason, talking about nothing in particular was once again possible with a plate of food in front of them and then all too soon, the coffee arrived and the tension returned along with it. They were now moments away from a rather crucial decision. "So are you expected home tonight?"

"I said I was seeing someone, not living with them. And why does whether I go up to your room or not have to depend on someone else? Why can't you just ask me?"

Alex looked at her, terrified and excited all at the same time. He took a deep breath. "Okay. Dani, will you come upstairs with me?"

"Yes I will."

8

Dani had been seeing Sean for a matter of months and already she had been unfaithful. It really was quite unthinkable but as dinner was in danger of being ready hours late, not to mention the fact that she hadn't yet showered or changed, she perhaps conveniently decided that this really wasn't the time to be dwelling on the fact.

She had left Alex in the early hours of the morning. When they'd reached his room, no more discussion had taken place. There had been no more debate about whether they should or shouldn't indulge in another wild session of uninhibited lovemaking. The moment the door was closed behind them, they had been in each other's arms, barely able to get their clothes off quickly enough, so overtaken were they with.....what exactly? With passion? Love? Lust? It really made no difference. Whatever it was, it was so all-consuming that for those initial mad moments, they didn't even make it to the bed. Sex somewhere between the bathroom and the main expanse of the room had only marked the beginning. It was several hours later before she had finally found herself able to leave.

It wasn't until she had returned to the normality of her desk the next day that she had realised something truly astonishing. She had felt all morning as if something wasn't right. Like an annoying itch that won't be sated, the feeling churned inside her, increasingly irritating her until finally the light bulb moment arrived. There was no guilt. She spoke to Sean and laughed with him as she always did, arranging to see him that night. She continued to smile long after she had hung up, believing that he represented what was real in her life, while Alex was something completely separate. She loved Sean, it was that simple, while Alex had her locked in some kind of spell and, while she continued to think of it that way, believing Alex's hold on her was out of her control, she gave herself the perfect excuse not to have to explain it further.

"Dani, for God's sake, they'll be here in half an hour!"

It was Saturday and Dani was losing control of her well-planned dinner party and it hadn't even started.

"It's all going wrong!" she despaired. "Perhaps we should go out for dinner?"

Sean took hold of her by her shoulders and kissed her. He felt the tension slowly slip away and then relieved her of the wooden spoon in her hand. "Right, leave it to me and please go and get ready!"

When Billy arrived, Dani had been ready for exactly two seconds. She threw her arms round him and for the first time felt a pang of something and tears briefly stung her eyes. While she had managed to successfully compartmentalise her relationship with Sean and her affair with Alex, bizarrely it seemed incredibly cheap to be deceiving her best friend. Supreme honesty between them was something she had always cherished.

"Hello neighbour!" she beamed, pulling herself together as she took his arm and led him into the lounge. She shouted for Sean who emerged from the kitchen looking slightly harassed. Billy smiled.

"You must be Sean. Unless Dani's done us all a favour and hired a chef for the evening?"

Sean smiled back and put out a hand. "Right first time I'm afraid. It's good to meet you Billy."

Billy took his hand warmly. "You too. And far be it from me to spout clichés within minutes of meeting you but I've heard so much about you I feel like I know you already."

"Likewise. Perhaps we should compare notes? What about a drink first?"

"Great, a beer if you have one."

And with that they continued to chat, oblivious to Dani, who was feeling immediately superfluous to the proceedings, watching on from the sidelines. Keen to appear useful, she disappeared off to the kitchen where everything seemed to be back on track and then Amanda arrived.

Dani heard her chatting with the boys and then did a double take as Amanda finally came looking for her in the kitchen. Amanda was well-known for her individual style. If she wore orange, you could bet it would be the brightest orange you had ever seen. If her lipstick was red, you could guarantee it would be deeper and richer and more striking than any shade you'd ever tried. Her legs were longer, her laugh louder, her hair wilder and yet tonight, everything was different. Her long red hair was pulled back into a smooth ponytail, her make-up was positively minimal and her clothes were simple and subtle.

"Bloody hell, what happened to you?"

"What do you mean?" Amanda said, her look suggesting she was unsure whether to be concerned or insulted.

"Did your mother finally get her way? No, I know, aliens snatched the old Amanda on the way here and replaced her with a new one!"

Amanda looked confused. "What on earth are you talking about?" She picked up an almost empty bottle of wine. "Did you drink all this already?"

"Look at you! You look fantastic!"

Amanda definitely now looked hurt. "Don't I always?"

"You know what I mean. You look different, that's all. I really like it."

Amanda relaxed with a smile. "Okay, so I decided it was time for a change of image. Time to calm things down, show off the more mature me."

As Dani struggled to find a suitable response, Billy appeared at the door. "This was meant to be a dinner party wasn't it? Or was that just some kind of joke?"

"Meaning?"

"Meaning I'm starving!"

"Relax, everything's ready."

Billy looked at Amanda for a moment. "Did I tell you how great you look tonight?"

"Yes you did," she said with a faint blush.

"Not that you don't always look great, it's just I haven't seen you for a while and I remember you differently."

Amanda moved a little closer. "Well that depends how close you were looking."

Billy smiled. "Not close enough, obviously."

Dani looked on in amazement, aware of a horrible sinking feeling. "Do you mind? I'd like to at least get some food inside me before I contemplate being sick, if it's not too much to ask? Go and sit down."

And so began hours of eating, chatting and general merriment. The conversation flowed freely and naturally with Sean providing great entertainment as always with his endless tales of chasing celebrities and showbiz parties.

"Don't you ever feel responsible if bad stuff happens on the back of your pictures?" Sean smiled at Billy. It was a question he'd been asked many times.

"The short answer is no, I don't. The truth is the majority of it's set up. How many times have you seen a celeb seemingly photographed without their knowledge, working out in some skimpy get-up with rolls of flab on show? And then a few months later, there's the fitness DVD showing how you too can go from flab to fab with just one small purchase." He shrugged. "It's business. In your world, if you want to push a product you stick it somewhere where it can't be missed, or lower the price to encourage folk to buy it. If Dani has someone with a TV show to promote, she shoves them out there in exactly the same way."

Billy looked at Dani with a playful smile. "Ruthless bitch."

She raised her glass by way of acceptance. "Although to be fair, I spend a fair amount of my time trying to keep people out of the papers."

"I guess so." Billy seemed unconvinced, unable to quite see how you could lump together a living breathing human with a stack of breakfast cereal you needed to shift but Sean was warm and infectious and Billy had no desire to push what he genuinely thought was a fascinating subject and risk offending.

As the evening progressed, it was becoming increasingly obvious that Billy and Amanda really liked Sean, although Dani was starting to think they liked each other more and if she was honest, she wasn't exactly sure how she felt about it. After all, Billy was her soul mate. They had been friends for years now and he knew absolutely everything about her, including stuff on Amanda. And what of Amanda? They'd known each other even longer. They were like sisters but if tonight was anything to go by, Billy and Amanda would soon know each other better than she knew either of them.

"Earth to Dani, come in please!" Dani dragged herself back to the moment and realised there were three faces staring at her. "Are you with us?"

"Sorry, I was miles away."

"So we noticed. She was always doing this you know Sean. Every lecture I ever went to with Dani, she was

109

always off somewhere, paying no attention whatsoever. I'm sure the only reason she became my friend was to get access to my pristine notes!"

Dani's face immediately elongated, eyebrows shooting up as her jaw simultaneously dropped, her eyes widening in the process. "As if anyone is going to believe that! If you hadn't copied every word I ever wrote, you'd still be there now doing retakes."

"How dare you!" The others laughed as Billy managed to look both hurt and outraged, a wicked glint in his eyes. He declared a silent war and turned to Sean. "Do you know, when we were at college Dani was so uptight you wouldn't believe it."

"I was not!" Dani objected firmly. "I went there to learn and worked hard." She shrugged. "What's wrong with that?" Billy and Amanda looked at each other and smiled. "Okay, stop right there!" Dani was keen to make sure this didn't escalate into a 'who has the most embarrassing or insulting story to tell about Dani' competition. "I knew it was a mistake getting you two here together."

"Believe me, it was the best decision you've made in a long time." As Billy continued to smile at Amanda, Dani was convinced that some unsavoury touching and fondling was now going on under the table. "Now I am going to be sick," she said as she stood up. "Would anyone like some coffee? Go and sit in the lounge and I'll bring it in," she said without waiting for an answer.

Sean hung back as Billy and Amanda did as they were told and then felt Dani relax as he folded his arms

110

around her. "They're only playing", he said. "It's been a great evening. I really like them both. And they obviously like each other. I thought they already knew each other?"

"They've probably met half a dozen times in as many years, that's all."

"Well I think this could be the start of something. You may soon be adding matchmaker to your list of skills."

Dani watched him disappear to join the others with a frown slapped all over her face, failing to see why this was something she should be celebrating.

It was another few hours before Billy and Amanda finally left - together. Dani was sure they wouldn't get further than Billy's flat as it was decidedly nearer. She felt strangely lonely as she watched them go, hoping this didn't mean she'd lost even just the smallest part of her two best friends. The part that was exclusive to her, the part she could tell anything without fear of it becoming dinner table chatter, or pillow talk for that matter. She sighed and turned her attention instead to the debris they had left behind them, glad to have something else to concentrate her mind on for the time being at least.

The next morning, Sean was up and out early. He had heard that Selfridges was opening specially for an American visitor. He didn't know who but with that kind of influence, it had to be someone huge. Dani, meanwhile, had arranged to have a relaxed Sunday brunch with Billy in a nearby café. When he arrived shortly after her, she couldn't help noticing how particularly tired he looked.

"I wasn't sure whether to increase the booking to three?"

He kissed her and smiled as he sat down. "Is that something they teach you? That art women seem to have of putting together a few well-chosen words and say them in a way that could cut stone?"

Dani raised her eyebrows. "I don't know what you mean?"

"You could just ask the question?"

"I did ask you a question."

Billy took a sip of the coffee Dani had already ordered for him, knowing that he always needed time and plenty of caffeine to wake up on Sundays before he could contemplate food. He laid the cup down and looked at her. "In order to speed this up a little, yes Amanda did spend the night with me, yes we did have sex, yes I am very happy about it and yes, we will be seeing each other again."

Dani forced an unconvincing smile. "Well obviously. I merely wondered if she would be joining us."

Billy laughed. "You're unbelievable! No, she's gone home. She didn't want to intrude."

"Well I'm sure that won't last. I'd better enjoy you while I still can."

Dani picked up the menu and hid behind it, aware that her last comment had been edged with something slightly unpleasant. Something that Billy felt he just couldn't ignore. "Meaning what exactly?"

"Meaning nothing. What are you going to have?"

"Dani come on! I thought you'd be happy for us?"

You just have no idea do you, she thought? No idea at all. No conception of what this will mean to us, of the change that is now inevitable. How much time will need to pass before meeting alone is just completely unacceptable, she wondered? Before there's no such thing as Billy, only Billy and Amanda? Billy pulled the menu away from her face. "Dani? Talk to me!"

Dani smiled. "Sorry I was miles away. What were we talking about?" she said, hoping that he might already have forgotten.

Billy looked throughly bemused. "Amanda, I think we were talking about Amanda."

"She knows we used to share a bed, you know. She's probably at home now wondering if we ever actually slept together, if we're still sleeping together."

Dani was horribly aware that her eyes had filled with tears and that Billy was looking more and more con-fused. "What on earth are you talking about? Maybe I missed something. Did I miss something?"

Only the blatantly bloody obvious, she thought. "No, just ignore me. I drank too much coffee that's all. Let's order."

9

Monday morning and it was raining. The truly miserable, relentless kind that felt like it would never stop. Hard, therefore, for Dani to claim she was being followed by a black cloud as everyone around her was in the same boat, or perhaps ark would be more appropriate. The pavement was crowded, an uneven ceiling of umbrellas making it necessary to perpetually dodge and weave to avoid losing an eye. Her hands were wet and numb with cold, her trousers damp around the ankles and she could feel her hair taking on that unattractive fluffiness synonymous with soft, drizzly rain. Great.

Dani speeded up, the office door now almost in front of her and then just as she reached it, a large obstacle appeared in her way in the shape of Steve Preston. He held out a coffee with a smile as she stepped into the covered doorway, forced to stand uncomfortably close to her nemesis. It seemed a small price to pay to finally be out of the rain. "What do you want?" she snapped.

"I bought you coffee."

"I have one already," she said, holding up the cup in her hand.

"Well have another."

Dani hesitated and then decided the easiest option was just to take it. "Thanks," and taking the coffee, she disappeared through the door with Steve hot on her heels.

"Dani, wait!"

Dani stopped and turned to face him. "Oh I'm sorry. Was there something else?" She smiled at him but only with irritation and then waited, her eyes full of warning that she really wasn't in the mood for games.

"Look, I'm here to help." Dani's eyebrows shot up her forehead until they almost merged with her hairline, proof if it were needed that she found his claim just a little hard to believe. "I'm on my way to interview Harry. Some pictures came in last night of him looking all loved up with the singer, Melanie James. At least I think she's a singer? Anyway, he's agreed to do a full chat about his relationship with Polly and all the affairs, and why he's now a changed man since meeting Melanie."

"How lovely. I'm sure his sincerity will be truly heartwarming."

Steve put out his arm to prevent Dani walking away. "So what about Polly? I thought she might like the chance to respond, put her side of the story forward?"

Dani felt her shoulders slump slightly, pulled down by her slowly sinking heart. It was inevitable of course that this would happen so there was little point shooting the messenger, however satisfying it would be to vent her frustration on the man in front of her.

Her face softened. "I do appreciate the opportunity but the answer's no. Let Harry do what he's got to do but Polly won't be fuelling the fire."

"I'll be really sensitive, I promise. I like her. I just want to give her the chance to redress the balance."

"If you mean it when you say you like her then leave her alone and respect her right to some privacy. She's just trying to do a job she loves and she's happy to do press when she has a project to talk about but she's not interested in the rest of it. I know that's frustrating for you but that's just the way it is."

Steve shrugged. "Fair enough. I'll just say she declined to comment."

Dani attempted a more friendly smile. "Thanks for the coffee." And she quickly turned and walked away.

"See you soon," Steve shouted after her.

"Not if I see you first," she shouted back without turning around.

As Dani walked through the office, Sammy scurried up beside her. "Did I just see Steve Preston leaving the building?"

"Indeed you did. Is Polly going on holiday?"

"Yes, in two days."

"Bring it forward. Try to get her away today. Harry's going to be all over the papers tomorrow which means it'll kick off online tonight."

Sammy took off. "I'm on it. Fucking shitbag."

Dani took a swig of her coffee. "My thoughts exactly," she said, not sure to which shitbag Sammy was referring and caring not.

Discarding as many soggy items as possible, Dani headed straight for Bernie's weekly meeting where all the key agents got together to update and share. It was a bore but obligatory so, as she regularly reminded herself, there was little point bitching about it, however compelled she felt to do so.

Seven other equally damp people trooped into the company's boardroom - Bernie, his business partner Sarah Stacey and five other agents, all responsible for their own pool of talent. With boring, weekly monotony, each took their turn with a quick overview of what they and their clients were up to, with longer time spent on any issues that would benefit from input from around the table. Over time, Dani had perfected the ability to listen with one ear (she had been caught out once not paying any attention at all and was never going to let that happen again), allowing her the freedom to simultaneously review her notes, update her to-do list or think about what she and Sean might have for dinner, whatever seemed most pressing on the day.

All was going pretty much to plan until it was Hannah's turn. Everything about Hannah was hard - her face, her voice, her wiry body, her attitude. Dani didn't know her very well but what she did know, quite frankly she didn't like very much. Hannah kicked off with one of her biggest actors who had battled an alcohol problem for years. He was recently out of rehab (and not for the first time) which had been well documented, only to be snapped in a bar drinking shots looking anything but sober. The offending pictures were now scattered through the morning's tabloids. "The producers of his next film have been in touch questioning whether he's up to the job and his wife has well and truly had enough and is threatening to leave

117

him," Hannah announced to the group, clearly not very happy at all. And then Dani suddenly realised the majority of the eyes in the room were on her. She glanced down at an open newspaper a foot or so away from her and instantly knew why. There was Sean's credit waving up at her from the picture. Fuck, she thought. She looked up again, suddenly feeling very hot.

"Dani?" Hannah was glaring at her but Dani chose not to respond. She had waged an internal war for weeks now wondering if she should tell Bernie about her and Sean, convincing herself he probably already knew and would raise it with her if he felt it was a problem. She couldn't currently see him very well without turning her head which would be far too obvious but was convinced in that moment, she heard a shiny penny drop. Dani sighed. She really didn't want to say anything but feared if she didn't, they would all remain frozen in position and the meeting would never end. She took a deep breath.

"I can sense your frustration Hannah but I don't represent Sean and therefore have no control over his career choices." There was a pause and then, just as Hannah was about to respond, Bernie cut in.

"If the producers can't be reassured then let me know. And I don't think Rachel's ready to give up on him just yet so let's move on."

Twenty-three long minutes later Bernie declared the meeting over and the room slowly emptied. Unlike everyone else, Dani took her time gathering up her things, knowing what was coming next and deciding to make it as easy as possible for Bernie to talk to her privately without drawing any further attention to herself. Bernie stood quietly until the room was empty and then waited as Dani looked at him. His eyebrows were raised expectantly. She was going to have to start.

"I'm sorry Bernie. I should have told you."

"Yes you should."

He was giving nothing away so Dani took a deep breath. It was time to start digging. "I know it's not ideal and given a choice, I'd love Sean to have a completely unrelated job but I work such long hours that everyone I meet is connected to what I do. We've talked about conflicts of interest and I accept this will be hard to believe but we simply don't talk about work. Banal stuff yes, but not about artists. We've agreed we'll never ask inappropriate questions or favours of each other and, to be fair, this is the first time there's been an issue. But equally, Hannah didn't mention him last week when his very lovely pictures of Jessie were all over the papers so, as with any photographer, you just have to take the rough with the smooth." Dani paused for breath, barely able to see out of the beautiful hole she had now dug herself into. She looked at Bernie whose eyes twinkled as he smiled.

"I was happy to stop at you should have told me. But thanks for the bigger picture." Dani felt her face burn as Bernie left the room. She squirmed, her face contorting with the excruciating humiliation she was feeling at how badly she had handled the situation, only to be quickly replaced by anger at how stupid she must have made herself look. A double whammy. She shook her head to dislodge the agonising feelings as best she could, picked up her things and went back to work.

Billy and Amanda were on their fourth date. Billy knew this because, for the first time in his life, he'd actually been counting. It was a complete novelty for him to want to see someone multiple times and he had to admit it was a feeling he was very much enjoying. Not just the nervous anticipation of sex with someone he genuinely cared about which in itself was a new experience but this sudden desire to make plans – and good ones at that. Every time he'd seen Amanda he'd really thought about where he should take her. Thought about what they might talk about, not that conversation was ever hard. It was fascinating to actually be interested in someone to the extent that you want to know everything about them from a pertinent childhood memory to their favourite film.

Tonight he'd chosen a restaurant on London's Southbank and had gone to great efforts to secure a table with a spectacular view of the River Thames and the splendour of Tower Bridge. With two courses already consumed and washed down with a generous amount of wine, the conversation had turned to when they'd first met. It had been the moment when Dani's two worlds - home and university - had been brought together for what should have been a great celebration, her twenty-first birthday party. Billy rolled his eyes. "Not a party any of us are likely to forget in a hurry, sadly for all the wrong reasons."

"It's our Kennedy moment isn't it? How many times have you been asked where you were the moment Nick dumped her?" Amanda felt immediately uncomfortable at the quizzical look on Billy's face, fearing she may have used completely the wrong analogy. "Obviously just because you remember where you were. Not because of the significance of the event which is clearly unlikely to have the same impact on history as Kennedy's assassination." Billy smiled, loving the fact she'd felt it necessary to clarify before she continued. "So where were you?"

"Far enough away that I didn't hear what he said," Billy told her, his expression suddenly very serious, "but I could see her face. I watched the colour literally drain from her cheeks and her eyes fill with tears. I had no idea what had happened, I just instinctively ran over by which time Nick had already walked away. She was just standing there, completely frozen, with a group of embarrassed looking people around her not knowing what to do. I couldn't believe it when she told me and then I handed her to someone and went after Nick."

"I always wondered if anyone had spoken to him. I just wanted to punch his lights out."

"Likewise."

Amanda looked at him and then gasped. "You didn't?"

"I bloody did! Of course I did. I couldn't have been less interested in what he had to say. Punching him was far more satisfying."

Amanda giggled. "Blimey. Does Dani know?"

"She asked me if I'd spoken to him. I said no." He shrugged as if to say he hadn't felt the need to say anymore either then or now. "What about you?"

"I missed it too but was given a blow by blow account by someone who had a ringside seat - 'I can't do this anymore, you're not the person you were, it's over, I simply don't love you anymore' - and all delivered with a steely look in his eyes. I think he may have punctuated it with a 'happy birthday' or that may have been unwittingly added over the years. Either way, it was cold and very harsh. I'll never understand why it was so important to him to hurt her so badly and so publicly. Although I've been told many times over the years from various mutual friends that he massively regretted it."

"I hope he's suffered horribly. He certainly did a great job of screwing her up."

Amanda hesitated for a moment. "Well that's not strictly true. I know she happily paints him as the root of all relationship evil but I think her Dad probably wins the award for that one." She looked at the surprise in Billy's eyes that he immediately tried to hide but it was there nonetheless, however discreet. Clearly Dani had never discussed it with him but she had been there during the inevitable demise of Dani's parents' marriage and it hadn't been pretty. But it wasn't her place to divulge. A change of subject was definitely needed. "So did you even notice me that night?"

"Of course I did! How could I not? I'd already heard so much about you there was something quite strange about finally seeing you in the flesh."

Amanda laughed. "Strange? Not the kind of first impression I was hoping for!"

"You know what I mean. If I'm honest, I was slightly terrified. Dani always talked about you with obvious affection but created an image of this wild, feisty woman, picking up men at will and like a praying mantis, casting them aside once they'd served their purpose!" Billy's theatrical arm waving made his account all the more dramatic.

Amanda smiled and nodded. "Yep, that sounds about right! Although your track record puts you on a pretty similar path if what I always heard was correct?"

Billy thought for a moment, eager to make sure his answer was considered. "I can see how it might look - a fair amount of sex and not many relationships to speak of but I was always honest about what girls should expect from me. I just wasn't ready for a relationship. I was too selfish maybe and wrapped up in my own stuff but I never played games and always tried to be sensitive to people's feelings." He smiled a roguish smile. He had left behind him a string of broken hearts and they both knew it.

"So what about now?"

Billy took hold of her hand. "I always knew when the right person came along everything would change. The biggest surprise is how liberating it feels. Who knew being in a relationship could actually be so enjoyable!"

Amanda smiled, enjoying the rush of adrenaline that was setting her heart racing and her cheeks flushing, wondering if she now had the courage to ask the question that was not only burning within her but setting her insides on fire. And then she sat back, her confidence suddenly deserting her. "That's enough of that nonsense. You're in danger of putting me off my pudding and we can't have that!" She picked up the dessert menu and looked for a waiter, suddenly feeling almost embarrassed at such unfamiliar openness. She was still getting used to this relationship lark too.

After polishing off a mouth-watering plate of chocolate fondant, créme fraîche and a lone strawberry to make it feel vaguely healthy, they came out of the restaurant and started walking along beside the river. The evening was slowly taking hold and the lights from the restaurants, bridges, offices and residential blocks that surrounded them started to glow against the darkening sky, bursting into life like a luminous Mexican wave rippling into the distance ahead of them. The area was buzzing with activity. Billy looked at the streams of people milling about but doubted any of them could be as content as he was.

With their arms comfortably around each other, they headed across the Millennium Bridge and then stopped half way to take in the view. Amanda smiled as her eyes feasted on some of London's finest landmarks from St Paul's Cathedral to her left, to Tower Bridge in the distance up ahead, standing proud and steeped in history, flanked by the modern, architectural phenomena that was the Shard. It was easy to take it all for granted but, when you stopped and actually looked around you, it was hard not to be blown away by the sheer beauty of the city and soak it all in, one cultural spectacle at a time.

As her eyes continued their panoramic journey round to the Tate Modern on her right, she was suddenly aware of Billy beside her and watched him out of the corner of her eye, momentarily lost in his own thoughts. For Amanda, the burning question was alight once more, desperate to be asked so it could be ceremoniously extinguished. She suddenly felt horribly nervous but knew she would be unable to relax until she had asked it. She took a deep breath. "So, you and Dani?"

The sound of her voice snapped Billy back to the here and now. "What about us?"

"Did you ever sleep with her?"

Billy looked at her, his eyes narrowing ever so slightly. "She must have told you we didn't?"

"Yes she did."

"So why do you ask?"

It took all of Amanda's will to hold his look. She of course knew there had never been anything between them but whether sexual or not, she was horribly aware of the intimacy they shared. She couldn't really explain why but it made her feel insecure. "That would make you the only friends I know who've never had sex."

"So you've slept with Dani?"

Amanda smiled. "You know what I mean."

Billy studied her for a moment. The complexity of the female mind was something he had never got to grips with but then he'd never really tried. He was at a total loss to know how to make this go away. "What do you want me to say?"

"It bothers her you know, the idea of you and me."

"She'll get used to it," he said with a shrug.

"So she's talked to you about me?"

Amanda's expression was one Billy had not seen her wear before. There was a fear in her eyes that she was desperately trying to mask, coupled with a sense of embarrassment that she had raised the subject at all, which only made her compulsion to do so all the more pertinent. Billy sighed. He was starting to feel like a lone child in a fierce custody battle. It was time to nip this in the bud before it really took root. "Amanda, please don't. Dani's my best friend and that's never going to change. She's not a threat to us unless you turn her into one so please don't do that."

Amanda looked suitably chastised. "I just don't want anything to spoil things, that's all."

Billy pulled her into his arms and kissed her. "Neither do I and nothing's going to."

Amanda was relieved her eyes were hidden from him as he hugged her, fearing they might betray her failed attempt to appear reassured. She knew she was being silly but decided it was her prerogative. Wanting to be with someone as much as she wanted to be with Billy was a new feeling for her too. Billy took her hand and they started walking towards the nearest tube station.

Amanda looked up at him with a smile. "And by the way, she's not your best friend she's mine!"

"So now you want to fight me for her do you?"

Amanda laughed but only on the outside. Inwardly, her insecurity had made itself very comfortable indeed and was simply refusing to budge.

10

Dani was sending out tickets to a select few for a huge celebrity bash. It was an annual charity event and, despite their cost, tickets were always thin on the ground. The fact that there were actual tickets at all, and gilt-edged ones at that with fancy gold writing, was all the reminder needed that this was indeed not just an event, but one of the key events of the year. No one begrudged paying. Everyone liked to do their bit for charity and this was undoubtedly the most public way to show you cared. Dani was going herself and as Sean would be there in an official capacity, she had splashed out on tickets for Billy and Amanda too. She would be glad of their company, even if she would no doubt be going in the role of one green, hairy gooseberry.

With a sigh, Dani turned her attention to the envelope in front of her addressed to Mr and Mrs Cambridge. On your marks, get set, go! And then her heart was off, out of control in seconds. It's not like she hadn't known this would happen. She would just have to be professional as she looked Alex's wife in the eyes and told her how lovely it was to meet her at last. She felt bile rising, burning the back of her throat at the very idea. It was amazing they hadn't met already. At any other time it would be a fleeting moment of no real consequence. Not anymore.

A few days later, Dani met Amanda for the inevitable 'oh my God we have nothing to wear' panic. "What do you think?" Amanda emerged from the umpteenth changing room in a stunning midnight blue number, straight to the floor and virtually backless. She looked amazing.

"Yep, that's the one, without a doubt."

"Have you seen how much it is?"

"Well why did you try it on if you can't afford it?" Dani barked.

"I should just have made something myself. Why didn't I do that?"

"Because there isn't time. And we've had this conversation already!" Dani had given up even trying to mask her frustration. They smiled at each other through gritted teeth. So much for shopping being an enjoyable experience, which of course it normally would be but on this occasion, the stakes were ridiculously high. They were both painfully aware they would be competing with a bunch of celebrities who ironically would most likely be borrowing dresses from the nation's finest designers while they were buying theirs and still hoping to somehow blend in. It was therefore vital to make a confident purchase to avoid endless self-conscious fidgeting on the night. It was basically hell and they knew the sooner they both found something, the quicker they could relax and go back to being friends. In the meantime, they remained locked in a frustration-induced combat, snapping at each other like a pair of bad-tempered crocodiles.

"Okay, I'm buying! That's it, decision made."

"Thank the Lord," Dani sighed. They were half way there. "I'm going back to that green one. Come and find me there when you've paid."

By the time Amanda found her, Dani was standing in front of a tall mirror, the beads on her dress, catching the light as she moved. It had thin straps and fitted snugly to her hips and then opened out slightly to the floor, moving elegantly in perfect swirls. It was beautiful and looked stunning.

"Well you know what I think."

"Yes I do thank you." Dani knew she was getting horribly vicious and that Amanda was right. This was by far the most striking dress she had ever tried on. "Okay, it's a sale."

"Hallelujah!" Amanda had never felt more relieved in her entire life. "Can we please now get a drink?" she pleaded but Dani was already heading for the nearest bar.

When the evening finally arrived, Dani didn't think she had ever seen such a mass of famous faces as a line of huge black cars pulled up one after the other, each spilling out another few members of the world's glitterati. Each time it sent the mass of photographers into a complete frenzy, their flashes illuminating the entire area like a set of floodlights. The gathered crowd was enormous, people at least ten deep and squashed behind crash barriers, all cheering and waving. The surprisingly warm evening had brought them out in their droves, not to mention the tourists, tour maps in one hand, smartphones held high and on record in the other.

The surrounding roads had been closed causing even more people than normal to be trapped in hot, sweaty cars and buses as they struggled to get home, all of whom were no doubt cursing the rich and famous for inflicting such inconvenience on them and all for a night out.

Amanda and Billy looked in awe at the bank of photographers penned in like a pack of hungry wolves. They had chosen to walk the last few metres and had finally battled their way to the door. The extent of the preparation was unprecedented and Amanda looked suitably impressed as they made their way to the ballroom. No detail had been missed from the tasteful decoration to the perfectly dressed waiters, all finished off with a silver tray of champagne glasses, held with such ease that they appeared to be natural extensions of their arms. "Wow!" Amanda's eyes lit up as she tried to take in all the sights before her. The ballroom was huge, topped with the most ornate ceiling from which hung the biggest and most intricate collection of chandeliers she had ever seen. She watched as people milled around from one perfectly dressed table to another, stopping occasionally for a brief exchange of words before politely moving on. The dance floor was already starting to fill up, the guests enjoying the first of a series of bands that would entertain them throughout the evening.

"I'm going to see if I can find Sean. I'll catch up with you in a minute."

Dani left them as a huge grin broke out across Billy's face. "Come on Amanda, let's mingle!" And off they went, determined to relish every single, celebrity-packed moment.

Dani went in pursuit of a man with a tray, feeling more than a little on edge. Having successfully obtained a glass of champagne, she stopped to look around and suddenly realised Alex was looking at her. She smiled as he waved. Might as well get it over with early, she thought as he expertly wound his way through the groups of people currently separating them.

"You look beautiful," he said as he kissed her on the cheek and then held on to her hand as he studied her face, wondering what could possibly be going on behind those incredible brown eyes. Before he could say any more, a hand appeared on his arm and he simultaneously let go of Dani as he turned to see Victoria standing just behind him. Dani wondered if it was her imagination or whether he did actually flinch slightly as he pulled his wife gently forward. "Victoria, I'd like you to meet my agent, Dani. Undoubtedly the best in the business."

Dani put out her hand. "It's good to meet you at last Victoria. I'm very glad you could come."

"Yes, it's all very exciting! I had no idea Alex was quite so well known. I suppose I have you to thank for that?"

"Not at all. My role is a very small one in the scale of things."

Dani quietly studied her as they spoke, not wanting to miss a single detail. She wasn't a beautiful woman but there was definitely something about her. Her long blonde hair was piled on top of her head in a complicated knot and her dress was simple, if not a little frumpy. Or perhaps she was being unnecessarily unkind, unsure for a moment if that was an accurate summary of what she was actually seeing, or just what she wanted to see. As if Victoria being a little mumsy or lacking in style might vindicate her in some way for potentially destroying her marriage which was of course ridiculous. Before she had time to make sense of it all, a flurry of flashes went off behind her and Alex and Victoria smiled in response, the perfect celebrity couple. Sean slipped his arm around Dani and kissed her affectionately on the cheek. "There you are! Have you been here long?"

"Only a few minutes."

Alex's eyes slowly recovered from the sudden burst of light and he found himself confronted by an incredibly striking man. Tall, dark, almost model-like and most alarmingly, with his hands all over Dani.

"Sean, this is Alex Cambridge, one of my clients, and his wife Victoria."

Sean took their hands in turn and shook them warmly. "Of course I know who you are but it's great to have a formal introduction. How are you?"

Alex was unable to speak so Victoria happily chatted. "Fine thank you. We're having a lovely time! You must send me a picture if they turn out well."

Sean laughed. "All my pictures turn out well! I'll let Dani have one and she can pass it on."

"That would be wonderful, thank you."

Sean kissed Dani again and then made his excuses. "Sorry, I need to move around. I'll see you later. Good to meet you both." And he was gone.

Alex stood quietly, unsure if he would fall over if he tried to walk away. He had been so confident that he could deal with this but boy was he wrong! He doubted Sean could have had a more powerful impact if he'd punched him clean in the face.

"Will you excuse me for a moment? I need to find the ladies."

Alex watched Victoria leave then turned immediately back to Dani. "So that was him?"

With a challenging look in her eye, Dani slowly looked up. "Yes, that was him."

Alex took her arm and led her to the side of the room, the force of his grip making it impossible for her to do anything other than comply. "This is just terrible," he said, running a hand backwards and forwards over his eyes as if he could somehow erase the image of Dani and Sean together. "I can't bear it!"

Dani stood firm, her body rigid, her expression fierce. "Well I really enjoyed meeting your wife. Yes, that was a real treat." The words were harsh and clipped, struggling to be heard as they buckled under the weight of sarcasm. Her immediate reaction was to feel incredibly angry with Alex which seemed like a much easier option than dealing with her own conflicting emotions that bubbled in a cauldron of unpleasantness deep in her gut. She took a deep breath as she struggled to restore some composure. She may be horribly conflicted but a public brawl was definitely not on the agenda. "Look, don't give me a hard time. There's a simple enough solution."

Alex was finding it harder to control himself. "But a fucking paparazzi photographer! Jesus, it's almost funny!"

"I won't deny myself a warm and loving relationship while you go home to your wife every time we have sex."

"And if she wasn't on the scene, what then?" Alex said, his voice infused with a rising sense of panic. "What would happen then?"

"So this is where you're hiding?"

Dani turned around with a start to see Billy. By the look on his face he had been watching them for some time but had clearly reached the point where he could act as voyeur no longer. He raised his eyebrows at her, suggesting an introduction was necessary.

"Billy, this is Alex Cambridge."

Billy took his hand. "Good to meet you Alex. I'm Billy."

"Nice to meet you too, Billy."

Judging by the tension, Billy severely doubted he meant it but cared little. "I'm sorry to interrupt but I'm afraid I need to take Dani away for a moment."

"Of course. I'll see you later Dani."

As Alex reluctantly walked away, Billy turned on her, talking in an angry whisper. "So are you going to explain or do I have to work it out for myself?"

"Please don't do this. Not here. Not tonight."

Billy was impervious to her plea and carried on regardless. "I may not be the most intuitive of people but that didn't look like a friendly chat between two colleagues."

"You have no idea what that was about!" Dani raised her voice, terrified for a moment that she was about to unleash her confused emotion on Billy who remained perfectly in control.

"Believe me I have a very good idea. You're still seeing him aren't you? Jesus, what the fuck's the matter with you?"

"Hey you two, what's going on?" Amanda looked from one to the other, waiting for someone to say something. Dani looked at Billy, willing him not to say anything. Relieved, she watched him relax and smile at Amanda.

"I was just trying to persuade the miserable old cow to have a dance. Perhaps you would oblige?" Amanda smiled and gladly took his hand but as they walked away, Billy looked back at Dani. "We'll talk about this later." And then he let Amanda lead him away.

Dani did her best to mingle and be sociable but, not surprisingly, she had never felt less inclined to exchange fake pleasantries. Surrounded by a small group, she suddenly realised she hadn't heard a word that had been said to her and with all eyes on her, a response was clearly now expected. As she faltered, she noticed Sean doing his best to discreetly attract her attention. Perfect. "I'm so sorry, it appears I'm needed. Do excuse me" and, hugely relieved, she headed over to him.

"You have no idea how brilliant your timing is. Thank you thank you thank….". Dani stopped abruptly. She hadn't noticed the distracted look on Sean's face so immersed was she in the wondrous feeling of her timely escape but as he held his camera screen up for her to see, she immediately froze. Looking back at her was an image of Jake draped over a big-haired, big-breasted woman who most definitely wasn't his partner. Shit. Dani watched as Sean pressed the little dustbin icon and the image did that magical shrinking, whooshy thing and disappeared. She looked at him, the relief very obvious in her slightly watery eyes. "Thank you."

Sean smiled. "Next time it might not be me." And with that he went back to work.

Dani stood for a moment, wondering if the evening could possibly get any worse. Then, with a deep breath, she went in search of Jake. When she found him, he was snuggled at a table in a corner with his hands all over his new 'friend'. The pictures from his family holiday were due to appear in tomorrow's papers. The irony could not have been more profound.

"Taxi for Jake," she shouted as she literally pulled him away and dragged him to his feet. His eyes suggested there was more than just alcohol in his system as he started to slur his objection to the sudden manhandling but with momentum on her side, Dani just kept him moving and headed straight for the door. A line of taxis was already outside and, pushing him into the back of the first one, she gave the driver far more cash than was necessary and very clear instructions - he was to take Jake to the address she supplied and under no circumstances whatsoever was he to take him anywhere else. She waited until the cab had pulled away and then, resisting the overwhelming urge to jump in one herself, she headed back inside to the party.

It was after midnight by the time Sean was able to hang up his camera and join the party. His pictures had been dutifully released and now it was time to relax. Dani was extremely glad to finally have him firmly by her side as she handed him a beer. "Perfect, thank you," he said, immediately taking a few large gulps. "So come on, what have I missed?"

"Shouldn't I be asking you that? No one knows how to work a room the way you do." Dani paused for a moment. "Thanks for letting Jake off. He may be too stupid to appreciate it but I really do. I know I've compromised you and I'm sorry."

"Don't be. It's not a big deal, really."

Sean took another long gulp of his beer. It was only his second of the night and he was definitely looking to catch up a little. "Do you know what I'd really like to do now?"

Dani looked at him with a knowing smile. "Go on, surprise me!" She giggled as he leant forward and started whispering the most outrageous suggestions in her ear. Then suddenly there was a polite cough beside them and there was Alex.

"Sorry, I just wanted to say goodbye. We're off now." Dani looked to see Victoria dutifully standing by his side. What a cosy foursome we are, she thought.

"Bye Alex, see you again soon I'm sure," said Sean, stretching out his hand.

Alex smiled as he took it, an electric shock of jealousy shooting up through his arm until his eye twitched. He blinked a few times to hide the involuntary spasm and then turned to Dani. "I'll be in touch."

"Bye Alex. Good to meet you Victoria."

"You too. You must come and have dinner soon, both of you."

Dani was relieved Victoria didn't wait for a reply and watched them go with an enormous sense of relief.

Alex walked away hating Sean more than he'd ever hated anyone in his entire life. Not since Johnny Bates had so brutally bullied him in the school playground had he ever wanted to hit someone more. And the most frustrating part was, he had absolutely no right to feel that way, which made it all so much worse. I suppose

139

he thinks it's fashionable to wear a t-shirt under a suit, he thought angrily. The event was supposed to be black tie but then he wasn't a guest was he? He was a fucking photographer! And the worst possible kind, as far as Alex was concerned. The kind that follows you unseen, catches you unawares and then shares the discovery with the entire newspaper-buying, internet-surfing public.

Alex felt uncomfortably hot and bothered despite the fact they were now outside in the fresh air. He took a deep breath and couldn't stop himself picturing the moment when he had first seen Dani tonight. That now unforgettable moment when she and Victoria had stood close enough to touch, when his two worlds had come together for the first time and looked directly into each other's eyes. One knowing nothing, the other horribly aware of the painful significance. As his mind raced, he knew it had taken only a split second for him to realise that a choice did indeed have to be made. All he wanted to do was go back inside, take Dani by the hand and run away with her. Whatever it took to be with her, to get her away from that bastard, he would gladly do it.

The doorman whistled for a cab and Alex was brought abruptly back to the present. He helped Victoria into the back and then climbed in beside her. As they pulled away, Victoria smiled. "What a wonderful evening. I'm completely star struck. What an amazing collection of people! I've completely lost count of the number of stars I've met tonight. Just wait till the school run to-morrow afternoon! No one will believe it when I tell them who I danced with! Life really has changed hasn't it?" Alex chose not to answer and lost in her own excitement, Victoria happily continued regardless. "And the dresses! Goodness only knows how much was spent on all the amazing gowns, not to mention the jewellery. And so lovely to meet Dani at last. She was as lovely as I knew she would be. What a striking couple she and Sean make. He was absolutely charming. Those eyes!"

Alex had tuned out at the mention of Dani's name and was gazing out of the window, his eyes a blur as Victoria's inane chatter washed over him. He sighed, a slow, heavy-hearted, desperate sigh. They were staying in London for the night and then tomorrow morning he would be back to Ireland where his current drama was filming. At least there he would be able to have some time and space to try to get a grip of his life. In the meantime, he still had to get through the rest of the night and as Victoria snuggled up to him, her hand placed firmly at the top of his thigh, he knew he was about to put his acting skills to the absolute test as he prepared to play out the most challenging and demanding performance of his life.

Dani decided she'd well and truly had enough and leaving Sean to finish up his final obligations, she headed for the cloakroom for her coat. Much as she wanted to be alone, she couldn't think of an excuse quickly enough to avoid sharing a ride with Billy and Amanda who appeared beside her, so within minutes, she found herself sitting in an uncomfortable silence next to Billy in the back of a cab. Amanda sat opposite them, looking from one stony face to the other, wondering if she should attempt some conversation. She took a deep breath and smiled. "Well that was fun!" She waited. Nothing. Not even a glance in her direction. Maybe she should just focus on Dani. She looked at her but her face was giving nothing away. "You okay Dani?" As the cab sped past a street lamp momentarily flooding them with light, Amanda couldn't miss how Dani's eyes were glistening, a clear sign that her friend was most definitely anything but okay. But those glistening eyes remained in a fixed stare, focused firmly out of the window while her body language was yelling loudly that she just wanted to be left alone. Accepting defeat, Amanda sat back. She had tried.

The silence continued until the cab pulled up outside Dani's flat. She opened the door and, without a word or so much as a backward glance, she climbed out, closed the door behind her and headed inside. Billy watched her go as Amanda moved to sit next to him. She took hold of his hand and gave it a squeeze as the cab pulled away again. "You okay?"

With a look of pure exasperation, he shook his head slowly. "I'm just so angry with her. Watching the four of them chatting, two of them conspirators and two completely oblivious to the deceit. It's like some horrible farce but with people I really care about. And you just know it's going to end badly."

Amanda thought for a moment. "Once you've convinced yourself that all relationships fail, I imagine it's hard to accept that you might have found someone who is genuine and trustworthy and in it for the long haul."

"I can see that," Billy said, "but only a complete idiot would set about destroying a good relationship just to prove a point."

"Well I'm not prepared to lose all faith in Dani just yet. She has a good heart which is why we both love her as much as we do. She needs our support Billy."

Billy's expression remained unforgiving. "She needs a wake-up call, that's what she needs."

11

Sean's pictures were all over the front pages the next day with lots more inside and taking pride of place alongside them were pictures of Jake, Sadie and their beautiful baby Beau. The most popular pictures were of Jake lying on a sun lounger with Beau asleep on his bare chest and one of him holding Beau in one arm with the other draped casually around Sadie's shoulders as they walked along a perfect white, sandy beach. It was official. They were indeed the perfect family, for the time being at least. Dani picked up the phone. "Jake hi, it's Dani. There's a car on its way to you. I'm buying you breakfast."

"What time is it?" It was clearly an effort for him to speak.

"Time for a reality check. I'll see you in an hour." And she hung up.

Dani was already waiting when Jake arrived. He was looking remarkably alive all things considered. Despite that, he approached her with the look of a naughty school boy aware he was about to be scolded and rightly assuming a hundred lines was clearly not going to cut it. He sat down, his eyes also down, his shoulders even further down and then he waited.

"For goodness sake, I'm not your mother!"

He risked a quick glance up and was both surprised and relieved to see Dani smiling. "Trust me, my mum's nowhere near as scary."

Dani laughed. "I'm going to take that as a compliment." She looked around for a waiter and ordered him some coffee. "Do you want something to eat?"

"Full English and toast please." The waiter nodded and Jake waited for him to go before turning his attention back to Dani. "I'm really sorry."

"I don't want an apology. I wish I didn't care how you behave out of hours but that's the thing, there are no out of hours for you any more. I want you to have an amazing career and if that's going to be possible, you have to understand it's a twenty-four hour commitment."

With caffeine now slowly working its way through his body Jake was starting to feel more alert. He sat forward. "But everyone loves a bad boy don't they? I'm young, not bad-looking, I've got money to spend. I'm not doing anything that bad am I?"

Dani raised her eyebrows and sighed. Where to start? "Your mates may think it's great, girls like the one you were wrapped around last night might think it's great but producers and directors don't. They don't see loveable rogue. They see unreliable, untrustworthy and risky. Are you prepared to take the risk that if a part comes down to you and one other, even if you're better by a mile, you may miss out because they want the publicity to be about the role and not about how many drugs you're taking or how many women you can pull? And what about Sadie? How do you think she would have felt this morning if she'd seen pictures of you with your hands all over another woman? And not for the first time. I want to see your success being celebrated on Graham Norton's sofa, not see you doing a lie-detector test about your infidelities on the bloody Jeremy Kyle Show."

Jake slumped back in his chair as his breakfast was placed in front of him. "Okay I get it." And with that, he hungrily tucked in. By contrast, Dani could only nibble at the corner of a piece of toast, hoping beyond hope that at least some of what she'd said had sunk in.

She'd been back at her desk for a matter of minutes when Dani got the call she'd been waiting for with a dread so intense it was suffocating. "Dani, it's Billy. I'm buying you lunch."

"But.."

"No buts, I'll be there in half an hour."

Before Dani could protest, the line went dead. She was unable to take her eyes off the clock and exactly half an hour later he was in reception. He followed her out of the building without a word. "So where are we going?"

"Soho Square."

"Why on earth are you taking me there? No don't tell me, a picnic. How simply charming."

Billy chose to ignore her nervous sarcasm. "Assuming there's going to be a certain amount of yelling, it was the only open-air space I could think of."

"What the fuck is this?" Dani stopped dead in her tracks, a growing sense of panic suddenly rooting her to the spot. "You're in no position to judge me so stop it!"

Billy took hold of her arm. "Save it. I'm your best friend and that gives me every right I need to tell you exactly what I think. And whether you like it or not you're going to listen."

Keeping a firm hold of her, he marched her to the small green oasis and didn't stop walking until they were as alone as they were ever going to be. Dani watched in silence as he paced for a moment in front of her and then, when he was ready, he turned to face her. "So come on then, why?"

Dani willed herself to remain calm but the message clearly hadn't reached her knees. As the rest of her body rallied she felt herself wobble slightly. She only hoped Billy hadn't noticed as she did her best to stand firm. "Why are you so angry with me?"

"Don't change the subject!" Dani flinched. She had never seen Billy so furious. "It just doesn't make any sense to me. Sean is a fantastic guy and Alex is married!" He raised his hands upwards as if to say, 'isn't it simple?' but Dani was saying nothing. "I just don't understand. It's not even as if there's a choice - one of them isn't available and you're risking losing the one that is for… for what? An occasional shag!"

"Don't you dare!" she hissed angrily. "You have no idea what this is about!"

"So tell me!"

147

Anyone who had been in the immediate vicinity had now chosen to move away, embarrassed by the scene being created by these two people who stood feet apart from each other, worried if the obvious agitation was only going to escalate into something far more unpleasant. It was undoubtedly safer to find an alternative spot to enjoy lunch and a brief respite from the office. Except one woman, of course, who continued to use her book as a cover for listening in on such a fabulous row, desperate to know the full back-story and equally desperate to tell her friends about the amazing verbal brawl she was witnessing.

Oblivious to anyone and everything, Dani could stand no more and the first defiant tear spilled on to her cheek. "I don't know. I can't explain it, I really can't."

"So try." Billy had no intention of letting her off that easily.

"Okay I'm scared. Scared of admitting that Sean is all I've ever wanted and then watching it all go wrong, waiting for him to hurt me or let me down." She held Billy's eyes with a fiery defiance in her own. "There, I've said it."

"So you're just going to ruin it all to prove a point? Just so you can say all your relationships fail? Jesus, is that what they call feminine logic?"

Dani's words were suddenly quiet and hollow-sounding. "You asked for an explanation and I've given you one. I don't expect you to understand." She stood, her head lowered, her arms folded tightly in front of her in the only way she felt she could protect herself from

Billy's onslaught. As he watched the silent tears, rolling steadily now in little rivulets down her face and leaving smudgy track marks in their wake, Billy wondered if he should throw in the new information he had acquired that had been preying on his mind. He sighed, doubting there would be a better time to do so. "Do you want to talk about your Dad?"

Dani swung her head up, her surprise, anger and goodness knows what else all joining to form a look that literally made Billy shiver. "Why would I?"

Billy struggled for a moment. "I don't know, it was just something Amanda said, and I…" He was interrupted by the most sinister of laughs.

"Of course! Bloody Amanda!" Billy felt as if Dani's stare would literally pierce his soul as she continued, her voice low and bitter. "And so it starts. What did she tell you?"

"Nothing, nothing at all," Billy hurriedly replied, wishing desperately that he'd kept his bloody mouth shut. "When she realised I had no idea about what happened to your parents she changed the subject."

Dani remained quietly apoplectic. "Well I suppose I should be grateful for small mercies then."

"Why haven't you talked to me about him?" He might as well finish what he'd started.

"Would that be because you care about me or because you're pissed off that she knows something you don't?"

Billy chose to ignore the obvious challenge to his integrity and instead, elected to keep pushing. "I knew your parents had split up but we never talked about why. I'm assuming now there were affairs which would explain the trust issues." Billy thought for a moment and then nodded as he continued, almost as if he were talking to himself rather than to Dani. "Yes, I can see how that would make sense. Abandonment issues, anxiety, why the idea of a relationship would scare you. Maybe even why you chose a career in a world where affairs are almost a rite of passage."

As Dani listened, she was finding it harder and harder to keep control, her body visibly shaking. "Have you fucking finished?" This was way too much for her to take on board. She simply couldn't bear to hear another word. "Don't presume to know how I feel! Don't stand there and analyse me, you patronising bastard!"

Billy refused to be put off. "You need to talk about it."

"No, you need to back the fuck off!"

And then there was a standoff. Both stood like statues, unblinking, willing the other to either open up or shut up, depending on whose perspective you adopted. Eventually it was Billy who made a move. Ignoring the initial resistance from Dani, he took her into his arms, holding her tightly until she stopped fighting him and finally gave in.

"What am I going to do with you? I've thought about nothing else since I saw you with Alex. I care about you, that's all."

"I wanted to talk to you about this last night. Sean was busy sorting his pictures but when I called you at home, Amanda answered so I hung up."

Billy smiled. "Do you have any idea how much trouble I got into for that? Amanda was convinced it was another woman."

"It was another woman and I needed you. However you may feel about everything, my heart was breaking last night. Seeing Alex and Sean side by side, seeing the two worlds that I've somehow managed to keep separate in my head collide in front of me was like opening a box and unleashing all the guilt, the deception, the fear - it was like a physical biow to the stomach. But not only did I have to deal with Alex and Sean meeting, I had to face Alex's wife. How do you think that felt? You may think I deserve it but I've never felt so guilty, so disgusting and so lonely and I needed you. I'm losing you Billy and to my best friend which only makes it even more unbearable."

"I suppose it never crossed your mind that I might have felt I'd lost you too when you met Sean?" Billy led her to a nearby bench as he talked, sitting her down and keeping a tight hold of her hand. "I know what you're thinking. You're wondering why I never call you late at night any more, why I rarely just turn up uninvited. Well there's something to interrupt now. You see, it works both ways." Billy wiped the fresh tears from Dani's eyes. "Anyway, you slippery little bugger, I think we were talking about something else."

"Help me Billy. Help me sort it out."

"Yes, I'll help you. You know I will." Billy stroked her hair as he rocked her gently in his arms in an attempt to calm her down. What a dangerous can of worms he had opened and with such brutal force. He had unlocked the door to weeks, or more likely, years of pent-up emotion and now there was no stopping it. He had to help Dani get all the little worms back in the shiny silver can where they belonged. He sighed. Climbing Everest suddenly felt like a stroll up a hill compared to what undoubtedly lay ahead.

Once he felt Dani had regained some control, he gently took hold of her chin so she had no choice but to look at him as he decided to give it one last try to get her to see sense. "If you really want me to help, you have to finish it once and for all with Alex. Do the right thing and let him go." Her eyes immediately lowered. Clearly this was going to be even harder than he'd thought but he felt compelled to carry on regardless. "I can tell you it's just all wrong but I don't think that will make a difference. I can tell you I think Alex is a complete tosser and I can't believe you've been sucked in but I doubt that will make a difference either. The one thing I do know is it will undoubtedly end in even more tears if you don't get a grip of things and I suspect most of those will be yours. But you're my best friend and I love you dearly so I expect none of that will stop me picking up the pieces when your life suddenly shatters. Just don't be surprised if I tell you when that happens that I told you so."

Dani's eyes were swimming with tears again. "You're disappointed in me, aren't you?"

"Not disappointed but I'm not going to pretend I'm not surprised. I thought you hated women who had casual affairs with married men? And how would you feel if it was Sean playing away?" He watched her visibly stiffen at the idea. "But it's not too late to put it all right."

Billy studied her face and felt his gut tighten. This was nowhere even close to being sorted. What a fucking mess. Suddenly he was the one who felt like crying.

When Dani got back to the office, Amanda was waiting in reception. Dani came to an abrupt stop as she saw her. "Are you fucking kidding me? What is this? Seconds out for round two?" Amanda leapt up and fell into step beside Dani who clearly had no intention of waiting for an answer. She took Dani's arm and steered her towards the sofas by the office's kitchen, sat her down and went to make tea, choosing to forget for a moment that this was Dani's domain and she was the visitor, and an unwelcome one at that.

"You're like some fucking awful tag team," Dani muttered, her head in her hands as Amanda sat down next to her, two cups of tea now on the table in front of them.

"Billy's been to see you then?"

Dani's head jerked up. "Oh he's been to see me alright."

"He cares about you that's all. He's trying to protect you."

Dani's eyes narrowed. "So now you're telling me what he's thinking are you? Jesus, just when I thought it couldn't get any worse."

Amanda immediately looked uncomfortable. "That's not what I was doing."

Dani put up a hand. "Just say what you've got to say and go, please."

Amanda paused to take a deep breath then looked at Dani. "You don't trust Sean do you?"

Dani looked surprised. "Of course I do!"

"I mean you don't trust him to stay the course."

Dani looked away, unable to answer. A lump appeared from nowhere and settled uncomfortably in her throat as Amanda continued, her voice low and calm. "You can deny it all you like but I know you too well. And I can see it in his eyes even if you won't. He doesn't just love you, he adores you."

Dani found the courage to look up. "What's your point?"

"Don't fuck it up. That's my point."

12

"So what do you think?"

"Don't think I don't know why you're suggesting it."
It was a stalling tactic. The truth was Dani wasn't sure
how she felt about it.

"There's only one reason why I want us to live together and that's because I love you and I want to know that
every time I come home you'll be there or, if you're
out, I'll know you'll be back with me within a few
hours."

"That's three reasons. And what about the fourth? The
fact that every time you're here, there's always something you need from your own flat and that means a
frantic dash across London or hours of grumbling that
it's so inconvenient not to have all your stuff here?"

Sean did his best to look hurt. "How could you say
that? As if I would let such basic practicalities influence
such an important decision?" He smiled at her. "Seriously, what do you think?"

Dani put down the clothes she was moving in one of
her many desperate attempts to tidy her overcrowded
bedroom. More space would definitely be welcome but
that couldn't be the reason for saying yes. She suddenly
felt hot, like a heavy blanket of fear had been thrown
over her. "Are we ready?"

"You don't think we are?"

"That's not what I said. But it's a big step. I just want to make sure we've talked about it properly."

Sean clearly hadn't imagined any resistance and so was momentarily thrown. "It doesn't have to be a big deal. We'll find somewhere bigger to rent, you rent this place out and if it doesn't work out, you can just move back in." Sean punctuated this with a shrug, as if to physically stamp on it his firm belief that it was really nothing to sweat about.

"And what about your place?"

"It's rented anyway so I'll just let it go. I can find somewhere else if I need to. But I won't need to." Sean took hold of Dani's hand and smiled at her, searching her eyes for a hint of what was holding her back. "It's okay to say no if you're not ready."

"No I am ready," she said with a smile that almost reached her eyes but not quite. "I'd love us to move in together."

With a squeeze of her hand, Sean then quickly left the room. Dani followed him into the lounge as he grabbed his laptop like a man on a mission. "Now what are you doing?"

Sean glanced up at her, his face full of surprise at her question. "Isn't it obvious?" he said as he sat down, his first Google search quickly underway. "We've got a flat to find!"

"I'll join you in an hour or so," Dani said, feeling suddenly overwhelmed. "I need to pick up some food." And grabbing her jacket, she left him to it.

Within minutes, Dani was sitting outside a café with a large coffee, her focus firmly on the general hubbub around her while her thoughts circled ominously overhead. She was happy to wait for a moment while they gathered themselves into some semblance of order before she tackled them, their onslaught inevitable. It didn't take long for the first question to swoop down into her consciousness. What was she afraid of? The answer was she didn't know, or perhaps wasn't prepared to admit it to herself but there was no mistaking she was definitely afraid. Panicked even. Impatient now to be acknowledged, down swooped question number two. Was it Alex? Was it thoughts of him that were holding her back?

Dani was distracted by Amanda dropping herself into the seat opposite and watched as she happily took a few sips of the coffee that had also been waiting for her arrival, then she sat back with a concerned smile. "What's happened?"

Dani had called her the moment she'd left home. Despite her best efforts to sound casual and relaxed, Amanda had of course got the message loud and clear that her presence was urgently required.

"Sean wants us to move in together."

Amanda's face visibly lifted in preparation for the verbal enthusiasm she was about to unleash and then she stopped, the muscles in her cheeks slowly slipping back down again as she took in Dani's general look of angst. "What, you don't want to?" Amanda watched Dani struggle to verbalise what she was feeling. "You

157

can't agree on where?" She searched for a sign this might be the issue. No, it wasn't that but something seemingly trivial had felt like a good place to start. Wishful thinking at its very best. "You don't think you're ready?" Nothing. Amanda sat forward. "It's Alex isn't it?" Dani shot her a look, her eyes saying what her voice couldn't. "Bloody hell Dani!" She watched Dani flinch as she forced a slow, deep breath to quell her frustration, knowing she absolutely must remain calm. Since the fallout after the Charity Ball, any further talk of Alex had been silently deemed off limits. The first few times Amanda and Billy had seen Dani there had been an awkwardness of elephantine proportion, the look in Dani's eyes leaving no doubt that she did not want to talk about him, despite the subject hanging heavily and uncomfortably in the air. After a few weeks, the atmosphere had relaxed but, as Dani sat mute in front of her, Amanda knew there was no way Dani was going to admit how she still felt. No matter. She could do this on her own.

"So let me guess? You want to move in with Sean because deep down it feels right and you're ready to take the relationship forward. But I know living together's a big deal for you, which means absolutely drawing a line under whatever it is you and Alex are still doing." She paused, aware that there had been no objection so far, either verbal or otherwise. "But you don't want to accept it's over, do you?" Dani hung her head. There, it had been said, even if not from her own mouth. "If you tell Sean you're not ready you'll have to come up with a pretty convincing reason to avoid damaging the relationship and I can't imagine what that could be. You're not seriously thinking of taking that risk are you?" Pleading eyes suggested no, she wasn't. "Then it's simple. Mourn what might have been with Alex if you need to - although I think we both know there's really nothing to mourn - and get on with your life with Sean."

Amanda sat back again and picking up her coffee, she finished it in three large gulps. "I have to go. Lovely talking to you."

Dani watched her walk away knowing that of course she was right. She had felt enormously grateful that Amanda understood exactly what she had needed to hear without forcing her to talk about it. Their friendship was such that she could still seek the straight-talking clarity her friend was always able to find, even with the obvious strain Alex had brought to their relationship. But it was the sense of unfinished business that she knew she was struggling with. There had been no chance to see Alex before he had run away back to Ireland and that's exactly what it had felt like. Like he'd turned his back and fled the country, leaving whatever remained of their relationship behind him in a sorry pile of painful words and broken promises. There had of course been reasons to call each other but with busy schedules there had been nothing more than a series of messages left, often ending with pauses and stuttering as they both battled with the need to talk. But both knew that leaving heartfelt voicemails was as incriminating as any attempt to express their confused feelings via email or text and leaving any kind of traceable footprint simply wasn't an option.

For Dani, there was a sense it was over but not ended and it was the fragmentary nature of how things had been left that she had continued to grapple with, a constant low-level sense of unease sitting uncomfortably in the pit of her stomach as a result.

When Dani got home, Sean was exactly where she had left him. She headed past him to offload her shopping and took a moment to regroup as she quickly put everything away. What better way to cut any straggling ties to Alex than by moving things forward with Sean? And the sooner they got things sorted the better.

"I have an idea," she said as she sat down next to him. "We use a letting agent at work, mainly for short-term needs when someone's filming for any length of time. Why don't I see what they can do? They can probably find somewhere that's available immediately. And furnished to keep it simple. It would probably make the paperwork quicker too as Stacey Walker has such a long-standing relationship with them."

Sean immediately closed his laptop, having been unable to find anything vaguely suitable. "Perfect."

"So what are the key criteria? You need a room for your work. Some outside space would be a real treat. And maybe a second bedroom?"

"And somewhere close to town."

"Somewhere round here then?"

That clearly wasn't what Sean meant. "No, somewhere much closer. Surely that makes more sense? Think how much easier it would be for work."

"But I don't want to be any closer to work! It would just make it too easy to stay there all bloody night and then you'd never see me which makes the whole point of moving in together completely null and void. And what about Billy? I was the one who persuaded him to move where he did on the basis it was near me. I can't just up and move off to another part of London!"

Sean could argue that the way things were going, Billy and Amanda would also soon move in together which could take them anywhere in London. He severely doubted that Amanda would be so understanding if Billy said he wanted to stay close to Dani. He sighed. There seemed little point in digging his heels in. They were neither big enough nor sharp enough to take the firm stand needed if he was to win this battle.

"Okay, you win." Sean smiled, resigned to the fact that if this process was to go as smoothly as he wanted, giving in was something he might as well get used to.

Stacey Walker were significant enough clients that the property agency were only too happy to help. It took only a few days to come up with some options and by the following weekend, Dani and Sean were walking into the flat that, on paper, seemed to tick all their boxes. Neither spoke as they went their separate ways to look around, walking slowly from room to room; a spacious, comfortable lounge with a wonderfully high ceiling and huge windows and a kitchen that was tastefully fitted with a large table and a sofa making it a really comfy and sociable room. It was not dissimilar to her own which was surprisingly comforting. There was a massive master bedroom with its own bathroom, a second bedroom, a second bathroom and a good sized study.

"Sean, look at this!"

At first he couldn't find her and then seeing two glass doors open in the kitchen, Sean followed Dani out into the most beautiful garden. It was small enough not to require Monty Don on the household payroll and was dominated by a patio edged with huge terracotta pots, spilling with flowers. It was enclosed by high fences draped with climbing plants which also gave it a wonderful sense of privacy. "Wow, this is fantastic!"

Dani looked at him. "So what do you think?"

"I think it's perfect."

Finding the flat turned out to be the easy part. Both spent the next few weeks sifting through their possessions and slowly packing up their homes. For Sean, this was relatively straight forward. A serial renter, he really only had clothes to pack and a box or two of other personal stuff. His tenancy was coming to an end anyway so without breaking a sweat, the job was swiftly done. For Dani, however, it was a much bigger task. She was determined to make their new place feel like home for both of them equally so didn't want to dominate by moving in all of her pictures, ornaments and the general

162

Dani-ness that filled her own flat. Some things were therefore lovingly packed away, while those that made the cut were put in a box for the move. She did her best to include Sean in the decision making process but it was obvious he really couldn't care less - in a positive, loving way, obviously. She then decided to let the same agency add her own flat to their books. Until she and Sean made any long term plans, she decided she preferred the idea of some premium short-term lets managed by a company she trusted, rather than have some random cuckoo move in on her nest. She really did want to make this work with Sean but that didn't mean she was completely happy about letting someone take over a home she had invested in hugely over the years.

They took a couple of days off work to move in properly. The excitement was palpable, a wonderfully positive energy walking through the door with them and spurring them on to get everything in order as quickly as possible. In amongst putting his DIY skills to the most challenging tests, Sean spent most of his time in the study, the room assigned as his and his alone. He picked up a tatty old desk that he lovingly rubbed down to its bare natural beauty, hooked up his computer and all the necessary connections to make sure he could get his pictures sent out and then smothered the walls with his favourite shots.

By the time their first weekend was behind them, they were well and truly moved in.

On Monday morning, it was back to business as usual. "Come on gang, let's talk." Gathering up any relevant bits and pieces, Sammy and Toby duly wheeled themselves over to Dani's desk. "Sammy. You first."

Sammy lifted her pad. "Damien's back next week for a few days. He's got two days filming in London so I'm just waiting to confirm a couple of meetings once his schedule's set - one for that film we've been waiting on and the other for that US mini-series. They want to cast Gemma up against him which will be interesting. He says he's cool with it but either way it's bound to create a bit of a story."

Dani groaned. "Did she go back to her husband after their fling?"

"Yes and they're still together. For the time being anyway." Sammy paused for any further interjections and when there weren't any, she continued. "Polly's film's well underway. Some press visits are being scheduled on set so I thought I might go along too just to offer some support. Harry split with that singer he was seeing. After all that guff about being a changed man he cheated on her so I want to make sure Polly's prepared to deal with the inevitable questions. There's a contract renewal on the table for our favourite beauty vlogger and some other stuff brewing that I need to get my head around. And Martha and Wills both have call-backs this week so hopefully there'll be at least one more newbie in play by the end of the week." Sammy scanned her pad. "Think that's the key stuff."

"Great, thank you. Toby?"

"Some good news! Dave's got not one but two jobs. He starts filming next week with Damien - they finally made a decision and gave him the part. Then almost immediately afterwards, he starts on that new TV sit-com which is beyond fabulous so he's very happy indeed." Dani and Sammy laughed as Toby stood up to perform a little victory dance.

"Alright, alright, we get it!" Dani said in an attempt to stop him.

Toby sat down and checked his pad. "I've got some newbies in play too. Too early to be claiming any victories just yet but game on as always my lovely," he said, shooting a playful look at Sammy which she chose to ignore, "which just leaves Jake. He's gone a bit quiet which is starting to make me slightly anxious. No doubt he'll resurface soon." Toby laughed nervously and Dani smiled.

"Oh well, something would definitely be wrong if we didn't have at least one potential crisis looming. It's what keeps us on our toes." Sammy and Toby both twitched - nervous tics were sadly all part of the gig - as Dani picked up a file from her desk. "Well I have news too. We have someone new to welcome into our unique little fold." She handed out pictures and a biography as she continued. "Imogen Owen. Bernie's been courting her for a while and she's a great steal so I'm delighted. She's done loads of regional theatre and the play she's currently in is about to transfer to the West End so it's really good timing. Sammy - perhaps you could organise some tickets for us all and we'll have a drink with her afterwards?"

Sammy nodded. "Will do," she said as she studied the photograph. Imogen was very striking. Incredibly short blonde hair with big, wide green eyes and she was tall and willowy. "Why does she look familiar?"

"She was a model," Dani replied with a perfected nonchalance and then she watched Sammy as the penny slowly dropped along with her jaw.

"Of course. Never out of the papers. Dated the lead singer of The Antidote. Didn't her best friend die of a suspected heroin overdose?"

Dani refused to be drawn. "Yes she did. Are we done?"

Sammy stood up and pushed her chair back to her desk, muttering to herself as she went, "mustn't pre-judge, mustn't prejudge". Toby elected to wheel back and, with as much force as he could muster, pushed back from Dani's desk, propelling himself at speed towards his own. He crashed into it with a loud bang and an apologetic "oops." No one batted an eyelid. Despite lots of practice, the same thing happened every single time.

Dani turned her attention to catching up on Alex. He had three weeks or so left in Ireland and the producers of a new film were desperate to get out there to meet him. The script was already on her desk and the part, as was becoming the norm, was incredibly strong. Dani hadn't seen Alex for months now but this one couldn't wait until he got back. A meeting would need to be set up and she was already being chased for a date. It was a major American production team so she absolutely had to be there too. Her blood ran cold and she shivered at the thought of seeing him again after so long, a growing sense of trepidation causing her foot to tap nervously as she picked up the phone. Deciding there was no point calling his mobile if he was filming, she rummaged for his hotel number with the aim of calling to leave yet another message so was immediately thrown when she was told he was there and was put through to his room, her foot unable to keep pace with the surge of pure panic that coursed through her body.

"Hello?"

"Alex, it's Dani."

There was the briefest hesitation. "Dani! What a lovely surprise."

"I'm not disturbing you am I? You weren't trying to sleep?"

"Of course you're not disturbing me!" Another pause. "It's just so great to hear your voice. I've been so desperate to talk to you and yet suddenly I have no idea what to say."

Can he hear my heart thumping? she wondered. Is he aware that I can hardly keep hold of the phone for the thin layer of sweat on my palm? She took a deep breath, aware that the growing silence was about to become uncomfortable, if it were possible for the call to become any more awkward than it already felt. "I need to set up a meeting with some American producers," she blurted, hoping her news would get the conversation going. "They have a film about to go into production. The female lead they were after is suddenly available so it's all moving ridiculously quickly and they're really keen to get you on board."

"Wow, my first feature!" Alex was overwhelmed. "What's the story?"

"You'll love it. I have a script here. I'll send it over as soon as we're done. What's your schedule like over the next ten days?"

"Hang on a sec." Dani heard him lay down the phone, followed by some frantic rustling of paper and then he was back. "Right, let's see. This week's no good really - crazy days and a couple of night shoots but I'm off on Monday and Tuesday next week."

"Okay, I'll call you back but I'll try for Monday. They'll probably want to meet for lunch then we can be there and back in a day."

Will he or won't he? she thought. "Why don't you come out on Sunday night? It would be good to have a proper catch-up don't you think?"

She thought for a moment, knowing how disappointed she would have been if he hadn't suggested it, despite being horribly aware of the implications of her doing so but they really did need to talk. "Okay, I'll see what I can do. I'll call you back in a minute when the meeting's confirmed."

Monday was fine with all concerned and Dani agreed to go out on Sunday night. Things had changed and she knew it. She was living with Sean now which had to mean something about the way their relationship was developing. It was definitely time to get those loose ends firmly knotted, once and for all.

Going home that night, Dani put her troubled thoughts to one side and felt her excitement growing as she neared her new front door. She opened it slowly and waited. She could hear nothing and was momentarily disappointed, believing Sean to be out but as she shut the door behind her, she shivered. There was a definite breeze blowing through the flat and she smiled as she walked out to the garden. "So here you are!" She found Sean sitting on an old bench, smothered in cushions, his face turned to the cool early evening sun. "Where on earth did that come from?"

She bent down to kiss him and Sean immediately pulled her on to his lap. "Do you mean this fine piece of craftsmanship?" Sean gestured towards the bench as Dani waited for an explanation. "I found it in a park. Can you believe someone had just left it there!"

Dani gasped. "You didn't!"

He laughed at her, a look of complete horror on her face. "Of course I didn't! I bought it at that junk shop down the road. Billy helped me get it out here. Fantastic isn't it?"

"Is Billy coming back? Feels like I haven't seen him for ages."

"Not tonight. He dropped in to say he's away for a few days but he'll see you when he gets back."

Sean sat for a moment, keeping his arms firmly around Dani and for a while they just sat there, enjoying the last strains of daylight. "Isn't this great?"

Dani smiled. "Perfect."

"This was definitely the right thing to do. I have a very good feeling," he said with a contented sigh.

"As long as you pull your weight we'll be fine."

"Absolutely! I've even sorted out dinner seeing as though you've been at work all day."

"Are you serious?"

Sean nodded and gestured towards the kitchen. The temptation to see what on earth he'd been up to was too much and Dani headed straight to find out having seen or smelt nothing on her way through. And then she was smiling, aware that Sean was now watching her from the doorway. She turned to look at him, a colourful piece of paper in her hand. "A Chinese take-away menu?"

Sean smiled. "I hear it's excellent!"

Dani looked at her watch and smiled. It was finally lunchtime and she was meeting Billy. When she arrived at their favourite restaurant, a place only they ever went to, he was already waiting for her.

"Am I late? I'm sorry."

He kissed her warmly. "No, I was early."

They chatted for a while, catching up on the necessary day-to-day stuff - how was Sean, how were things with Amanda, how was work. With all of that out of the way, there was a slight pause. Billy looked at her, searching for any sign that would make his next question redundant but found none. "You know I have to ask?"

She looked at him, her eyes suddenly steely, her face expressionless. Every time they'd seen each other recently either Amanda or Sean, or both, had been there. She had found it vaguely amusing that he had been desperate to ask about Alex but had been unable to do so. "I haven't seen him since the Ball. I have a meeting with him in Ireland on Monday with a film producer, before which we will be telling each other what we both already know. That it's well and truly over. And as you chose coming here over going to a park, I assume that means you're done yelling at me?"

Billy looked back at her, not afraid to hold her stare. "Well if what you're telling me is true, then there's no need is there?" They smiled smugly at each other, Dani unwilling to talk about Alex further and Billy desperately hoping it really was all now in the past.

"Do you feel better now?" she asked with a hint of sarcasm. "I know you've been desperate to ask."

"Well this is the first time I've seen you on your own for weeks."

It was a throwaway comment but Dani leapt on it. "And whose fault is that?"

"Both of ours." Billy looked at her as she lowered her eyes, hugely frustrated this had come up yet again although this time he only had himself to blame. "I know what you're thinking and it's just not fair. We both have other people in our lives, not just me. Jesus, we've been over this a hundred times! My being with Amanda doesn't now and never will change our friendship."

Oh but it has, she thought sadly. The last time she had arranged to meet him, she had arrived to find Amanda with him. He had told her he was meeting Dani and Amanda had automatically decided that meant she was invited too. "Does she know you're meeting me today?"

Billy looked at her and sighed. "No, she doesn't."

"Why not?" You are quite incorrigible, he thought, trying to decide how to answer but Dani saved him the trouble. "I know she's jealous."

"No she is not! Why should she be?" Billy's patience was starting to show its first crack.

"So why didn't you tell her?" Dani waited. "Worried she would invite herself along again?"

"She's your friend too. She would have wanted to come and I just wanted to see you on my own for a change. What the hell is wrong with that?"

"That you couldn't be honest with her, that's what's wrong with it and now if she asks if I've seen you, I'll have to lie to her."

Billy dropped his knife and fork on to his plate, wondering if once again a park would have been a better option as Dani flinched at the unexpected clatter of steel on china. "I am not going to fight with you about this! Just eat your lunch or go back to work. Whatever you like, just stop pushing me!" Dani felt his frustration almost physically as if he were jabbing at her chest with a finger to drive home every word. "I'm not going to tell you that you're more important than she is.

You're both special to me. Just stop making me feel like I have to choose between you all the time!"

Dani sat back in her chair, feeling verbally stung, then picked up her bag and went to get up. Billy quickly took hold of her hand to stop her. "Please don't walk out," he said, his voice now full of genuine concern. "I've come between the two of you and I don't know what to do about it. It's not me you've lost, it's her and I don't know why that is and I'm sorry. If there's something I can do then just tell me and I'll do it."

Dani dropped back into her chair. She looked mystified as Billy's words slowly permeated her thoughts until she gasped. "Oh my God, you're right. I used to meet her after work and we'd just have fun together. Laugh at nothing, maybe flirt a little. There was never anything in it, it was just a bit of fun. But that's all changed. She's frightened of putting a foot out of line in case I tell you. She resents the fact I know you so well and that we have a past. There are experiences we've shared that she can never be a part of." Dani hesitated for a moment. "But it is different with you. I tell you things that I don't want her to know and I can't help wondering if you tell her. And I can't bear the fact that you might talk about me and the worst thing is, I can't bitch about her anymore!" Neither could manage more than a rather dampened smile, their eyes flooded with sadness. "Why her? Why did it have to be Amanda?"

He thought for a moment. "If only we could exercise that kind of control."

Dani could only lower her eyes, aware of exactly who he was talking about.

That evening, Dani and her faithful duo were off to a theatre in Hammersmith to see Imogen in action; her last stop before opening in the West End. Sammy was clearly the least enthusiastic but even she had to admit Imogen was brilliant. It was a serious play and Imogen was on stage for almost the entire show. Despite that, her energy and commitment to the role had never wavered once.

When she joined them in a nearby bar afterwards, she was make-up free and dressed very simply in cropped harem trousers, a t-shirt, denim jacket and pumps. Despite the casual attire, she still looked like she was on a catwalk as she sashayed towards them, all surrounding eyes drawn to her like she was some kind of sexual magnet. Introductions out of the way, they settled into an easy conversation.

"The play was amazing Imogen." Sammy had completely let go of her reservations and was already full of respect. This was one heck of a transformation.

"Thanks, I'm loving it." Imogen was warm and gracious and instantly likeable. "Doesn't mean I'm not terrified about moving into the West End though. You just know every opening paragraph of the reviews is already written."

"Having seen the play now, I really don't think you should worry," Dani chipped in and no one was happier about that than her. "They may not be able to resist a quick round-up of how life used to be but it will be hard not to enthuse about a great play and an outstanding performance."

Imogen looked like she desperately wanted to believe this to be true. "Do you really think so?"

Dani smiled her most reassuring smile. "Yes, I really do."

Imogen still looked a little anxious. "In that case, would this be a good time to tell you I'm seeing my co-star?" Dani felt her eye twitch as Imogen continued. "It'll probably run its course before anyone finds out." She hesitated again. "Before his wife finds out at least."

Dani forced a smile, aware that Sammy and Toby had momentarily frozen. "Well it's good to have a heads-up," she managed, desperately trying to convince herself that she really should have expected nothing less.

13

Dani hated flying at the best of times but she was finding this flight particularly challenging. As if she wasn't nervous enough about what lay ahead, the weather had been awful and the last half an hour's flying had been like the most terrifying roller coaster ride. She looked down at her hands, colourless and rigid and gripping the arms of her seat as if life literally depended on them maintaining their vice-like hold. She felt locked in a nightmare that showed no signs of abating and then, joy of joys, the voice of the air hostess announced their final descent into Dublin. She blew out a long, slow breath, relief sweeping over her in a deliciously cool shiver as she braced herself for landing.

Dani was glad she had managed to dissuade Alex from coming to the airport to meet her, enjoying the ride out into the Irish countryside in contemplative silence. Initially, she was only aware of a sense of pure delight at being back on terra firma, which made her immediately more aware of the sights around her. The scenery was quite breathtaking and Dani was particularly aware of the colours, the pastel shades of summer replaced with the rich, deep browns and reds of autumn. And then she indulged herself in thoughts of nothing, allowing the passing views to blur, her eyes glazed, her breathing deep and even, as an eerily calm sense of resignation wrapped itself around her.

It was over an hour later when the cab pulled through large iron gates and down a narrow tree-lined road, at the end of which emerged the hotel Alex was staying in, standing proud and imposing in acres of its own grounds. Alex had assured her that only a few of the cast and crew were staying there, most of whom had taken advantage of a well-earned weekend break and had subsequently disappeared for a couple of days. Of course, this should have been irrelevant and she had hoped the nod towards discretion had been force of habit and nothing more.

Dani checked in, made sure everything was set for lunch the next day and had only been in her room for a few moments when there was a knock at the door. She jumped. She hadn't wanted to acknowledge the growing sense of anxiety that had taken hold the minute she had stepped through the grand hotel entrance but its physical manifestation now made it impossible to ignore. She took a deep breath and exhaled slowly, willing herself to at least appear calm, whatever chaos now reigned on the inside.

As she opened the door, she was immediately hit by how well Alex looked. His hair had grown slightly and, despite a heavy schedule, he looked relaxed and well. He took her into his arms and for a moment they just stood there, enjoying the uncomplicated and welcome feeling of intimacy that came with the warm embrace.

It was Dani who pulled away first and she walked towards the window keeping her back towards him as he closed the door. Why was this so hard? Why couldn't it just be as simple as Billy and Amanda seemed to think it was?

"What a beautiful place."

"Yes it is." Alex stood just behind her. He couldn't see her face and the flat tone of her voice made him nervous. He had been so looking forward to seeing her that he had chosen to focus on that alone, squashing all memory of their last meeting, and instead had spent hours romanticising about their impending reunion, the images of which were now quickly fading. "How was your flight?"

"Awful."

Alex waited, his ears now horribly aware of a clock ticking loudly somewhere behind him. He had to say something, if for no other reason than to break the otherwise unbearable silence and take his attention away from the hypnotic tick tock, tick tock.

"Dani?" She stayed exactly where she was. "Look at me." Slowly she turned around and he was immediately struck by the sadness in her eyes. "I'm really sorry we haven't been able to talk properly since the Ball. It was awful, for both of us." He paused, suddenly feeling awkward just standing there facing each other with a huge impenetrable void between them. Looking for a way to make things feel more relaxed, he sat on the edge of the bed and tapped the space next to him. He was relieved when Dani sat down next to him but she was in no hurry to talk.

It was a few moments before Dani slowly looked up at him and then she felt herself immediately pull back at the look of fear in his eyes. She had expected sadness, regret maybe, even resentment that they'd inevitably reached this point but not this growing sense of panic that was clearly taking hold of him. It was like she was watching him finally accept that this meeting would mark the end of their affair.

"Is this where we say it was fun while it lasted?" Dani was hoping to make him smile but Alex could only shake his head, slowly and rhythmically. "Come on Alex, we always knew there was nowhere for this to go."

"I promised you nothing and I thought if I said that then everything would be all right. That we could somehow keep our feelings out of it. I certainly thought I could but I was just being so naive. I've been such a fool!" He paused for a moment and then took hold of Dani's hand. "I always said I'd be honest with you, so here it is. I've fallen in love with you. I suppose I always knew it but when you told me you were seeing someone, I've never felt more desperate in my entire life. I was watching you slip away and there was nothing I could do to stop it. I thought when I saw you today…"

"No Alex," she said, quickly pulling her hand away. "You're not in love with me, you're jealous!"

"I just needed a wake-up call that's all. I didn't want to admit it to myself but you have to believe me Dani, I love you! Surely this changes things?"

"It changes nothing." Dani resisted the temptation to shout, delivering each word slowly and calmly. "I'm still with Sean. You're still married."

"But I can't bear the thought of not seeing you, of not touching you." He gently pushed her hair back from her eyes as he spoke. "It was never just sex. Something happens when I'm with you." He thought for a moment. There seemed no point in holding back now. "When I started to ask what if Victoria was out of the picture, I really meant it. Seeing the two of you together, I knew I just wanted to be with you."

Dani waited, searching his face for a clue as to what was coming next. "But?"

"Victoria's pregnant again." Alex was suddenly unable to look at her, then found himself rambling, feeling an urge to try to explain. "It was the night of the Ball. I hadn't slept with her for months but that night, in a huge hotel room, it was just too difficult to find an excuse not to. I…"

Dani put up a hand to stop him. "Spare me the gory details. I know how it happens." And then she shook her head in disbelief. "You're fucking unbelievable! How can you go from telling me everything's changed because you've suddenly decided you love me to that? Surely having another child is what changes things?" Alex said nothing. "Well Sean and I have moved in together, so I guess things have moved on for both of us."

"So what are we saying?"

How typical that it's up to me to actually say the words, thought Dani, as she took a deep breath. "We're saying it can't continue. If it does, we'll both lose everything. And there's just too much to lose." There, she had said it and in a strange way, she felt better. Alex put his arms around her and hugged her tightly.

"I'm so sorry Dani."

"For which part exactly?"

Alex smiled as his arms loosened. "Not for having a relationship with you. Despite everything, I'll never regret that. Sorry for being naive enough to believe we could carry on seeing each other and conduct our lives as normal I suppose. Sorry for being such a completely stupid bastard." And then he kissed her. He expected Dani to pull away but when she didn't, he kissed her again. "So it's over?"

"Yes Alex, it's over." Dani let him ease her down until they were lying beside each other.

"You're sure?" Alex unbuttoned her shirt and gently kissed her shoulder.

"Yes I'm sure." Dani watched as Alex pulled off his jumper and she closed her eyes as she felt his skin next to hers. He never stopped kissing her, her face, her neck, anything he could get his lips to.

"I do love you Dani."

"I know you do." And then there was nothing else to say.

When Dani woke the next morning, Alex was still asleep. For a while she chose to just look at him, enjoying the sense of innocence that sleep brought and the calm absence of conflict. She was horribly aware that as soon as he was awake, their bubble would be burst for the last time. She subsequently felt weak, a horrid, sick feeling in the pit of her stomach.

It was the noise of the shower that finally caused Alex to stir. He stretched and smiled at the memory of the previous night and then felt the warm and secure sensation that nestled in his stomach, slowly turn to one of fear and resignation. He was just as aware that as soon as they stepped out of the room, the spell would be broken, perhaps forever.

Dani appeared back in the room, her head and body smothered in huge white towels. There was an air of embarrassment almost, an awkwardness that they hadn't experienced before. "You should get back to your room before people start moving around." Obediently Alex got up and pulled on his clothes. He sat on the edge of the bed for a moment and then reluctantly headed for the door. "Alex?" He turned around slowly. He knew what she was going to say but that didn't mean he wanted to hear it. "It is over."

He smiled. "I know. I'll see you at lunch."

14

Sitting at her desk a week later, Dani was still finding it hard to concentrate. She was trying to focus on the fact the meeting in Ireland had gone really well and just erase the other stuff but it was a challenge she simply wasn't up to. And then she could hear Amanda. Don't fuck it up, she had said. She felt bereft, so impossible was it to deny she was doing a supremely efficient job of fucking it up and right royally at that. She jumped as she realised Toby was shouting at her, desperately trying to grab her attention. Dani looked over and followed the line of his frantic gestures in time to see a rather weary looking Sammy walk back to her desk and slump into her chair with a sigh. She had been out doing interviews with Imogen to promote her West End debut.

"Oh dear. Someone doesn't look happy." Toby stood up as he spoke. "Don't worry. A cup of my very special tea is on its way."

As Toby disappeared, Sammy looked over at Dani. "What happened?"

"It was all going brilliantly until the last interview. I was literally grabbing my coat thinking we were done when the final question came." Dani raised her eyebrows in anticipation. "'Just one final question', he innocently said. 'What did you have for lunch?'"

Dani gasped. Any normal person would be forgiven for looking confused at this point but for someone who started life as a model, for someone trained to be super paranoid about all things to do with body weight, terrified of gaining even a tenth of a gram, for this person, this was the mother of all no-nos. Dani was therefore horribly aware of the significance of the question. "Oh shit. What did she say?"

"I'd love to be able to tell you she coped with it perfectly, that she was composed and professional but sadly that is not the case." Toby arrived with a mug of tea and handed it to Sammy. She held it in her hands for a moment, taking some comfort from the heat and the sweet smell that she took a moment to breathe in. Toby had rightly assumed this was a situation requiring plenty of sugar.

"Sammy?" Dani was starting to twitch. "What did she do?"

"She leapt out of her chair, screaming she knew exactly what Phil was trying to do, that he was an insensitive fucker not interested in the slightest that she was trying to move her life on, that if he thought she was fat he should take a long hard look in the mirror, that…"

Dani put up her hand. "Okay, I get the picture. Wowser. Safe to say she didn't handle it well then. How was she when you left her?"

Sammy blew on her tea and took a large satisfying slurp. "I let her swear her head off for five minutes then calmed her down, then she vowed she'd never do any more interviews. And before you ask, I've sorted it with

Phil. He genuinely enjoyed the play so thinks her ability to really act is a bigger story than the fact she's clearly nuts so he said he'd leave it out. It was a really good chat before then which helped."

"Good girl. Clearly she needs a bit more media training."

"But I rehearsed all this with her! That's why I'm so pissed off," Sammy cried, the desperation and frustration strangling her so that her voice was nothing more than a high-pitched squeal. She swallowed hard. "We knew this was likely to come up one way or another and we covered it all. She doesn't need training, she needs therapy. But the damage is done. He may not print it but Phil will tell the story a million times. You just know it will come out at some point." Her voice trailed off as she started scanning through the stack of unopened emails that had accumulated in her absence.

"You're okay then?" Sammy nodded, her eyes now fixed on her computer screen, already moving on to the next challenge. Dani smiled. Either she had trained her seriously well or she needed to find out exactly what Toby was putting in his 'special tea'.

Half an hour later, Dani stepped out of the office and flinched at the immediate wall of noise that hit her, sticking close to the building to avoid being swept along the pavement by a constant flow of people. She took a moment to take in a deep breath of the freshest air London was capable of offering and then she headed towards Amanda's shop. Billy was right. It was her friendship with Amanda that had taken the brunt of her recent frustration. If she was honest, she realised now it was Amanda she was angry with. She had wanted Billy for herself which was both selfish and greedy and she had been punishing Amanda which was as inappropriate as it was childish and pathetic. Shame on me, she thought as she quickened her step, stopping only briefly to pick up a lovely selection of sushi, a small but lethal selection of chocolatey cakes and a bottle of chilled wine.

Dani entered the shop as Amanda was bidding farewell to a customer carrying a suitably large bag of purchases. The woman disappeared out the door and Amanda's big smile widened further as she saw her friend and then she looked at her watch. "Hello slacker. Shouldn't you be at work?"

"I brought you some lunch," she said, holding up the bag as if proof were needed.

"Fantastic. I'll get some plates." Amanda disappeared into the back of the shop, leaving Dani to settle herself into one of two huge leather armchairs normally reserved for the male companions of customers who, knowing their partners were sitting comfortably, were immediately able to relax into their browsing, or for friends waiting to give their opinions as items were tried on. The well-worn chairs had subsequently paid for themselves many, many times over. There was a small table between them stacked with magazines which Dani now removed to make room for their lunch and then she waited. She had decided against any kind of clumsy explanation or apology for her withdrawal and for all the resentment and anger she'd been struggling to contain since Amanda and Billy had got together. Just getting things back on track, back to the way they used to be seemed far more productive. A spontaneous lunch and a long overdue chat with just the two of them was clearly the best way forward.

With a slight tinge of sadness, Dani was suddenly able to see how much she had missed Amanda but before she had time to get too maudlin, she was forced to quickly pull herself together as the sound of Amanda's clattering increased until there she was, sitting in front of her, armed with plates, glasses and cutlery.

"Well this is a lovely surprise," Amanda said as she laid everything out. "It's ages since we've done something like this."

Dani started to unpack her wares. Amanda watched her carefully, studying her face and the haunted look in her eyes and then she sat back. "You slept with Alex again didn't you?" Dani stopped what she was doing, her eyes immediately filling with tears and she nodded. Amanda was unable to hide her distress. "Jesus Dani! What the fuck?" She couldn't think of anything else to say. Dani put a hand up to cover her face, the shame she was feeling compelling her to hide her eyes at the very least. "I just don't understand," Amanda continued and then she thought for a moment. "Actually I do understand. The point is are you ready to?" Dani looked at her and Amanda immediately felt her own eyes flood with tears. She had never seen anyone look so traumatised, so vulnerable, so terrified. And then finally Dani found her voice.

"I just can't bear to blame him for everything. It's such a dreadful cliché."

"But how could you possibly not be affected by it? It's just ridiculous to think your dad leaving hasn't had a lasting effect on you. I was there remember? I saw what it did to you."

Dani's parents had only been together for a few years when her father had his first affair. Dani had been two years old. Perhaps helped by the fact the affair was short-lived, her mother had been prepared to forgive, convincing herself it was probably her own fault, spending too much time on her child and therefore neglecting her husband. They picked themselves up and managed to get things back on track and, for several years, had what many would consider a good, solid marriage. But for Dani's mother, there was always a degree of anxiety as she watched her charming and outgoing husband mix at parties and work-related functions, an ever-so-slight nervous tic developing as she watched him chat with all sorts of women, eyes alive, tactile hands touching, lips lingering a little bit longer than necessary on flushed cheeks, the odd quiet word whispered in ears. The fear never quite went away that it could happen again. Which of course it did. And not just once but again and again and again.

On the final occasion, Helen, Dani's mother, started to have the now familiar suspicions but, as always, immediately dismissed as paranoia any notion that he could be betraying her again. It worked for a while but when one of her friends, pained and embarrassed looking, told her she'd seen Ed in a restaurant with a young woman and described vividly the way they were behaving together, she knew she had to do something. It was one thing to suspect but quite another to hear that he was publicly humiliating her. That very same night, she had confronted him and to her horror, he had been relieved, almost happy, that it was now out in the open, his face suddenly relaxed, his eyes annoyingly bright. He clearly hadn't had the courage to admit he'd strayed and now he didn't have to. He felt released and without offering any explanation or, perhaps worse, any attempt at an apology, he opted to leave her with her thoughts and went out for the evening.

Over the following week the initial relief that it was all out in the open was then replaced by extraordinary anger on Helen's part and a completely unfathomable determination from Ed that they should just carry on as they were. Night after night they argued, Helen screaming at Ed, Ed resolute that he loved his daughter and wanted to stay around, unwilling to even consider why they couldn't just adjust and crack on as they always had done. He promised to be more discreet, wasn't that enough? No, was obviously the short answer. The longer version was far more painful, involved endless rows, rivers of tears and hours of sad, desperate silence.

Dani, now ten years old, listened to every word from her bedroom, curled up in a ball behind her bedroom door, her hands clasped tightly around her knees and able to hear every painful word. She watched her mother function on autopilot during the day, her smiles unable to mask the sadness in her eyes and watched her father do his best to behave as normal. It was like being in some kind of bizarre play with people adopting roles they clearly didn't believe in, their performances subsequently unconvincing. While it was incredibly tough to witness, the hardest part for Dani was how to manage her own feelings. She desperately wanted to comfort and protect her mother, that part was easy. The torment came when she thought of her father. A man who had hurt her mother to her very core and who therefore deserved nothing better than pure hatred. But he was her father and she loved him, loved everything about him.

As Dani struggled with her own feelings, her parents continued to argue at night and move awkwardly around each other during the day until Helen finally snapped. It was a Friday evening and one that Dani would never forget. She was sitting comfortably on the sofa, a Friday treat of ice-cream in a bowl on her lap. When her father came home from work, her mother pounced and in seconds, voices were raised. Putting the bowl to one side, she put her hands over her ears, willing it to stop until she couldn't stand it any longer. Running into the hall, she screamed at both of them, "Stop it! Please just stop it!"

Helen and Ed froze and in that moment, they both knew they couldn't carry on the way they were. A brief look at each other was all that was needed and then Ed hurried upstairs while Helen desperately tried to encourage Dani back into the lounge. Rising panic took over. "What's he doing? What's happening? Mum, make it stop, please make it stop!" Of course she knew exactly what was happening and moments later, there was her father whom she idolised, standing with a bag in each hand, his face dripping with sadness. "Dad, please!" Dani was hysterical, her heart breaking, her world crumbling.

"I'm sorry Dani." And with that he opened the door and slipped out.

Amanda stood up and heading to the door, she flipped the 'open' sign to 'closed' and turned the lock. This was definitely not the time for interruptions. As she sat back down, her mind easily slipped back the twenty something years to that fateful night. She had innocently turned up as she did every Friday for a film and some ice-cream and had witnessed the carnage first hand. She had been terrified by Dani's hysteria, unsettled by Helen's tears and at a complete loss to know what to do. Eventually, she had merely told Dani that she would hold her hand through all the turmoil and that's what she had done, literally. She held her hand on the way to school, in the classroom, at playtime and on the way home. She held her hand as they watched television together and as they made their Saturday trip to the local shop for a magazine and a bag of sweets but, while she could act as a physical prop, what she couldn't stop was the emotional withdrawal. She knew Dani was aware of the other mums looking at her with what she could only interpret as pity, overhearing on a regular basis how angry they were with Ed, how despicable he was and occasionally, how they had witnessed him with one woman or another as he played out what was obviously some terrible mid-life crisis. This was almost better than those desperately trying to reassure her mum that it was only a matter of time before he would realise how idiotic he had been and that he'd be back. She knew whenever Dani heard this, her face lightened slightly, wondering if tonight would be the night when she would once again hear his key in the door.

Amanda remembered how tormented Dani had been when several years later her relationship with Nick developed into something that mattered and how anxious she had been about admitting how strongly she felt about him. Of course she had never stopped to consider why. It all seemed so obvious now. She looked at Dani opposite her, always confident and charismatic, smart and wily, determined and strong. But not today. Today she was the terrified ten year old; fearful, confused and emotionally disabled. Amanda leant forward across the small coffee table laden with untouched food and stroked Dani's knees. "Talk to me."

Dani slowly looked up. "Everyone was always so condemning of him, so vocal about the lives he'd ruined, the mess he'd caused. It just felt like my job was to defend him. Someone had to. He was still my dad and I just couldn't bear to consider for even a moment that he might have damaged me too."

"I get that, I really do but of course he did! I don't know, maybe you're trying to understand him better, prove that it is possible to love two people at the same time. Maybe Alex reminds you of him in some way and that's why you're so drawn to him. Or maybe you're still traumatised by the fact he was prepared to leave you too. Who knows? But you're not your dad and neither is Alex." Amanda stopped as Dani's tears finally started to spill onto her flushed cheeks and then they both jumped as the front door rattled, their heads sweeping round to see a woman knocking on the door. They had been aware of a few people wandering up to the shop and then obediently retreating on seeing the closed sign but this one wasn't to be so easily put off. Dani immediately sat up, wiping away her tears as she hunted for a tissue in her bag to tidy up her mascara-soaked face. "It's okay," she said, "let her in."

Amanda hesitated for a second and then stood up to open the door. As the determined shopper came in, she ushered Dani to a quiet corner. "Hang around for a while. I'll get rid of her."

"No, I need to get back to the office."

"Really? Five more minutes, please." Amanda was desperate to hang on to her but Dani was already checking herself in a mirror, horrified at the puffy mess that looked back at her. She did the best cover-up she could and then putting the mirror away, she looked at her friend. "Thank you. And I'm sorry…"

Amanda stopped her. "No, don't be sorry. About any-thing." She took hold of Dani's hand. "Shall I walk you back?"

They both smiled, aware of the significance of the gesture. "No, I'll be fine."

Heading back to the office, Dani felt numb. So the truth was finally out there. She was a crazy mixed up kid. And a thirty six year old one at that. How very dis-appointing. Although she wasn't quite sure for whom. She'd tried so hard to lock it all away but now that she thought about it, she had no idea why. What had she possibly hoped to gain by denying such a fundamental part of her childhood? Especially when it had obviously had such a profound effect. The part of her psyche that governed her relationships was clearly contaminated. She shuddered at the sudden feeling of being diseased in some way, poisoned by the ghosts of divorce past.

And it definitely wasn't how she'd imagined lunch would play out. That said, she had left Amanda feeling incredibly close to her so job done she supposed, even if it was in a way that had left her emotionally ragged. She hadn't even had the chance to tell her the affair with Alex was over. Oh well, she thought, convinced that Amanda wouldn't have believed it anyway.

As Dani pushed open the doors to the office, she hesi-tated for just a moment, shaking off the sense of tor-ment in an attempt to leave it behind her. Sitting back at her desk a few moments later, she stared at the client board. The active section was looking strong and her growing gang of influencers were doing great business but, as always happened, there were a number of newbies that just weren't getting even remotely close to making that giant first step into gainful employment. The harsh reality was that for every one that made it, there were always countless more who, for whatever reason, just couldn't break through. It had been on her mind for a while now and she had been successfully batting away any thoughts that some action was needed but enough was enough, it was time to let some of them go. As it seemed impossible to feel any worse about herself today, now seemed as good a time as any to make the cut.

When Dani didn't respond to Sammy's third attempt at attracting her attention, it was obvious something was wrong. Sammy got up from her desk and stood between Dani and the board and waited quietly until finally Dani acknowledged her. "You're in my way," she said, her eyes still fixed on the board even if she couldn't now see it properly.

"Is it time?" Sammy took the absence of an answer as a 'yes' and pulled up a chair, telling Toby to do the same. Looking now like they were waiting for some kind of lecture, they sat in front of the board while Dani slowly walked over, her eyes flitting from one mugshot to another. Eventually she pointed at a girl called Molly who'd been signed up over a year ago. She had been to countless castings but didn't seem to be making any impact at all.

"No, not Molls!" Toby cried. "It will happen, I just need more time!"

"If she sits there any longer she'll take root." Dani unpinned her picture and put it at the bottom so that poor Molly now hung precariously off the edge of the board. Another moment and she was joined by Mike and then quickly by Tony, both talented and engaging but seemingly unemployable at the same time. Sammy went to say something but stopped herself. They all knew how it worked. Eventually you just had to accept that the time invested in no-hopers - harsh but true - was time that could be spent on those who were already proving to actually stand a chance. None of them liked it but that was simply the way it was.

Dani clearly hadn't finished. Two more mugshots were moved to join those already condemned and then she stood back. "Thoughts?" Sammy and Toby pulled suitable faces to show their regret, their disappointment and ultimately, their approval.

"Before you ask, I'll do it. And before you say anything," Toby quickly continued, knowing interruption was imminent and eager to stave it off until he'd finished, "I know my role in this unique trio of ours is to provide some well-needed jollity to proceedings but I can be sensitive when required, and ruthless too. So let me tell them."

Dani smiled warmly. "Well Toby Brader, I think you may just have graduated to a fully-fledged grown-up. Of course you can do it. And I have no doubt you'll handle it with confidence and sensitivity."

Toby was immediately on his way back to his desk. As he sat down, he pulled a handkerchief from his pocket, shook it open and then placed it carefully on his head.

"Bloody hell," Sammy said under her breath. "He's delivering some bad news, not sending them to the gallows." She watched him sit up straight, take a deep breath with eyes closed and then slowly exhale. "What the hell's he doing?"

"Composing himself."

Sammy was unconvinced. "Maybe I should do it?"

"No," Dani replied calmly. "He'll do just fine."

Shaking her head, Sammy reluctantly headed back to her desk, persuaded more than ever that she was the only one amongst them who hadn't completely lost the plot.

15

Dani was already awake when her alarm went off the next morning. The office had provided the perfect distraction for a few hours the evening before but, with Sean out, she had found it impossible to settle once she had got home. Whatever she had tried, her conversation with Amanda kept swimming in her mind, round and around and around. She had felt horribly twitchy, unable to focus on anything, finding it impossible to sit in one place for more than a few minutes. Going to bed early had only meant even longer spent lying awake staring at the ceiling, the search for peace fruitless, the desperation to be asleep backfiring until she was so wired, any notion of rest was as far out of reach as the answers she so desperately wanted.

She reached out to turn off the alarm and then continued to lie where she was, her body heavy with tiredness, Sean sleeping peacefully beside her. She had no idea what time he had crawled into bed and knew he was unlikely to wake up. He had perfected the art of sleeping through her alarm and not even the shower, the sound of her opening and shutting wardrobes or clattering around for a specific pair of shoes, provoked even the slightest stir. She was grateful today that this was the case.

Several minutes passed before she sat up and then reaching for her phone, she emailed Toby and Sammy to say she wouldn't be in but would catch up with them later. They could cope on their own for a day.

Without a word to Sean, Dani got herself dressed and an hour later she was on a train. However guilty she felt at not telling him what she was up to, she knew he would have wanted to come with her and she didn't want to have to explain why she needed to make this trip on her own. She would have time on the way back to work out how she would explain herself.

Settling back into her seat, Dani stretched out her legs as best she could and pushed aside the stack of magazines she had bought as she'd flown through the station. She had thought the unchallenging reading matter would be perfect for the ninety minute journey but now that the train was actually moving, they held little appeal. She turned her attention instead to the window and immediately reached for her sunglasses. The light was bright against the glass pane and hurt her tired eyes. With London now behind her, she was amazed how still everything looked as the countryside sped past. Every tree was completely static and there was no sign of life in the occasional cluster of houses. Dani imagined a bizarre game of musical statues was in play, wondering if the music would at some point restart, causing everything to become animated once again. While she waited for this phenomena to take place, her eyes were automatically drawn to anything that moved; a woman walking a dog along an otherwise deserted path, a sudden burst of activity from a small herd of cows, a tractor slowly working its way across a field, its path perfectly mapped out in the shape of thick tyre tracks in the earth behind it. And then she caught a glimpse of someone sitting on a bench in an empty playground, their head in their hands and her heart contracted, imagining a kindred spirit, another tortured soul desperately searching for resolution.

Dani picked up one of the magazines and started to flick through it, her eyes flitting but settling on nothing beyond a few words here and there. She closed it and turned back to the window for a while and then chose another magazine but still found nothing to grab her attention, eyes drifting back once again to the window. The agitated pattern continued until the train finally pulled into her station.

Dani was the first to disembark. It felt strange to walk a platform she hadn't been on for far too long, normally choosing to drive straight home, allowing for minimum contact with memories of a life left behind. Her eyes were drawn to the colourful array of plants in well-kept troughs that lined the way, replaced by hanging baskets as she reached the ticket office. It was a level of care and attention that, like everything else around, felt alien. As she stepped outside, she couldn't help a quick nervous survey of the horizon, checking for any familiar faces but was relieved to see none. Ignoring the line of waiting taxis, she then slowly set off on foot, preferring the fresh air to forced conversation with a driver glad to have some company after a long, silent wait.

The pavements were quiet as she passed by rows of independent shops, resisting the urge to browse, each window doing its best to tempt her in. Maybe on the way back, she told herself as her ears tuned in and out of the sounds around her - people chatting on street corners, the clatter of plates as café tables were cleared, the hum of an occasional car. The relaxed pace, something she had hated as a perpetually bored teenager, was surprisingly soothing as she wove her way down the high street, through the square in the centre and on out the other side until she reached her destination.

As Dani sat down opposite her father, she took a moment to gather her thoughts. It was time to try to find some understanding, time to try to layer the maturity and experience of adulthood over the raw black and white emotion of the child she once was. Eventually she looked up. "So I had an affair. I know! Talk about hypocritical." She paused for a moment. "I mean what was I thinking? I had a ringside seat to the fall-out after you and mum split up. I've never lost that feeling of abandonment, feeling like I didn't matter enough to make you stay. I've never really forgiven you and yet here I am, wrecking other people's lives with the same selfish disregard."

The silence was deafening but Dani was perfectly calm. In a bizarre way, she felt closer to her father than she ever had. She wondered what he would make of it all as she studied the gravestone in front of her, sitting cross-legged on the ground, knowing there would be no response, no words of wisdom to release her from her own guilt. She looked at the carved inscription - Loving Husband and Father - and she laughed. "What does that even mean?" she asked, continuing to speak out loud. "Loving husband to which wife?" There had been three all told. And then she stopped. He may not be able to hear or reply but that didn't stop the inner child wondering if she'd gone too far. At least there was some small comfort in knowing he was father only to her, although she wasn't sure why that mattered. Her eyes were drawn to the flowers left by whom she wondered? "I didn't bring you flowers," she said, her voice suddenly less confident as her chin wobbled and then she sat in contemplative silence, desperate to feel a connection that she knew, despite everything, would make her feel safe and loved.

Thoughts overtook any sense of time until eventually Dani stood up, brushing the dusty, dry earth from her jeans. She looked at the headstone, reaching a hand out to touch it, tentative fingers brushing over its surface and she stayed there, her heart swollen in her chest forcing brief, shallow breaths, until she finally found the strength to turn her back and walk away.

"You sounded subdued on the phone. Is everything alright?"

Dani had headed straight for the place that truly deserved the title of home and within minutes was settled in the lounge, a cup of tea on a table placed carefully beside her by her mother. She was the only person Dani knew who still had a nest of coffee tables, one of a few bits of furniture that had survived over the passing decades. Dani took a moment to familiarise herself with the room. It had evolved over the years with the wallpaper and fussy prints of the eighties giving way to the fabulously ridiculous paint sponging craze of the nineties, with one too many fake silk flowers on show. The noughties brought with them the comeback of wallpaper (only for a feature wall, obviously) and finally to the more neutral shades it wore now, with a careful selection of house plants that were once again real. Money had been tight so the classic three piece suite had been forced to stand the test of time, protected at various points by patterned, colourful throws and eventually re-covered by a friend on the cheap. When her father had left, Dani knew exactly the moment when her mother had accepted there was no chance of a reconciliation when she came home from school one day to find her parents' bedroom swathed in Laura Ashley florals from top to bottom and everything in between. Her father would have hated it.

Helen sat opposite her daughter and waited for Dani to answer her question, her smile encouraging. She couldn't remember a time when Dani had come to see her midweek and was desperate to know what could possibly be so important to justify the uncharacteristic visit. Not that it wasn't lovely to just sit and look at her; her beautiful daughter who made her so proud and whom she missed terribly. The visits were few and far between, which had only got worse over time as the pace of Dani's life had accelerated to a rate Helen sim-

203

ply couldn't understand. The pressure terrified her but she knew there was nothing she could do. She had been relegated from the front row seat she had cherished through childhood to the restricted view of the upper circle, able to do nothing more than observe from a distance.

Helen left it for as long as she could and then provided a prompt. "Dani?"

Dani snapped herself out of her thoughts and as she looked at Helen, her expression changed, her distress suddenly fully on display. "Oh Mum, I don't know where to start. It's all such a horrible mess."

Again Helen waited and then gradually, it all came out. The affair with Alex, how she felt about Sean and yet despite her strength of feeling for him, how she still struggled with the idea that she'd let Alex go. And then of course there was Alex's wife and children and her blatant disregard for them all. "What's happened to me? You know better than anyone how I feel about affairs and how long I've dreamed of finding my soulmate and when I finally do, I cheat on him! I still can't quite believe it. Even when I say it out loud, there's a part of me that still thinks I'm talking about someone else." She looked at her mother's loving face. There was no trace of disappointment or anger, just warmth and concern. Dani felt tears sting her eyes as Helen thought for a moment, quickly trying to catch up.

"Yes I do know how you feel about affairs but that didn't stop you getting involved with Alex which speaks volumes in itself."

"So you think I should be with Alex?"

"That's not what I'm saying at all," Helen smiled gently. "If you finished things with Sean do you really think you could go through with pulling Alex away from his family? Assuming of course he could actually be pulled away."

Dani shook her head. "I don't know. If he did leave his wife that would only be the start of it. His career is really taking off which means he's away a lot and surrounded by temptation in the shape of who knows how many gorgeous women. He's done it once so why not again?" She looked at her mother for a moment. "I'm so sorry Mum. This must be really hard for you."

"Why? Because of the way your dad behaved? It isn't a case of one size fits all. Some people make mistakes, realise they're married to the wrong person and go on to find happiness with someone else. Of course, we'd all prefer it if that could happen without an affair to speed up the process but that's inevitably the way it goes."

"You're surely not putting Dad in that category?"

"No. He was more of a serial offender. Someone who had multiple affairs with no intention of ever trying to be faithful."

Dani's eyes were drawn to the various framed photographs dotted around the room. "So why do you still have a picture of him?"

Helen turned to look at the picture of her ex-husband and child, wrapped around each other and brimming with happiness. "Because without him, I wouldn't have

205

you." Helen looked at Dani. "I know you hate grey but there's no black and white here I'm afraid. If things hadn't come to a head as they did I wouldn't have met Mike. Truth is, I could never have been this happy and secure with your dad."

"What, so he did you a favour?"

Helen stood up. "How about a biscuit?" she asked as she headed back to the kitchen without waiting for a reply. With no time to prepare for this conversation she needed a moment to gather her thoughts if she had any chance at all of actually helping Dani. Sometimes the pressure of being a parent felt crippling and it certainly didn't get any easier. She smiled to herself as she remembered how desperate she had felt when, at five years of age, Dani wouldn't do anything she was asked. It had seemed monumental at the time as she'd watched other children behave so much better, filling her with shame at her seemingly inadequate parenting skills. Oh how she would happily have that problem back! She knew that, as always, Dani expected her to have the answers, to be able to shed light when she obviously felt lost in the dark but, on this occasion, it was just too much to imagine she could conjure up a simple solution. As time went by, the problems that needed solving only got bigger, along with the stakes that came as part of the package. She hadn't forgotten the years of insecurity, the hurt and the shame she'd felt that her marriage had failed but it was clear to her more than ever that Dani bore the scars more than she did and she had no idea how to put that right. She felt a pang of regret painfully stab her chest. A sharp, wretched reminder that she knew exactly what Dani needed - to have it out with Ed. To thrash, vent, argue and listen until she found some peace with it all but that could never happen now. A sudden heart attack five years earlier had caught them all unawares and no one understood better than Helen the significance of the event for her daughter. Apart from the obvious sense of loss, the closure that Dani so desperately wanted had immediately become forever out of reach.

Armed with a plate of assorted biscuits, Helen headed back to the lounge. She watched Dani, lost to her thoughts, as she placed them beside her before sitting back down. "I can see you're traumatised about the affair with Alex but it's not really about him is it? Or Sean for that matter. You've always been so determined in your condemnation of your dad's behaviour. It must be unsettling at best now that you've seen how easy it is to cross a line you thought was impenetrable."

Dani looked at her with a bittersweet smile. "Bullseye."

"You're not a bad person. Anything but. It was a tough way to work out that your dad wasn't either. Stupid yes. Arrogant definitely. And thoughtless too." Helen shrugged.

"I should have talked to him about it. That would have been a less complicated and painful way to go."

"Or it might have made it worse for you."

"How is that possible?"

"Because you would have wanted answers. I'm pretty sure that any explanation he might have given you would have infuriated you rather than appease you."

"Maybe."

A heavy silence descended. Dani wondered for a moment why she had come or, more importantly, what she had expected to leave with. A new level of understanding perhaps? Some new insight or information that would explain or perhaps even justify her moral inconsistencies. She felt thoroughly ashamed.

"Are you okay darling?" Helen watched as Dani slowly massaged her temples, her fingers moving in small, gentle circles. Eventually she stopped and looked up.

"I hated what Dad did to you and despised the women he cheated with more. It's hard to accept that I'm no better."

"Maybe you saw something of your dad in Alex?"

"Or maybe I'm more like him than I thought?"

"I'm pretty sure he never had similar moments of self-reflection. Learn and move on Dani. Beating yourself up won't undo anything but it can change how you behave in the future. You're in control. Remember that."

16

Dani picked up the copy of the Sunday Times Magazine with a smile. There on the cover was Alex, Victoria and Bethany, the newest edition to the Cambridge household. Inside were eight pages of the deliriously happy couple at home with their four children, all perfectly polished for the camera. Over the past few months it had been almost impossible to pick up a magazine or newspaper or go online without seeing pictures of Alex, so in demand by producers and the media alike. He had been on every major television chat show and Dani was already trading on his name, occasionally only confirming his appearance or an interview once she had a slot for one of her lesser known artists. They might as well all bask in the Alex Cambridge glory. He had well and truly been taken into the hearts of the nation, so attractive, so charming and so committed to his family. The irony was pure poetry.

Dani's workload had become unmanageable and she had finally had the go-ahead to bring an assistant into the team. Her name was Caroline and she was an unflappable young woman whose twenty-three years belied her extreme confidence. She was perfect for Dani and her working life had never felt more organised and under control. She had also waved a fond farewell to her merry band of influencers, now safely housed in a department of their own under the guidance of a new agent whose background in social media made Dani look like a complete novice, which she had to admit by comparison she absolutely was.

Her contact with Alex had been minimal. When he'd left Ireland, he'd gone straight on to do the film with a demanding schedule in a host of different locations. There had been a few meetings as she worked to line up future projects but with his time under so much pressure, there was certainly no room to add in any extra-curricular activities even if she had wanted to, which of course she didn't. In between, and normally just when she'd hit a point where she'd stopped thinking about him, flowers would arrive or a small gift. Something he'd seen that he thought she'd like. And it always was something she liked which only made it worse. He might as well have sent a shroud of sadness as each left her feeling thoroughly wretched and consumed by the very worst sense of melancholy that she always struggled to shake off. She continued to strike his deals but there was no need for any hard sells any more. Alex had an assistant of his own now too which gave her another excuse to leave the detail to others to manage. Then there were the awards; a BAFTA already now under his belt and a momentum-building rumour of an Emmy nomination after the surprise success in America of one of his first TV dramas.

Thankfully, life was too busy to dwell on what might have been. Sean was doing extremely well and he and Dani had never been happier. They enjoyed an enviable lifestyle with great holidays, an invitation to any party they wanted to attend and a level of pure contentment that was hard to put into words. They had managed to achieve and hold on to that perfect combination of a relaxed contentment that came with so much time spent together but, at the same time, they had never lost the spark of passion. If work kept them apart for a few days, it wasn't unusual for one to literally wait behind the front door, pacing up and down in anticipation of the other one coming home. They had possibly had sex in the hall as many times as they had in their bedroom.

"Dani, Sean's on the phone. He can't remember what he's supposed to be getting for tonight." Caroline smiled as she watched Dani pick up the call, her eyes raised to the ceiling.

"You are completely useless! What happened to the list I wrote you?"

"I left it at home."

"Brilliant. Just get some wine and I'll get the rest at lunch time."

"Red or white?"

"Both. Can you manage that?"

"Consider it done! I'll see you later."

When Dani got home, her arms felt inches longer after a mammoth struggle with several overloaded bags. Sean followed her into the kitchen and then saluted. "Private MacDonald reporting for duty!"

She smiled at him. "Time check?"

He looked at his watch. "Six forty five."

"Our guests' ETA?"

"Eight o'clock."

Dani handed him a knife. "Well I'm going for a bath. You can get chopping."

Dani lay in the bath, luxuriating in a mass of gorgeous smelling bubbles. As often happened in moments of pure relaxation when the minutiae of the day-to-day slowly melted away, she found herself thinking about Alex. As soon as they had stopped seeing each other, the guilt had finally arrived and judging by the amount of luggage it brought with it, Dani had known it was planning to stay for some considerable time. Occasionally she shed a tear, unable to comprehend that she had behaved with such malicious selfishness, with such incredible deceit and all with such ease. Most often, she just lay in the bath and went over everything again and again, her heart heavy. She had thought often of her mother's words about being in control of her future, a mantra she was desperate to embrace but she knew that would only be possible once she'd found peace with the terrible decisions she'd made that now defined her recent past.

Her thoughts were broken by the arrival of Sean at the door. "I've chopped everything I could lay my hands on. The chicken's in the oven, the vegetables are perfectly arranged in saucepans ready to be switched on, I've made the starter so the salad and the dressing just need to be formally introduced at a strategic moment, you already made dessert, the white wine is chilling and the red wine is breathing. Now what?"

Without waiting for a response, Sean was already pulling off his t-shirt and undoing his jeans. "What are you doing?"

"Having a bath. What are you doing?"

Dani squealed as the water slopped over the side of the bath as Sean stepped into the soapy water and then nestled himself between her legs. He relaxed back to lie on her chest and she squeezed her legs around him, kissing the side of his head. They lay there together, as happy chatting about this and that as they were just relaxing in a comfortable silence until reluctantly, Sean climbed out again, standing in wait with a huge towel for Dani, a familiar glint in his eye. She smiled as she stepped out of the bath and let him gently start to rub her dry. There was only one way for this to go now which would undoubtedly mean a last minute panic to be ready in time. Never mind, she thought, breathing in deeply as Sean wrapped the towel around them both. It would be worth it.

When the doorbell rang, Sean was just buttoning up his shirt. He quickly ran his hands through his short hair a few times and left Dani frantically waving a hairdryer in the general direction of her head, while she struggled to get dressed at the same time.

As Billy and Amanda sat down in the lounge, Dani appeared just behind them. She looked stunning, her hair long, straight and shiny, her clothes as simple as ever, her eyes bright and alive. Billy was on his feet again immediately and took her into his arms. "You look fantastic. And you're ready! I feel extremely honoured." Dani smiled, aware that she was fast earning a reputation for always being late.

She exchanged a mischievous glance with Sean as he busied himself getting drinks for everyone, idle chatter starting up with a vengeance. Billy immediately began recounting an amusing story, one of his unique 'it could only happen to me' tales, while Amanda as always questioned Sean about where he'd been and who he'd seen. Dani watched them with a warm smile but with a certain apprehension. She wasn't sure why but there was definitely something in the air. She couldn't put her finger on it. It certainly wasn't tension but there was undoubtedly something there.

They sat down to eat and the wine flowed freely. As they took a pause before dessert there was a sudden break in conversation. Whatever it was, thought Dani, I think I'm about to find out. "Come on Billy, I know you're dying to tell us. Spit it out."

"You really know how to steal a man's thunder don't you?" Dani shrugged her shoulders with a smile while Sean looked on, confused.

"What's going on?"

Dani raised her eyebrows. "Billy?"

"Okay, okay!" He took a deep breath and smiled. "Amanda and I are getting married."

Sean leapt out of his chair and kissed Amanda, then took hold of Billy's hand and shook it almost violently, immediately overtaken by genuine excitement. "That's fantastic news! Thank God we've got some cham-

214

pagne!" And he hurriedly disappeared in search of a bottle and some fresh glasses.

"You'll be my bridesmaid?" Amanda looked eagerly at her friend.

"Of course I will!" Dani said, feeling suddenly quite overwhelmed.

Sean rushed back into the room and with some clumsy unwrapping and twisting, the champagne cork exploded and Amanda screamed, laughing with Sean as he desperately tried to catch the flow of liquid that was already spilling from the bottle. She jumped up to offer her help leaving Billy and Dani alone at the table. He took hold of Dani's hand and they smiled at each other. Goodbye forever my most trusted friend, she thought and then bit her lip in a desperate attempt to stop the tears that she so badly, and selfishly, wanted to cry.

Oblivious, Sean handed out glasses of champagne. "To Amanda and Billy," he said. "And to the lifetime of happiness you both hugely deserve." They all raised their glasses.

"Thanks mate." Billy smiled but Sean was already thinking ahead, seemingly lost in his own thoughts. "Sean?"

"How wonderful. Before the wedding comes the stag do!"

Amanda looked immediately horrified. "Now just a minute! If you're imagining chaining him naked to a lamp post or putting him on a train to Scotland, you can think again!"

215

Sean ignored her playfully, his attention only for Billy. "So how long have I got to make plans?"

Billy smiled. "Well provided we can get everything booked, we thought September which gives you about six months to come up with something truly original!"

A look of panic swept over Amanda. "Dani do something!"

Dani laughed. "Drink some more champagne and relax. He's only winding you up," she said as she looked at the men, their voices now lowered as they plotted in a conspiratorial huddle. "At least I think he is."

For the remainder of the evening, the conversation was dominated by discussions of whether they should have a small or large wedding, where they should hold the reception and whether Amanda would be struck down by a bolt of lightning if she chose to wear white.

17

Dani was horribly aware of the lunch she had just eaten as it desperately tried to claw its way back up her throat, fighting against her frantic swallowing. Alex was in London for a few days and he wanted to see her but there was no business to discuss. He had a couple of weeks off then a brief spell in America for a series of meetings that would coincide perfectly with the Emmys. Dani had wanted to make sure he was available for publicity if the nomination came off but had no wish to embarrass him by sending him on a wild goose chase if it didn't. Thankfully, the timing had worked out perfectly but there was certainly nothing for them to talk about until the meetings in America were behind him.

The message had said for her to meet him for dinner at eight o'clock. Taking a deep breath and desperate not to let her overactive imagination get the better of her, she picked up the phone to call Sean to let him know she wouldn't be straight home.

The afternoon was soon behind her and suddenly she was alone in the office, sitting in silence, watching the clock on the wall by her desk slowly work its way round to seven thirty when it would finally be time to leave.

Dani chose to walk to the restaurant, feeling a need to try to clear her head. As she walked the last few blocks, a taxi pulled up beside her and Alex climbed out. Without a word, he took her hand and whisked her down an alley and into a doorway. She was sure he was saying something but she couldn't hear him as he took her in his arms and kissed her. She was only aware that she was kissing him back, breathing in the smell of him until she thought she would pass out, aware that her heart was in danger of bursting and that something uncontrollable had taken over her, giving her no choice but to just go with it.

Dani had no idea how much time had passed when Alex finally pulled away from her. They looked at each other, neither knowing what to say. What could they say? However incomprehensible it may seem, however ridiculous, they were just unable to resist each other and it now seemed like a miracle they had managed to stay away from each other for so long. Eventually, Dani smiled. "I thought you invited me for dinner?"

"Who wants to eat?"

"Well we can't stay here!"

Alex sighed with frustration as he took in their surroundings. Overflowing dustbins, the smell of stale urine - not exactly an atmosphere conducive to romance. "Well come back to my hotel with me then?"

"I thought it was never just about sex? And what if someone sees us?"

He smiled at her. "Like you don't want to? Come on." And grabbing her hand, he ran back to the main road, hailed a cab and bundled her into the back.

As the taxi expertly wove its way into the flow of traffic, a distant voice at the back of Dani's mind, one that instinctively she tried to dismiss, refused to be silenced and instead shouted louder and louder until it could simply no longer be ignored. "Stop the car!" she shouted, the words literally bursting out of her mouth. Dani suddenly felt horribly claustrophobic, beads of sweat breaking out on her palms and forehead, her lungs struggling for air. She leant forward and tapped on the glass that separated them from the driver. "Stop the car!" Her voice was now full of panic.

"Dani, what are you doing?" Alex was understandably confused as the taxi pulled over to the curb. Dani clambered over him and opened the door as Alex sprung forward and grabbed her in a desperate attempt to try to stop her. "Dani, for fuck's sake! What are you doing?"

What Dani was doing was having what she would later refer to as her epiphany moment. A moment of absolute and indisputable clarity when all she could see was Sean, all she could feel was how much she loved him and all wrapped up in a desire to protect what they had at all costs. Her conversations with Amanda and Helen had had a profound effect but it had never really felt like her relationship with Alex was over. Until now. All that mattered now was that, in a flash of consciousness, it felt like her true belief systems were back in check, her self-esteem had been restored and her faith redis-

219

covered. Or simply put, the time had finally come when she knew she had to stop doing her best to fuck it all up.

With the cab driver wondering what on earth he was witnessing, Dani turned to Alex. "Let me go." Three simple words that said it all. Alex went to say something, anything that would make her stop, horribly aware of the significance of what was happening but Dani stopped him. "Let me go Alex." Her voice was calm and determined.

If it were possible for time to stand still that was exactly what it did and then, finally, Alex let go of the breath he had been holding and let go of Dani too. She immediately got out of the cab, shut the door and started walking away as fast as she could, not stopping to watch Alex's desperate face staring from the back of the cab as it disappeared back into the evening traffic.

18

Dani was sitting at her desk waiting for Amanda. They were comfortably back in the swing of impromptu nights out and it felt really good. Nothing like a bit of spontaneity to make you feel youthful and carefree. Or so they kept telling themselves. Tonight they were on their way to a TV studio to watch Dave's sitcom being recorded, now in its second series and doing really well for him. The script was very funny which obviously played to his strengths but it was surprisingly subtle and sensitive too at times. To Dani's absolute joy, it had therefore proved to be the perfect vehicle to show he could actually act. She was under no obligation to go along but, apart from wanting to show her support, she hadn't seen Dave for ages and as she and Amanda couldn't think of anywhere to go - so much for spontaneity - it had seemed the perfect solution.

When her phone rang, Dani assumed it would be Amanda saying she was on her way. She groaned as she saw Steve Preston's name instead. "What do you want?"

"Lovely to speak to you too! How are you? How's your day been?"

Dani couldn't stop herself smiling but refused to be put off. "As I said, what do you want?"

"I wondered if you fancied dinner tonight? I have a table at the Grand."

Dani's eyes widened. "Wow! You must have booked that weeks ago. Who let you down?"

Steve hesitated for just a second while he decided whether to just be honest or to start spinning what would no doubt turn into a web of epic proportion. He quickly settled on honesty. Might as well save himself the embarrassment of being exposed as an exaggerator, a fantasist or worse, a liar. Heaven forbid. "Okay, you got me. Some bastard, that's who. But how flattering to be the first person I called when they bailed?"

"That's one way of looking at it. Sadly I have plans. I'm going to see Mercy Street recorded."

"Can I come?" Steve sounded genuinely excited at the prospect.

Dani laughed. "No you can't. But let's organise lunch soon."

Steve was momentarily thrown. "What, you actually want to arrange to see me?"

"Why not? And I'm paying. That way I don't have to feel obliged to give you anything. But if you don't want to…."

"No I do, I do! Of course I do! You're inviting me and paying? Of course I do!"

"I'll send you some dates. Now sod off and leave me alone."

"A story or two would still be good though….." Steve was left wondering if she'd heard him as the line went dead. She had hung up already.

When Dani and Amanda arrived at the studios they went straight to the Green Room. Dani was hugely relieved to recognise absolutely no one in it. What a joy not to have to engage in banal small talk. As she grabbed them both a drink, the door opened and Dave burst in. "You're here!" he said as he kissed Dani warmly on both cheeks.

"Of course I'm here! Dave, this is Amanda."

Amanda joined them with a smile and Dave kissed her too. "Friend? Journo? Fellow luvvie?"

Amanda laughed. "Friend."

"Great. We're definitely all having a drink later then! I'll meet you back here," he said as he disappeared with a huge smile and a wave.

"Come on, time for us to go too." Dani and Amanda downed their drinks and headed for their reserved seats in the studio. Tempting as it was to drink their way through the courtesy bar, it seemed pointless to come all this way just to watch the show on a television.

Meanwhile across town, Billy and Sean were out for a beer, a fairly regular occurrence now and, as always, they had chosen a bar within staggering distance of home. Billy had asked Sean to be his best man which had somehow sealed their friendship. As she had already given Billy up to Amanda, Dani had felt it was simply a natural progression to let Sean have his share too.

The two men chatted for a while about general stuff and then Sean's eyes suddenly darkened as if a cloud had quite literally come over him, casting an immediate

223

shadow that sent a cold shiver down Billy's spine. "Can I ask your advice on something?"

Billy knew there was no time to debate whether it was possible to say no to such a request and instead forced out an enthusiastic, "Of course!"

Sean thought for a moment, giving Billy time to start feeling really nervous. "I've had a tip-off about someone and I've done a bit of asking around. I think it's genuine."

"I thought that was how you got all your pictures?" Billy attempted a relaxed smile. Jesus, he thought, where the hell was this leading?

"Yes but this is a little more complicated. It's Alex Cambridge."

I bloody knew it! thought Billy, struggling with every inch of his being not to look as terrified as he now felt. "What about him?" he said, posing the question as casually as he could.

"You know he's famous for being so loyal to his wife?" Billy nodded. "Well I'm hearing that he's having an affair, or at least he was. It seemed like the moment had been missed but now it looks like it's all on again."

Billy felt his bowels turn to water. "So what's your problem?"

"It's Dani. She represents Alex and she's worked really hard for him. It's possible that he's just about to really take off in America and I'm not sure she would thank me if I got him slapped all over the tabloids with another woman."

No, thought Billy. She definitely wouldn't. "And you're sure you could get the pictures?"

"Absolutely. Thursday night at the Knightsbridge Hotel to be precise."

Billy rubbed his hand across his face. All he wanted to do was run to Dani and warn her. Then he would scream at her like he'd never done and shake her until she came to her senses once and for all. When the hell had it started up again? Jesus, this is a nightmare, he thought. The worst fucking nightmare imaginable.

"So what do you think? The pictures would be worth a fortune and the timing's perfect. Shit! When did I get a conscience? It can only be downhill from here." He smiled at Billy. "So what do I do?"

Why me? thought Billy, horribly aware that Sean was staring at him, eagerly waiting for an answer. He sighed, knowing he had to say something. He took a moment, his face suitably contorted to suggest he was considering the dilemma and then with great internal effort, he pushed all thoughts of what he already knew to one side and tried to think with a clear and fresh perspective. "At the risk of oversimplifying, why would you do something that you know will hurt Dani? And why aren't you talking to her about it?"

Sean scratched his head roughly. "We always had an agreement that we wouldn't let our relationship interfere with our work, knowing there would be disagreements and the occasional conflict of interest. I can't ask her because she'll tell me not to do it and that's not fair."

"Well something like this must have come up before? What did you do then?"

"Surprisingly it really hasn't. Not on this scale anyway."

An uncomfortable silence settled over them. Billy was already pretty certain Sean knew exactly what he would do but clearly having Billy's approval would make him feel better about it. Offering his blessing was definitely out of the question and Billy started to feel slightly irritated, angry even, that he was being forced to play a part at all in the decision making process. "I can't tell you what to do," he eventually offered. "If I say do it and Dani goes mad, you'll blame me and if I say don't do it, you'll hate me anyway for losing you so much money." Billy shrugged, the anger starting to swell. "Or just to be really out there, why not think about Alex instead of Dani? Or his wife?"

Sean's eyes narrowed. "Meaning?"

"Well it might cause Dani a couple of difficult days at work but what about Alex and his family? I'd hazard a guess the repercussions may be a little more permanent for them."

Sean used his drink as a stalling tactic, slowly swilling the mouthful he had just taken around his mouth before swallowing it and then he looked at Billy. "I won't patronise you by saying he's asked for it. But do you know what, in a way he has." He shrugged. "You just can't pick and choose when it suits you to be in the papers."

Billy went to say something and then he stopped himself. There was nothing to gain by having a moral argument about the line between promoting something and blatant intrusion. He knew he'd started it but right now, he didn't give a shit about anything other than reaching a point where they could change the subject. Billy watched Sean who was lost in his own thoughts for a moment and knew it was time to ask. "So what will you do?"

Sean drained his glass. "I'm gonna do it." He banged the empty glass down on the table as if to seal the decision and Billy flinched, Dani's life flashing before his eyes as Sean smiled, relieved to have finally said it out loud. "One for the road?"

That would be the road that leads straight to hell would it? Billy thought as he nodded, gladly accepting the offer of another now well-needed drink.

Billy didn't get much sleep that night and was waiting for Dani when she arrived at work. He pounced on her the minute she reached the door. "Billy! For Christ's sake you scared me! What are you doing here?"

He grabbed her arm and led her across the road to a café. "What are you doing? I have to get to work!" She watched with her mouth open as he pulled out his mobile, dialled a number and waited. "Oh hi Caroline, it's Billy. Dani's been held up on her way in. No, everything's fine. She'll be with you in about an hour." He put his phone back in his pocket and opened the café door.

227

"Okay, enough! What is going on?"

Billy gestured to a table right at the back. "Go and sit down while I get us some coffees. Believe me this is an emergency."

Dani did as she was told and then launched at Billy the minute he sat down. "You're scaring the shit out of me. Just tell me what's happened?"

Billy looked at her and sighed, not quite sure where to start. "So you're seeing Alex again?"

"For fuck's sake Billy, I thought someone had died!"

Billy was clearly furious. "Well I might just have a fatal coronary before the sun sets! What the hell are you doing?"

Dani looked at him for a moment, looked at the anger and disgust in his eyes and gave herself a moment to align her own struggling emotions. Up first was a massive sense of disappointment. As she spoke, her voice was low and calm. "You couldn't even ask me if I was seeing him again? You just chose to assume I was. Well here's a newsflash for you. He did want to start it up again and I turned him down." She almost spat out the last few words, her bottom lip starting to quiver as she desperately fought tears.

Billy's eyes immediately widened, his expression a mixture of shock, relief and remorse. Hurting Dani's feelings was not something he had imagined he would suddenly find himself guilty of. There was an immediate struggle as he reached for Dani's hand. She of course resisted but he was physically stronger and he simply refused to let go. "Dani I'm sorry. I'm really sorry."

"Maybe you could have trusted me when I said it was over? Had a little faith in me?"

Billy looked at her but as his mouth opened slightly to say something he stopped himself. He was happy to admit he was incapable of knowing what he should say to that. The truth was, her behaviour had made it hard to trust her and have faith in her. As he watched her shoulders relax and felt her hand soften in his own, he knew Dani knew that too. "Look, I'm truly sorry but when Sean said he thought Alex had been having an affair but it was done with and then heard it was all back on again, what was I supposed to think?"

"He said what?" Dani's cheeks went from red to grey in a nanosecond. In a very quiet and frightened voice, she then dared to ask. "Tell me what he knows."

"He knows Alex is having an affair with someone, or was. He doesn't know it's you but he knows he's meeting someone this week and he knows where and when. He was in a right state about whether or not he should go after some pictures in case he might hurt you but he talked himself round and he'll be there, with his camera poised and ready for action."

Dani was immediately fighting to remain in control, a sense of extreme panic quickly spreading and desperate to take hold. "Jesus, what am I going to do? I can't let it all come out now. Not when it's all over."

"Well just cancel the date."

"It's not a date! It's work and it's important. I'm trying to distance myself from him and it will happen over time but I can't just stop being seen with him."

Billy looked at the ashen face before him. Dani had her head down, her hand on her chest, desperately trying to control her breathing and stop herself crying. If nothing else, he was in no doubt now how totally committed she was to Sean and there was an ironic cruelty to the timing of this but equally, he couldn't help acknowledging she only had herself to blame. Not a thought he would be sharing right now. He wasn't that stupid. "Let's leave it for now. I'll meet you after work once it's all sunk in."

Dani gathered up her things on auto-pilot and headed for the office. She found it incredibly hard to concentrate on her work and, for the first time in her entire history at Stacey Walker, the time just limped by. Each second seemed crippled as it painfully struggled passed, causing Dani to wonder if the day would ever come to an end or if she was to remain locked in some kind of punitive time warp.

When she arrived back at the café, Billy was already there. She sat down opposite him, feeling horribly ashamed and genuinely scared about how this would all play out. She looked at him and he smiled, a warm, reassuring smile. "I'm sorry Billy. So incredibly sorry. I've been so stupid! What I've done is just so awful and even worse is the thought of what might happen next. I've put the relationship I dreamt of having at such extraordinary risk." She shrugged. What else could she say?

"Come on, enough feeling sorry for yourself." Billy did his best to sound positive.

"I really am sorry. Particularly that you've got so involved."

"Will you stop apologising!" Billy smiled at her and once again, took her hand across the table. "We've got more important things to discuss, like how the hell we're going to get out of this." Dani felt reassured by his use of the word 'we'. It was hugely comforting to believe she wasn't in this alone. "You have to cancel. As long as there'll never be another chance for him to snap the two of you, then game over."

Dani looked unconvinced. "I just can't believe it can be that simple. He won't give up that easily, not for something like this. He'll keep on hunting until he gets what he wants."

"You're surely not suggesting there will be other times when he can catch the two of you at it?"

"Of course not! But I can't take the risk of him, or anyone else for that matter, asking questions and ferreting around. God knows what he might uncover." A shiver whispered down Dani's back as she struggled with her thoughts.

"I know!" Billy was suddenly animated. "We could send someone else in your place. Get them to hold his arm, whisper in his ear, anything that could look intimate. Sean will get some pictures, the story will run and then it will be over."

Dani shook her head. "We can't do that! Forgetting for a moment that we'd have to find someone daft enough to actually do it, what about Alex? What about his wife when she opens her morning paper?"

Billy winced at the pain in Dani's eyes, eyes that had never looked darker. "This is a no-win situation. If we start worrying about Alex and his wife, we'll be here all night and still not have the answer."

"No, I won't do it. I've done enough damage without knowingly sacrificing their marriage to save myself."

Billy sighed. "So now you get a conscience?" He rubbed his eyes roughly. "Just cancel and be done with it. Provided you never see Alex romantically again, there'll never be anything incriminating for Sean to photograph."

"But people have seen us and will continue to see us! That's the whole point, I work with him! Whoever's talking could be in a hotel, a restaurant, anywhere! Perhaps everywhere. What happens the next time we appear at a function? One of these people takes Sean to one side and says, 'There's your girl, mate. That's the one he's been seen around with'. And then what?"

"But you said yourself, you work together! Sean would just think it had been business."

Dani looked up slowly. "Not if he's talking to a hotel maid, or someone that saw us kissing or …" Dani suddenly remembered some of the screaming rows as frustration had overtaken them. Anyone overhearing them would be under no illusion about the nature of their relationship. How far did these sources go?

Billy looked at her. "Boy, have you been careless! What have you been doing? Fucking in glass elevators or something? Jesus, it just gets worse!" He ran his hands through his hair for the millionth time and was horrified to see several strands still in his fingers as he pulled his hand away. He sighed. I'll be bald by the time she sends me to that early grave, he thought. He watched the hairs slowly float towards the floor and then deciding he needed a break, he stood up. "I'm going to get a proper drink."

Dani watched him go and tried desperately to pull everything back under control. Any minute now I'll wake up from this frightful nightmare, she thought. She pinched herself. Nothing. She pinched herself again, harder and winced at the pain. She tried again and again. Nothing.

"What are you doing?" Billy put his beer on the table and a large glass of wine in front of Dani and sat down. "I really don't see how self-harming's going to help at this stage." And then suddenly they were laughing. It started with a snigger and within minutes they were screeching, tears running down their faces. Every time they looked at each other it just got worse. Gasping for breath, they fought for control and then one caught the other's eye and they were off again. Putting his head between his legs and therefore completely out of Dani's eye line, Billy took a few deep breaths, wiped his eyes and sat up, satisfied that whatever had possessed him, whatever it was that had caused the so badly needed release, had now moved on but when he looked at

Dani, his heart lurched. The tears of laughter had turned to tears of utter distress. Billy immediately pulled his chair around the table towards her until he was right by her side, his arms around her, his words gentle and comforting. "Come on love, it'll be all right. Just think of it as character building!"

"I'm sorry I didn't listen to you," she stuttered through her tears. "I should have been stronger."

"Just don't turn up. I'm not doing anything on Thursday. Come out with me instead?"

Billy gave her one final squeeze and moved back to his chair and smiled. "Well one thing's for sure. Wherever we go, we always put on a good show!"

Dani looked around them and blushed. Everywhere she looked there were tables full of people, desperately trying - and in most cases failing - to look as if their own conversations were more interesting than what was going on between herself and Billy. And then the colour suddenly drained from her cheeks again. So violently this time that Billy thought she was about to faint. "Dani, what is it?"

"You just said you'd take me out on Thursday?"

"Of course Thursday!"

"And that's the night Sean said he was going to catch Alex?"

Billy looked newly confused, unsure why they were suddenly back at the beginning. "Yes! Thursday night at the Knightsbridge Hotel."

Dani gasped and closed her eyes as she saw the last foundations of her crumbling life turn immediately to the finest dust. "But I'm not seeing Alex until Friday. And we've never been to the Knightsbridge Hotel."

Billy shook his head as he struggled to take this on board and then almost physically waved 'bon voyage' to the weight of this hideous problem that slowly released its vice-like grip on him and floated away from his shoulders. "That's fantastic! That's fucking fantastic! Whether you deserve it or not my girl, you have been saved!" Billy laughed, never having experienced such relief in his life. And then he realised Dani wasn't joining in. "Dani?"

She looked at him, still as pale, her eyes a blur behind a wall of tears. "So who the fuck is he meeting on Thursday?"

19

Alex was running late. He had left the hotel to do some shopping and had lost track of time and now he couldn't find a cab. Just as he thought he was going to have to walk, he finally spotted the familiar orange glow of a 'For Hire' sign and ran.

Sean was only minutes behind him. He had been following him in his car all afternoon, just in case there was a change of plan. He smiled as he pulled out after the cab. With Joe Public reaching for their phones at every turn, taking pictures and uploading videos without hesitation, it had been a while since he'd played this game and he'd forgotten what it felt like. There really was nothing like the thrill of the chase.

He watched Alex go back into the hotel and left his own car with a doorman to be parked. He waited a few minutes then walked past the hotel's glass fronted restaurant. He smiled as he saw Alex sit down, order a drink and then look around him. Yes, you may well look nervous, he thought, as he took a few snaps. They would be nothing more than establishing shots but it felt good to get started. He would get the close-ups he needed when Alex and his dinner date enjoyed their intimate dinner and then later, when they parted company, whatever time that might be. He could imagine eager reporters letting their imagination run wild as they built their own picture of how the intervening hours would have been spent. Sean looked around and headed off in search of a coffee. He would make sure he was back for the good stuff.

As he walked away, the air of nervous anticipation around Alex evaporated and he stood up as he saw her stroll towards him. "I didn't think you were coming."

Dani smiled at Alex as her heart flipped over. Some things remained impossible to control. "Just because I kept you waiting for a while? I decided it was your turn to sweat a little."

Dani looked at him. How can you be so brazen? she thought. How can you laugh and smile with me, when it's all just been a game? She had called him and said she needed to change their meeting to Thursday, choosing to ignore his desperate attempts to insist they went ahead as planned. She had been horribly aware how quick he was to say he already had plans and could only therefore meet her for an hour, making no attempt to hide his disappointment that they would not now be spending an evening together. How easy that second call would have been, Dani had thought. 'Sorry darling. Have to delay for an hour. My agent needs to see me.' She wasn't really sure why she'd even called him. Was it just to disrupt his plans? Perhaps she just needed to look into those eyes and try to accept the joke had been on her all along before the shit well and truly hit the fan. For a moment, she could hear herself telling Billy she wouldn't sacrifice Alex's marriage to save herself. She felt herself stiffen. Things were different now. She had told Sean, as casually as she could manage, that she would be catching up with Alex briefly before she came home. He had of course waved it away saying, equally casually, that he would be out working anyway.

"What's the matter Dani?"

She snapped herself away from her thoughts. "Nothing. Why?"

"Unless I'm mistaken, we've slipped back into polite conversation mode." He looked at her, waiting for her to say something.

"Oh, I don't know. People are looking at you."

Alex scanned the room. "No they're not. That's why I'm staying here this time. It's way too expensive for autograph hunters. The people that eat here only watch the news and select documentaries. I promise you, no one knows who I am."

"If you say so." I almost believe you, she thought. It couldn't have anything to do with the fact that we don't come here I suppose? That it's me the staff don't know and that's what's important?

Dani gave her head a little shake and forced herself to focus. It was time to do what had to be done and just get the hell away. She pulled a selection of scripts and schedules from her bag that they needed to go through but Alex clearly had his own agenda. "We need to talk."

"No, we need to work," she said as she continued to put the paperwork in order.

"But we haven't had the chance to talk since you ran out on me. I've thought about you constantly since then. That's why I wanted to see you, just to see once and for all if it was just the fantasy of what we had that haunted me or if it was real. And it is real. You know that don't you?"

Dani stopped what she was doing. "If you're about to say what I think you are, please don't. It'll only make things worse."

"It couldn't possibly! I can't go on living with a woman I no longer want to be with. It's you I love. I want to be with you!"

What was happening here? Dani struggled again to remember why she had wanted to gatecrash Alex's date. Something had compelled her to look him in the eye before he deceived her, desperate to see something that would suggest he had indeed been genuine, that there had been something meaningful between them. Whatever her motivation, she knew now she had made a terrible, terrible mistake. "I can't listen to this."

Alex was starting to look desperate. "Come upstairs with me."

"No!" Dani blushed, afraid that her response may have been a little louder than was polite for such a grand setting but this was unbelievable! Alex, on the other hand, was oblivious to their surroundings, becoming louder and more animated by the second.

"You can't back out on me now!"

"I have backed out on you!" The large silver cutlery rattled loudly as Dani banged the table, the eyes of the room now discreetly on them.

"But I'm ready to leave Victoria! Ready to give it all up if that's what it takes for us to be together!"

Dani looked at him coldly and shook her head. She could say it was over a million times, all a pointless waste of breath if he wasn't prepared to listen. She stood up, gesturing to the pile of papers on the table. "I have to go. Have a look through these and we'll talk about them another time."

Alex grabbed her arm. "Stay!" Dani tried to pull away but Alex just intensified his grip, their eyes locked together. He lowered his voice to an almost vicious whisper. "I won't let you walk out on me again!"

"Can I get madam something to drink?"

Neither had seen the waiter approach whose expression made it clear he had no interest at all in knowing whether madam wanted a drink or not but he definitely wanted madam to either leave or sit down and for them both to be quiet. The sudden interruption made Alex jump and his hold on Dani loosened enough for her to break free. Horribly embarrassed, Dani did her best to look composed. "No thank you. I was just leaving."

The waiter nodded and walked away. Dani waited until he was out of earshot and turned to Alex who was now slumped in his chair with the look of a man defeated. "This can't happen again Alex. Have a good evening." And with that she was gone.

When Alex finally stepped out of the large hotel doors, Sean was more than ready for him. He watched through his camera lens as Alex stood for a moment, holding the hand of a woman, her hair long and dark and blowing slightly in the cool night air. Alex used his free hand to gently push her hair away from her face. Sean couldn't have stage-managed it better if he'd tried. As he continued to fire off shot after shot, Alex looked around a little nervously and then kissed her briefly before seeing her into a cab but, however brief the kiss, it was perfectly long enough to get the necessary job done. Sean put down his camera and smiled. "Gotcha!" he said in a loud, satisfied whisper. The intimate exchange of words, the kiss, his hand on her face, a great close-up of her and then Alex, standing alone as he watched her go, plus the earlier pictures he had of them dining together. The press would have a field day piecing it all together until a picture of betrayal and deception took shape. What alternative conclusion was there? He looked at his watch. Just enough time, he thought. It was time to start making some calls.

When Sean got home, Dani was fast asleep. An assumption he made based on the fact her eyes were shut and she didn't stir when he gently called her name. He had hoped she would be awake so they could get any row out of the way tonight. Not that there was any going back. The pictures were out and the papers would be hitting the streets at any moment. He wouldn't be surprised if they were already online.

For a moment, he paced up and down the room and Dani could barely breathe as she nervously waited for him to decide what his next move should be. And then the pacing stopped. Dani desperately tried to place him in the silence and then she opened her eyes with a start as suddenly Sean was shaking her. "Dani, wake up."

"What is it?" Sean turned on the light and she immediately screwed up her eyes. She had been lying in the dark long enough that the reaction was genuine. "What's going on?"

Sean sat on the bed next to her, his head in his hands. "I've done something tonight that you should know about."

"What are you talking about?"

Sean took a deep breath. "I photographed Alex Cambridge with another woman. Every tabloid and online news site took at least five pictures. It'll be all over the place within a few hours." Dani pulled the duvet over her head and groaned as Sean continued a little nervously. "It probably won't do any harm. Just a flash in the pan. It'll be forgotten by Monday."

Dani sat up, suddenly finding herself genuinely angry. "And what about his wife? Do you think she'll have forgotten about it by Monday?"

"Of course not! But it wasn't me skulking around in the early hours with another woman was it?" He held her eye until Dani could bear it no longer, sinking her head back into the pillow, desperate to forget the look she had just seen in his eyes. "If you want to be angry with someone, get angry with Alex. I only snapped what I saw." Sean waited for a moment and then sighed. "I'm sorry."

Not as sorry as I am, she thought. Nowhere near.

20

The coverage couldn't have been worse. It swept around the online world like wild fire, with all forms of social media immediately flooded with comments and opinions, the audience multiplying with every like and share. Six newspapers carried it with two tabloids deeming it significant enough to feature pictures on their front pages. The pictures definitely told a story but it was made all the worse by the several people who had been quoted saying they had seen the couple together, along with a list of their favourite haunts. This was clearly way more than just a one-off liaison. Dani had only ever been to two of the six places mentioned so the phrase 'rubbing salt into the wound' not surprisingly sprang to mind. She sat at her desk in a slight daze, her phone diverted to voicemail, her mobile switched off. She'd had a ridiculous amount of calls already and Steve Preston had taken up residence in reception. It was nothing less than she had expected but, as she wasn't planning on returning any calls, she didn't know what to do with herself. She knew what she should do. She should go to see Alex but she desperately didn't want to. Instead she twitched and fidgeted in her chair, with regular nervous glances at the phone. Eventually she picked it up but then immediately replaced it, deciding instead to go and talk to Bernie.

As she got up from her desk, it was impossible to avoid Hannah's stare. As Dani caught her eye, Hannah raised her eyebrows in a smug, knowing fashion, clearly relishing Dani's misery having fallen foul of her own boyfriend. Dani couldn't have heard the 'I told you so' any louder if Hannah had actually bellowed it across the office. Dani sighed. It was a fair cop.

It was a relief to find Bernie more pragmatic. He was far too grown up to blame the whole incident on Dani's choice of boyfriend. Like any industry, this was an incestuous one and while personal relationships might add another dimension to a situation, he was fully aware that Sean was just doing his job whether they liked it or not.

More pressing was whether or not they should issue any kind of response. After discussing some ideas, they decided to offer a simple 'no comment' but the first thing Dani had to do was speak to Alex, something they both knew she should have done already. She panicked and turned back to Bernie as she was leaving his office. "Bernie, you know you said I could always ask for help?" He raised his eyebrows and Dani felt herself blush. "Would you talk to him?"

"Why?"

"Because he'll accept what you say without question. He'll be more emotional with me. I think it would be better coming from you."

Bernie shrugged. "Fair enough. I'll need the number."

Dani called it out as Bernie dialled and then sat down again to listen to the call. Bernie had to demand to speak to the manager before he succeeded in getting through to Alex who had obviously switched off his mobile and Dani was already extremely relieved it was him doing the yelling and not her. When he finally got Alex, he was in a terrible state. Bernie handled him perfectly as Dani had known he would. He had him on speaker so she could hear too and her heart leapt to her mouth as she listened to his terrified voice. Bernie calmed him down, telling him over and over again that it would be all right. These things inevitably happen. The skill was to deal with it and then put it behind him. He told Alex he had no desire or need to know the truth. As far as he was concerned, it was a casual meeting with a friend. The quotes would be brushed off as complete nonsense. Pure fabrication that wasn't even worth bothering about.

"Have you spoken to Victoria?"

"For about an hour."

"And?"

Dani listened as Alex sighed. "I told her it was rubbish, just a meeting and late drinks with friends. That the pictures were just a tiny snapshot of how the evening had actually played out. I think she believes me. She always knew that someone would eventually turn on me. I don't know of anyone who's had nothing but positive media coverage. She's more worried about the photographers outside the door. She can't go out."

"She must, Alex. Tell her to put on a killer outfit, slap on some make-up and her best smile, then just stroll out there and laugh it off. Can she do that?"

"I guess we'll find out soon enough."

"If she hides away, you're guilty and they'll just say your marriage is over."

Alex managed a hollow, bitter laugh. "You mean it isn't?"

"One thing at a time. It'll all blow over, I promise you."

There was a pause. "Is Dani there? I really need to speak to her."

Bernie looked across the room and Dani shook her head in a way she hoped didn't give away the immediate sense of panic she felt at the prospect of speaking to Alex, which under the circumstances was clearly massive enough without the added bonus of Bernie listening in. If he did notice, Bernie chose to ignore it. "She's busy dealing with the fallout. I'll get her to call you."

"Please. Or better still, tell her to come to see me. I could do with some moral support."

"Okay, whatever you want. Call me if you need me."

"Thanks Bernie, I appreciate it."

Bernie hit a button that released the call and turned to Dani. "Looks like you better get over there. Talk to someone and go in the back. There's no point drawing attention to yourself. We don't want the next wave of coverage to report panic meetings with agents." Bernie starting scrolling through emails. His mind had already moved on. "Don't worry about it," he said without looking up. "It's just a storm in a tea cup. It's really not a big deal. Now go and hold the silly boy's hand and make him feel better."

Dani walked back to her desk feeling physically sick. As she picked up her bag and coat, horribly aware that she now had absolutely no choice but to go to see Alex, she stopped for a moment to turn her mobile back on. It immediately went into overdrive as endless voicemail messages and texts came flooding through in a symphony of bleeps and pings. And then it started ringing.

"Hey Billy."

"Finally! I've been trying you for hours. You okay?"

"I'm not sure yet. Bernie's spoken to Alex, there's a horde of press outside his home ready to pounce on his wife, Sean keeps apologising to me which is unbearable and now I have to go and see Alex."

"Oh shit."

"My sentiments exactly."

"Well call me if you need me or just want to talk."

Dani slipped her phone into her pocket and gestured to Sammy to help her deal with the next hurdle. As Sammy walked into reception, Dani held back, positioning herself strategically out of sight. When Sammy reappeared a moment later with Steve Preston in tow, Dani wasted no time and slipped out behind them.

"If you just wait here a moment Steve. Oh hang on a sec." Sammy stopped to answer her phone. "Oh hi. Yes, okay, I'll tell him." She looked back at Steve with her best apologetic smile. "Sorry, Dani's had to go out."

"But where's she gone?"

Sammy was already steering him back through reception, making suitably sympathetic noises to his desperate complaints at having waited for hours, hoping she had enough momentum going to see him straight out the front doors.

Dani called the hotel on her way there and after they had checked with Alex, they let her in through a back entrance, admitting as they did that at least five women had already tried to pass themselves off as her in an attempt to get in. You can't blame a journalist for trying.

All too soon, Dani was standing outside his room. When she finally unearthed the courage to knock, she thought for a moment that she might actually throw up and then he was standing there, his face white except for two huge, dark circles around his eyes. His hair was ruffled, his t-shirt creased. He walked back into the room, leaving Dani to close the door behind her. She followed him nervously and waited, desperately trying not to focus on the bed as she fought off painful images of what had undoubtedly happened in it only hours before.

As Dani felt an eternity go by, Alex finally turned to face her. He was furious. "How could you? How could you do that to me?" Dani said nothing. "You sold me out! You fucking sold me out! You and your fucking photographer boyfriend!" Dani watched him pace backwards and forwards in front of her. "Does he know about us? Was this your compromise? He still gets his pictures and you get left out of it?"

"Hang on a minute. Last night you told me you loved me and wanted to leave Victoria to be with me and then hours later, you were having sex with someone else!

And when you get caught, it's immediately my fault! You are priceless!"

"But you must have known Sean was there? You could have warned me!"

"And you could have been honest with me." Dani's voice was suddenly strangely calm and for a moment they just looked at each other. It was Dani who finally broke the silence. "Sean still has no idea about us."

Alex was barely able to speak. "So you get off scot-free! My marriage is as good as over, not to mention my reputation and you just walk away?"

"Walk away? Yes that's right, I just walk away. With the knowledge that I was completely taken in by you. Someone who I believed really felt something for me. But then you are an actor after all, aren't you? So if you're expecting some sympathy and support, I'm afraid you called the wrong mistress."

"Don't you dare say that to me!"

Dani's jaw dropped slightly under the weight of disbelief. "In case it had escaped your notice, you completely selfish bastard, last night's liaison was a revelation to me too. Believe me, I got no pleasure from discovering Victoria isn't the only one you've been cheating on." Alex went to say something but Dani quickly stopped him. "And if you're about to remind me we agreed our relationship was over then don't you dare! You've had me dangling on a string for months." Alex suddenly had nothing to say, his head hanging in defeat. "I mean how long have you been seeing her? Were you shagging me at the same time?"

"It really wasn't like that. There is an explanation for all this you know."

"Maybe there is but that's one Oscar-winning performance that's about to be denied you."

Alex could only watch as Dani headed for the door but then she stopped and was suddenly heading back towards him again. Before she had time to collect her thoughts, the words were already spilling out of her mouth. "I never told you I loved you because it was the only thing I felt I could hold back. My way of convincing myself that I was still in control. But, for what it's worth and despite everything that's happened, I did love you." She paused for a moment. "More fool me eh?" and then she turned around again and this time didn't stop until she was through the door, closing it loudly behind her.

Alex stayed exactly where he was. The anger and the hurt took a momentary reprise and then he just felt numb. He had wanted Victoria out of his life and there was every chance that had been sorted out for him but he had been so stupid! There had been others apart from Dani, he was hardly in a position to deny that now but there had certainly been no one else before her. When he and Dani had first attempted to end their relationship he had felt hurt and bitter that they couldn't be together. Hardly a convincing excuse for walking straight into the arms of another woman but that is what he had done, again and again and again.

What he should have been able to recognise so much sooner was that it was only his own weakness that had kept him away from Dani. He had talked about leaving Victoria on more than one occasion, dangling the words in front of her like a bunch of rotten carrots but what had he ever done about it? Nothing. Perhaps if he'd had the strength to leave Victoria, he might be with Dani now. Perhaps if he'd had the courage to admit all those years ago that he didn't actually want to marry Victoria, that he wanted more from life and wasn't ready for marriage and a family, then his life would look very different now. He sighed. Perhaps, perhaps, perhaps.

He poured himself a large drink and slumped into a chair. The truth was he had meant every word spoken the night before. He was ready to leave Victoria, not just talk about it but actually do it, for the simple reason that he really did love Dani. He had always wanted her and yet, despite that, he was horribly aware that the only emotion he felt for her at this very moment was hatred. He hated her for choosing to save her relationship with Sean over being with him. He hated the fact that she would never believe now that he did really love her. But most of all, he hated the fact she'd chosen now to tell him that she loved him.

Billy stopped for a minute to look at Dani sitting on a park bench, her head in her hands. She had sounded totally bereft when she called him but as she looked up, suddenly aware that she was being watched, he was relieved to see she now looked fairly composed. He sat down next to her. "So how was he?"

"I think you can probably imagine."

"I'm imagining something close to a complete nervous breakdown."

"That sounds about right." Dani thought for a moment. "Do you know, I think he was more upset that he thought I'd played some part in all this than he was about being found out."

Billy looked at her. "And what about you?"

"What about me?"

Billy sighed, wondering if Dani did this deliberately, always pretending that she had no idea what he meant. Getting her to talk was sometimes like pulling teeth. Big bloody molars that had no intention of shifting without jaws being broken. "How do you feel?"

She thought for a moment. "I feel like someone who cheated on her boyfriend and then in some way cheated on her lover. After, that is, finding out that my lover had already been cheating on me. I feel like shit. Like some cheap, heartless bitch. I feel selfish. I hate myself. Are you getting the picture?"

"A veritable Picasso."

Dani's anger and frustration at herself were now really ramping up. "I mean how could I have been so stupid? How could I have been so superbly sucked in? It's not like I don't see it every day and see it for exactly what it is. Endless insecure actors making themselves feel worthy and important by shagging anything that moves. And yet I still fell for it." She shook her head in utter disbelief. "I mean, it's simply ridiculous!" She was working herself up into quite a frenzy.

252

"Dani," Billy made an attempt to interrupt the manic flow.

"I've behaved like some kind of lovesick teenager for God's sake. How is this possible? Where the fuck has my head been all this time?"

"Dani!" She jumped as Billy raised his voice in a second attempt to stop her. "So now what?"

Dani slumped and then she shrugged. "I have no idea. Alex will probably want me sacked just to draw a final close to everything but he can't because then he might have to explain why."

"What about Sean?" Billy really wasn't interested in hearing any more about Alex. "What about the two of you?"

Dani went to speak and was then forced to stop as the tears that suddenly flooded her eyes momentarily choked her. "I think about losing him," she stammered, "and it fills me with such a terrible fear." She shook her head, unable to say any more, so overwhelmed was she with frightful thoughts of what might have been and how differently this might have turned out. Billy took her in his arms.

"Time to put it all behind you. It's all over now."

When Sean got home, Dani was already there. He found her on the terrace, curled up in the far corner of the bench. It was really too cold to be sitting outside and she had a rug pulled over her knees which made her look even more vulnerable, her hands pulled up inside the sleeves of her jumper. Despite the cold, she had needed to be outside, wanting to be in the fresh air and have the cool wind wash over her in some desperate attempt to feel cleansed and be rid of any scent of Alex.

Sean stood nervously in the doorway, waiting. When she said nothing, he slowly made his way over and sat down next to her. "Do you have any idea what kind of day I've had?" Now it was Sean who had to turn away. "I had to slip in the back of the hotel and be yelled at by one very unhappy actor. And don't think you weren't mentioned. Betrayed by his agent's boyfriend who had no doubt earned a stack of cash in the process."

"It's no secret what I do for a living. If it hadn't been me it would've been someone else."

Dani looked at him. Whoever had first discovered that attack was the best form of defence had been no fool she thought, horribly aware that she was deliberately trying to make Sean feel guilty, knowing all the time that she was the one who should be apologising, begging for his forgiveness. Slowly she leaned forward and taking his face in her hands, she kissed him. "You did what you had to do. Let's just forget it."

Sean kissed her and as he put his arm around her, she nestled into him, soaking up his warmth. I do love you, she thought, concentrating really hard not to think about how close she had come to throwing it all away.

When Dani heard that Alex had indeed been nominated for an Emmy, he was half way across the Atlantic. The press were already starting to congregate at the airport, eagerly checking every incoming flight from London. They hadn't spoken since Black Friday, as she had chosen to call it. When Alex had finally ventured home, she had been able to watch his arrival on every news item she saw. He handled it well, an air of nonchalance that he had no doubt been rehearsing with a furious passion, as if the best role of his life depended on it.

Alex had a full team of people working for him in America led by an agent and a publicist. Dani had emailed them the appropriate cuttings and wishing them luck, had happily handed Alex into their care for the time being. At least they would have no trouble at all getting people to interview him.

Two weeks later, the attention was back at Heathrow where Victoria, resplendent in dark glasses, was boarding her own flight, off to spend time with her husband in the run up to the ceremony. She laughed as she was asked if she would be standing by her husband. Of course she would be, she had said. There was no reason not to. Dani smiled. How quickly she had perfected such a polished act for the cameras, forgetting for a moment which one was the actor.

Within a few days and a flurry of consistent attention, the press soon got bored of photographing Alex out with his wife and when one of the showbizziest nights of the year finally arrived, Alex was under no illusion that he was most definitely, the rank outsider. No one was really that surprised when he didn't win the award.

21

Billy and Amanda's wedding was getting closer by the minute. To Billy, it was a month or so away. To Amanda, it was thirty-four days, plus a certain amount of hours, minutes and seconds depending on exactly when you asked. To say Amanda was getting boring on the subject would be the understatement to end all understatements. It wasn't that she was being difficult or unreasonable about anything. The event had just become so all-consuming that she was literally incapable of thinking about - or talking about - anything else.

"Dani, should you be eating that?"

Dani froze, a huge spoonful of delicious hot chocolate fudge cake and ice cream now suspended an inch from her mouth. "Why not?"

"Your bridesmaid dress, of course! There really isn't much room to spare you know."

Dani laid down the spoon and pushed the plate away, her appetite immediately deserting her.

"What's wrong Dani? Don't you like it?" Billy returned from the kitchen with another bottle of wine and Sean quickly interjected, aware that Dani would be only too pleased to tell him.

"Nothing's wrong! Eyes bigger than her belly, that's all." Sean squeezed Dani's hand under the table, afraid to look at her in case he lost his sight to a flying dagger, as Billy banged the bottle loudly on to the table.

"If you're talking about the fucking wedding again, believe me I'll cancel the whole fucking thing! Jesus Amanda, you're like a stuck record!" Amanda's eyes immediately filled with tears.

"Is that the time already? We should be going Sean." Dani kicked him as she stood up.

"Oh yeah, time to go! Thanks for a lovely evening."

"Now see what you've done? You've driven our best friends away and who could blame them for wanting to go?"

"Calm down Billy! It really is getting late." Dani took hold of his arm and pulled him away from the table. "Go and find my coat."

Dani waited until he had left the room and then put her arm around Amanda, the tears now flowing freely down her cheeks. "Don't cry honey, he doesn't mean it."

"Oh yes I do!" Billy reappeared, his face flushed. Dani glared at him, pleading with him with her eyes to calm down. When it was clear he was in fact only just warming up, she looked at Sean, standing helpless in the middle of the room, unsure what he should be doing.

"Why don't you come and sit with Amanda for a moment Sean?" At last, thought Sean, a constructive role to play. He moved in to replace Dani as she turned to Billy. "Come on you. We're going for a walk." Sean's face fell. He hadn't planned on being left alone with

257

Amanda but it clearly wouldn't be appropriate to protest. Instinctively putting his arm around her, he watched Dani swiftly usher Billy out of the room, with Billy muttering and grumbling as he went.

With the front door safely closed behind them, Dani practically pushed him down the steps to the pavement and then grabbing his arm, marched him off down the road until she was satisfied he'd inhaled at least half a dozen large breaths of cool, fresh air. "What's the matter with you? You can't blame the girl for getting excited about her wedding, even if it is you she's marrying."

Billy shook his head. "Excitement's one thing but it's all starting to drive me insane. We don't seem to talk about anything else. There are endless lists of things to do and check. One minute I'm not doing enough, the next I'm interfering." If it hadn't been for the desperate look in Billy's eyes, Dani was sure she would have laughed. It was all so ridiculous. "Is this what it's going to be like? Because if it is, then I've made one huge mistake."

"Of course it won't be like this! It's just nerves. She just wants everything to be perfect. Everyone gets wound up before their wedding and I think Amanda's actually been quite low-key about everything. You're the only one who's getting hysterical."

"Since when were you such an expert on marriage? I thought your speciality was breaking them up?"

As Dani hit Billy across the face, she only hoped that it hurt him more than it did her, her fingers immediately stinging, the echo of the slap ringing in her ears. Billy threw his hand to his face and clutched his cheek, tears pricking his eyes. "I think you just overstepped the mark, you bastard. You don't deserve Amanda!"

Billy looked at her, immediately hating himself. "I'm sorry, I didn't mean that, I really didn't." Dani's expression remained fixed. "Forgive me. I'm upset, I don't know what made me say that."

It was clear he was genuinely sorry and Dani had to admit she'd made herself an easy target for such jibes. It didn't make it hurt any less though. "You're never going to let me forget are you? You're the one who keeps telling me to leave it all behind and then you never miss an opportunity to remind me what I've done. You're incredible."

"I'm sorry, it was a flippant remark. I didn't think. It's just that everyone keeps saying it's nerves making Amanda uptight but what about me? I'm terrified! It's like suddenly finding myself in a cage and any minute some vicar's going to lock the bloody door and that's it. No escape."

Dani sighed. "Something must have made you ask her? No one was forcing you."

"I know, I know! It felt like the right thing to do at the time but what if I am making a mistake?"

Dani looked at him and gently stroked his cheek. Billy winced slightly, his face still smarting from the slap. "I'm sorry, I didn't mean to hit you quite so hard."

"I deserved it."

She smiled. "Yes you did."

They looked at each other for a moment, Billy desperate to say something more, Dani afraid that he might say something he would regret and then they walked for a while, both lost in their own thoughts. What was it, he wondered, that had made them stay friends, never tempted to try something more? Although that in itself wasn't quite right for there had been many times when he had indeed been tempted. The nights when she had slept beside him and he had lain awake for hours just watching her, his imagination running wild as he had wondered what it would be like to have sex with her but then Nick had always been there, lurking somewhere in the background. She had trusted Billy implicitly and he had never wanted to risk losing that, even in his wildest student years. If he was completely honest, there had been a fleeting moment when he had thought his move to London might see the start of something. Of course that was before he had known about Sean.

As for Alex, he had initially been more incensed at the sense of compromise than at the deceit; the fact that Dani had been prepared to accept so little, when he would have given her everything. As the relationship had developed, he had wanted only to protect her. Nothing else had mattered as long as she was all right.

In his current heightened emotional state, Billy was now starting to question his relationship with Amanda. Did he really love her or had being with Dani's best friend been the next best thing to being with Dani? Maybe that had played a part at the beginning but surely not now? Not now they were only weeks away from getting married. Weeks away from making a commitment that was for life. Billy squeezed his eyes shut and shook his head in an attempt to end the self-torture. It was too late for all this! He could tie himself up in knots or just take a deep breath and get on with things. What choice was there?

They walked in silence for a while longer and then Dani stole a look at him. "What are you thinking about?"

Billy sighed. "Nothing you would want to hear about."

"You know I thought I was going to lose you forever when you announced you two were getting married." Billy felt a hand squeeze his heart, making breathing difficult. "And I know I've given you a hard time about Amanda in the past." She shrugged. "I guess deep down I was jealous. I didn't like the idea of there being a more important woman in your life."

"But you never wanted me." Billy struggled to get the words out, not sure if he had asked a question or merely stated the obvious.

Dani stopped walking and looked at him. She could say he had never asked but there seemed little point at this stage. Instead she smiled. "I wanted you as my friend and I should never have doubted that you wouldn't be there for me." She stretched up and kissed him on the cheek and in a moment of complete madness, Billy was just considering grabbing her and running off into the sunset, when she turned and walked back towards the flat. "Come on," she shouted over her shoulder. "You've got some making up to do."

When they walked back through the front door, the first thing they heard was Amanda laughing. They looked at each other, neither able to hide their surprise. As they slowly walked into the lounge, it was Sean who looked up first. "We were just wondering where you two had got to."

Dani was unconvinced. She didn't think they had been missed at all. "What are you doing?"

Sean lifted up a box by way of explanation. "Scrabble, but with a difference. Only rude words allowed!"

Amanda giggled as she placed three more letters on the board. "I had forgotten I had such a filthy mind!" And then she looked at Billy, her face suddenly serious. "I'm sorry Billy. I've been a prize pain in the arse but I promise it's going to stop." Billy was too stunned to speak. Nothing made any sense anymore and he had neither the strength nor the inclination to do anything about it. Instead he simply opened his arms to Amanda as she came towards him, wrapping her arms tightly around his neck.

Dani sat down next to Sean and kissed him "Well done, you're a complete miracle worker."

"Not really," he whispered. "Anything was better than actually having to talk to her."

Dani and Billy found themselves getting dragged into the ridiculous game and it was several hours later when Dani and Sean finally got home, both completely exhausted and desperate to be lying down. "God what an evening," Sean said, already taking off his clothes as he followed Dani into their bedroom.

"You did a great job calming Amanda down. I was ready to thump her myself, which is why I took Billy out. I hope you didn't mind?"

Sean was now in bed. "Of course not. What did you talk about?"

"Oh nothing much. He just needed some space. They're both nervous and winding each other up something chronic."

Sean laughed. "Who'd get married, eh?"

Dani turned to face him, wanting to know what he meant but Sean was already lying with his eyes shut, looking instantly peaceful, his breathing low and even. Dani quickly changed and then disappeared into the bathroom. She cleansed her face of make-up and the trials of the day and then looked in the mirror, staring deeply into her own eyes, something she still found difficult to do. She stayed there, motionless, as if in a silent standoff with herself. Why do you still think about Alex? she silently asked herself. Why can't you just leave it all behind and be done with it? She watched her mouth slowly form a rueful smile, knowing her anger at her own stupidity at falling for all the lies and empty promises had now been replaced by a sad desperate disappointment that she simply hadn't been special enough to stop him sleeping with others too. However irrelevant, however self-indulgent, it hurt to accept that.

She forced herself away and as she slipped into bed beside Sean she found herself wide awake, lying in the dark, her mind still racing. She took in a deep breath and quietly let the air seep out, forcing her shoulders to relax and willing the tension to leave her neck. And then she was thinking about Billy and she smiled. Despite those occasional looks, those unspoken words, those moments of anger that could so easily have been masking sexual tension, she knew they were always meant to be the very best of friends. There were no regrets on her part that there had never been anything more and deep down, she knew Billy felt the same. It was a comforting thought and closing her eyes, she finally drifted off to sleep.

Two weeks before the big day, there was another reason for celebration and Dani for one was delighted to have something else to plan for. As always, Sean had maintained he wanted a quiet birthday - no fuss, no frills and definitely no party. Although he wouldn't say it, Dani also knew he really didn't want to celebrate it with Amanda and Billy, so convinced was he that he would be pushed into the background to be replaced by yet more wedding talk. Dani felt she had the perfect solution and was feeling incredibly pleased with herself having told no one but the key people at work of her plans.

When the day finally arrived, she got up early to enjoy a few moments of calm before she tried to wake Sean. Having collected the day's papers on her way to the kitchen, duly delivered to the door every morning, she sat with a cup of coffee and slowly started to work through the pile. Only scanning the headlines and pictures, she quickly settled into an easy rhythm, a crackle of paper as she turned a page, a brief silence as her eyes scanned left to right, followed by the same again and again until one by one there was a thump as each discarded paper was dropped on to the floor beside her. By the third one, her pace had quickened with little new to read but as she pulled forward the fourth, she was suddenly unable to stop her mouth falling open slightly, the efficient process abruptly brought to a halt. Seeing the story flagged on the front page, she quickly turned straight to the centre spread, her eyes struggling to take in all the pictures and words at once. Alex had been caught on holiday with his family and there was a series of shots of him kissing Victoria, whispering in her ear or touching her, anything and everything that spelt intimacy, as their children happily played around them. As far as the paper was concerned, this was all the public needed to confirm that Alex and his wife were most definitely together, their marriage well and truly intact. Dani smiled. This was no accident. At last it seemed Alex was learning how to play the game, accepting his role in a stunt that would have been executed by his American team, clearly designed to convince any remaining doubters that all was well in the Cambridge household. Pushing aside her annoyance that she hadn't been told about the feature in advance, her eyes lingered on his face and her smile slowly weakened. She quickly closed the paper, throwing it on to the floor with the others, sending any thoughts of Alex with it. She had far more important things on her mind today.

Heading back to the bedroom, Dani sat down on the bed, willing Sean to wake up so she could finally share her surprise. As she rocked impatiently, he opened an eye and after a glimpse of Dani's grinning face, immediately shut it again. "I saw you! You're awake! Stop pretending to be asleep!"

He groaned as he reluctantly opened his eyes and then sat up, unable to stop a boyish grin from slowly spreading across his face. He had no idea why yet but he was aware of a growing fluttering of excitement, a spontaneous reaction to Dani who was clearly struggling to contain her own growing sense of delight. "So come on then, what have you done?"

Saying nothing, Dani handed him a box. Sean opened it slowly and there, hidden amongst endless strips of paper, was an airline ticket and a page from a travel magazine. His jaw immediately dropped as his eyes tried to take it all in. Unless he was mistaken, they were headed for a week of glorious sunshine on a secluded Caribbean island. He looked at her, unable to speak. "I thought we could do with some time away together. No interruptions, no distractions. Just me and you."

Sean was still struggling to find any suitable words. A simple and rather obvious, "I'm speechless," was all he could manage until his brain finally caught up. "I had absolutely no idea! When did you do all this? How did you manage it? How could you possibly keep it to yourself?" Dani leaned forward and kissed him, for no other reason than to stop the barrage of questions. Sean pulled her on top of him, wrapping his arms tightly around her. "Thank you," he whispered in her ear. "You are truly amazing."

"I know! I just can't help myself!" she said, the heat of his excitement flushing her cheeks and warming her heart as she pulled away from him.

"Where are you going?" Sean watched as she opened the wardrobe and pulled out two suitcases, already packed.

"Well we're all ready to go and you have about an hour to check I've packed everything you need and get yourself sorted before the cab gets here."

"We're going now?"

"Of course we're going now! By this evening, we'll be sipping cocktails on the beach!"

With that, Sean was out of bed like a streak of lightning, completely caught up in the sheer spontaneity of it all. He only hoped he wasn't dreaming and about to wake up to find yet another photo album waiting by the side of his bed. He had never been able to work out why so many people throughout his life had felt this was the perfect gift for him.

The next few hours passed in a complete blur and when that same night, they walked barefoot across warm white sand, the moon sending a perfect shimmer of light across the sea that lapped on to the shore in a series of gentle caresses, Sean was more convinced than ever that he must be dreaming and he never wanted to wake up. "Isn't this beautiful?" He took a deep relaxed breath and smiled with pure contentment. "It's paradise. Absolute paradise." Turning back towards the hotel to see how far they had walked, he could see nothing but a small cluster of lights, his ears vaguely aware of the very distant hum of chatter and music. A look ahead revealed nothing more than sand and more sea and the darkest sky he thought he had ever seen. He stopped walking and pulled Dani close to him, his hands more than able to feel her body through the thin layer of linen that covered her. And he wanted to feel her. Feel his bare skin on hers with the gentle sea breeze caressing them, with nothing more than the warm sand to support them.

"What are you doing? Someone will see us!" Sean had already removed his t-shirt and unbuttoned her dress as he pulled her down on to the sand, taking off the rest of their clothes as he did so. He was unable to remember the last time he had just enjoyed looking at her naked, at the way her body so beautifully curved in and then out again, marvelling at the smoothness, the suppleness and the raw sexuality that emanated from every pore and then he was kissing her again, making any further protests impossible.

The next afternoon, after a day spent swimming in the sea, lying on the beach, reading, chatting and drinking an endless variety of cocktails, they sat in a beach bar, their faces aglow with the wonderful shock of hours spent in such glorious sunshine. They sat in contented silence, enjoying nothing but the simple sound of the sea rolling slowly and gently backwards and forwards and behind them, the sound of their new friend Rico shaking up yet another irresistible concoction.

Sean checked his watch. "Okay, you ready? Three, two one, go!"

Dani laughed as Sean handed her her phone and watched as she efficiently started scanning emails. They had agreed half an hour a day for her to check in with the office so Sammy and Toby knew they had one small window of opportunity to share any important news and ask any questions. They subsequently packed everything into one email each, making the whole process as quick and painless as possible. Sean knew it was churlish to expect complete radio silence but, at least this way, it was only a small interruption each day. He watched as Dani's facial expression changed every few seconds like some kind of bizarre freeze-frame montage, recorded and then comically played back at high speed. Having digested the news from her team and read a few other cherry-picked communications, she switched to reply mode and typed a couple of quick messages back and then in a flurry put the phone back on the table with a big smile. "How was that?"

Sean looked at his watch again. "Seventeen minutes. Not bad at all! Anything juicy?"

Dani's contorted work-face returned. "Dave's been passed over for a really good part but Imogen's got a great new role so that's something."

Sean waved his hand to stop her. "I said anything juicy."

"Of course, silly me thinking you might be interested in the important stuff," Dani said with a wry smile. Sean refused to look apologetic and merely waited, eyebrows raised in anticipation. "Okay. Polly's in a new relationship." She paused for obvious dramatic effect. "With Damien. How's that for starters?"

Judging by the smile spreading across his face, that was indeed a great start. "Well that's got disaster written all over it! Has the woman learnt nothing?" he said with unashamed amusement. Dani was clearly less enthralled. "So if that was for starters, what's the main course?"

Dani rolled her eyes, desperately not wanting to share but knowing she had to. "Imogen's in a new relationship too."

"With?"

"Damien." Dani said the word then visibly flinched in anticipation of the huge roar of laughter that was now spilling forth. She watched, expressionless, waiting for him to pull himself together.

"Oh come on! You have to admit that's funny?" Dani sighed, failing to see anything funny about it at all.

The week literally flew past in a perfect haze of lazy mornings, more days spent lying in the sun, evenings enjoying wonderful meals and dancing into the early hours or long walks in the moonlight. As for the sex, Dani doubted she would ever be able to capture in words how truly amazing it had been, from spending hours in bed together to Sean pulling her into a seemingly quiet corner, aware they could be discovered at any moment. She happily decided the word 'perfection' had been invented purely to capture this moment and then suddenly, it was time to go. "Come on Sean, you've hardly packed a thing!"

"It's a protest, I don't want to go home, ever."

Dani stopped what she was doing to kiss him. "I know. But we have to get back. Billy and Amanda would never forgive us if their best man and only bridesmaid decided to stay on holiday and miss their wedding."

Sean fell back on to the bed. "That's it, I'm definitely not going back."

"Yes you are! And just to get you back into the swing of things, you can write your speech on the flight home."

As Dani stood at their bedroom door for the last time, she took a moment to look around and then rummaging in her bag, she pulled out her phone and took a final picture, never wanting to forget this room with all its wonderful memories. With one last glance, she closed the door behind her with a contented sigh. She had felt the need to whisk Sean away to remind herself why she loved him so much. Now she didn't just know why, she could feel why in the very pit of her stomach, in every single nerve end, in every heartbeat. She smiled to herself. Mission well and truly accomplished.

"Come on Sean, we're supposed to be inside now!" Billy was starting to get anxious. "That's if you can tear yourself away for just two sodding minutes!"

Sean gave Dani one final kiss then took hold of Billy's arm and walked him into the church.

"What's got into you two? You can't keep your hands off each other. You're like a couple of irritating teenagers." Sean could offer nothing in response but an annoying grin spread from ear to ear. "You have got the rings haven't you?" Sean patted his top pocket. "And you've written a speech?" Sean pulled out two neatly folded pieces of paper from his inside pocket and waited.

"Anything else?"

Before Billy could answer, the vicar nodded towards them and the organist hit his first powerful chord. For a moment, Billy was afraid to turn around and then suddenly, Amanda was beside him. A vision in pure cream silk, a spray of beautiful flowers in her hands and in her hair. He was aware of no one else as he looked at her, watching her smile at him through a thin veil, knowing only that he loved her. The ceremony began and Dani was unable to stop a tear escape as she listened to the beautiful exchange of words. I wish you so much happiness, she thought. Especially for you, my dear sweet Billy, feeling not one single ounce of regret or envy as he sealed his commitment to Amanda with a simple, 'I do'.

I do, thought Alex, as he impatiently boarded a plane to finally start his journey home. I absolutely and totally love her. He had stayed on in America which had been the most amazing experience. It had also provided the perfect distraction and, until now, he had successfully managed not to give Dani a thought. Having given himself a mental break from it all, he was amazed how simple it all now seemed. He had gone to such incredible lengths to save his marriage and prove to Victoria, and indeed to everyone, that there had been no affairs and that he was as committed as he had always been to his wife and family. The energy he had expended in doing so had been enormous and it had worked. For a while, even he had been fooled. He had brought the whole family over for a holiday during a week off. As he thought about that now, he was unable to think of one single reason why he had done it, other than to further perpetuate the myth. He realised now that he had only managed to make things worse, make the pretence seem even more devious and cruel, assuming that was humanly possible. Indulging himself for the first time in months, he slowly rewound and replayed the events of the past and realised beyond any doubt that the energy spent had been hugely misplaced. He had fought to save his relationship with Victoria when he should have been fighting for Dani. He had managed somehow to convince himself that his marriage was worth everything when it was really worth nothing compared to how he felt about Dani. And he had made love to his wife when he should have been celebrating his love for

Dani, convincing her beyond any doubt that she was all he had ever really wanted. There had been no further indiscretions. No one-night stands. No emotionless sex just to help pass the time. He knew it would be of no interest to anyone else but he had had something to prove to himself - that he needed or wanted no one but Dani.

The long flight was pure torture. No film could hold his attention. He flicked through the in-flight magazine but nothing really caught his eye. He played mindless games on his phone but quickly got bored and frustrated. He couldn't eat, his stomach churning with nervous energy and even several glasses of wine did little to smooth the edges off his agitation, so pronounced that he imagined himself prickly to the touch. For the last hour he stared at the seat belt sign like a man possessed, willing it to life until finally it illuminated with a satisfying ping marking the final descent into London. He sat back in his seat and sighed, his heart pounding and aware of only one remaining thought. He had to be with Dani. Absolutely nothing else mattered now.

22

"Caroline, where did this meeting come from?"

Caroline stopped to look over Dani's shoulder at her diary. "Oh it was a producer who said he hadn't spoken to you for a while but wanted to talk to you about a new project for Alex. I told him Alex was taking a break and then going back to America for another film but he still wanted to have a catch-up with you. He was fairly insistent. Said he wanted to talk about Dave and Imogen too."

Dani shrugged. She was meeting Amanda later and the meeting would ensure she got away on time so she might as well hear what he had to say. She looked at the name again. Peter Campbell. She said it to herself a few times and then finally she remembered. They had met at a dinner some time ago and he had talked about some projects he was working on. He had a formidable reputation and had said he would be in touch as soon as he had something concrete to discuss. Dani felt a building sense of excitement. That moment must finally have arrived.

The meeting took her to a quiet road in Mayfair, to a freshly painted door and then to a rather severe looking porter in a grand foyer. He took his time to study a piece of paper in front of him as she gave him her name and then told her to head for number 37 on the third floor.

When Dani found the appropriate door it was already ajar. She paused for a moment and then pushing it open, she stepped into a wide hallway, calling out a tentative "hello" as she did so. When there was no response, she had a quick look around and decided to head for the only open door ahead of her, suddenly feeling slightly apprehensive. This hardly felt like a place of business. As she walked into the room, Dani immediately felt how she had as a six year old on the day she had run into the patio doors believing them to be open only to discover, somewhat painfully, that in fact they were not. It wasn't just the surprise of seeing him. It was more the sense that she had been lured somewhere, that she had been tricked, leaving her feeling immediately angry and out of control. "What are you doing here?"

Alex sat on a huge dark sofa in a grand room. The walls were covered with beautiful paintings and the furniture all looked very expensive. There was a low, very solid looking coffee table, a thick sumptuous rug and a smattering of other well-chosen pieces but it was a cold room, each purchase clearly made as a statement of wealth with no regard given to comfort or homeliness. Dani felt a shiver whisper down her spine. It was all too much for her to take in. Alex, on the other hand, looked relaxed and slightly tanned and Dani thought he may have lost a little weight too. And then she remembered she had asked a question that still hadn't been answered. "Alex?"

"I wanted to see you somewhere quiet. I'm sorry. This seemed the only way." He stood up and Dani found herself taking a small step back. "Can I get you a coffee?" She nodded and Alex immediately headed for the kitchen. "I won't be a moment. Sit down," he said, gesturing to the large sofa.

Dani surveyed the room again and chose the safety of a chair instead. From her new position, she could see out of the huge windows that dominated one wall. The view was quite stunning. A perfect square of tall white buildings, all incredibly well looked after with a colour-rich garden in the centre that was equally well-kept. The kind of garden protected by high iron fences and locked gates, reserved for the highly privileged and subsequently completely empty.

"Here we are then." Dani jumped as Alex reappeared with a tray and two mugs of coffee, a milk jug and a sugar bowl, all matching. It was like something out of the pages of Homes & Gardens. He handed her a mug before sitting back down on the sofa then watched and waited as Dani took her time to stir in a couple of spoonfuls of sugar. When she couldn't justify making the simple task last any longer, she finally looked up.

"So how was America?"

"It was good thanks. The film looks great and I'm looking forward to the next one."

"I'm sorry you didn't win the Emmy."

Alex smiled. "I never really expected to but it was fun going to the ceremony and being surrounded by so many of my heroes. Thanks for sending those scripts over and the other bits and pieces. I quite like the idea of doing the British film next summer but it seems a long way off at the moment."

"Don't worry. There's really no hurry. They just want you to come on board early so they can use you to get the final funding they need."

"How cynical you are!"

She shrugged. "It comes with the territory. And with experience."

An uncomfortable silence followed as they both sipped at their coffees, both momentarily lost in thought while at the same time, desperate to know what the other was thinking. For very different reasons, both were reluctant to ask. Finally it was Dani who decided enough was enough. "So how do you know Peter Campbell and why are you in his home?"

"I was there when you met him. I was hoping you might remember his name and would be at least vaguely interested in seeing him. It seemed less dangerous than picking someone you would know better and might be tempted to call."

"You could have just called me. Asking for a meeting with your agent is generally seen as quite standard." Alex said nothing. "So whose flat is it?"

Alex looked at her, his face calm and collected. "It's mine."

Dani looked confused. "I don't understand."

"I live here Dani. I've left Victoria."

Dani lost all feeling in her fingers and the mug she had been holding fell to the floor, the last of her coffee spilling on to the rich, soft carpet. Dani jumped to her feet. "Oh I'm so sorry. Where's the kitchen? I need a cloth."

Alex stood up. "Please Dani, don't worry about it."

"Quick Alex! A cloth, before it soaks in!"

"Okay, if it makes you feel better." He disappeared for a moment and then returned, cloth in hand. She watched him as he knelt down, gently mopping up the liquid and then giving it a quick rub for good measure, he stood up again, standing uncomfortably close to her for a moment. He smiled. "See? Nothing to worry about."

Dani felt horribly hot and flustered, wanting desperately to put some distance between them. As Alex stood firm, she chose to cross the room to the sofa and sat down. "I'm sorry."

"Sorry for what? Spilling the coffee or because I've left my wife?" Alex sat down where he was, the majestic coffee table resuming its position as a solid barrier between them. Dani looked at him, leaning forward with real purpose, a look of determination in his eyes and suddenly, she felt angry.

"Are you being deliberately flippant about this?"

"I just expected some kind of reaction from you! Aren't you going to say something, anything?" Dani was unsure if it was nerves or frustration creeping into his voice. She held his eye.

"Why should I say anything? As far as I'm concerned, how you choose to conduct your personal life has absolutely nothing to do with me. Although you really should have let the office know you've moved." She watched him hang his head for a moment and then she stood up. "Was there anything actually work-related you wanted to discuss because I have to be somewhere?"

Alex looked up. "Oh come on! You can't just hear that and walk out?" The look in his eyes made it crystal clear it was nerves that were troubling him. This obviously wasn't how he had imagined their meeting would go.

"Why can't I? You said you'd never leave your wife for me so you must have done it for someone else. I don't see that it has anything to do with me." Dani looked at him, wanting to leave but not quite ready to head for the door. To her great surprise, she realised she actually felt sorry for him. She watched him run his hands through his hair, slowly and deliberately, his head down as he clasped his hands behind his neck. And then slowly he looked up.

"I left Victoria because I don't love her and I was sick of pretending."

"If that's what you felt was right for you then that's great. Just don't be surprised if Sean suddenly starts wanting to take your picture again." She waited for just a split second and then picked up her bag. "Now if that's it, I need to go," she said as she headed for the door.

"Dani wait!" Dani turned around as Alex leapt to his feet and came towards her, stopping just in front of her, their faces only inches apart. There was a desperate look in his eyes. "You said you loved me!" Dani looked away immediately, away from those piercing eyes that were now pleading with her. "I know you meant it."

Dani sighed and then slowly shook her head. When she raised her eyes to look at him, she was finally able to see him. Really see him. This man who had sucked her in so expertly that she had lost her way for a while. Lost all sense of perspective, so impenetrable had the bubble been. But her eyes were open now, the bubble long since burst.

"Stop it Alex." Her voice was calm and deliberate. "It's not really me you want. It's just that I said no. I've seen it a million times. You just need to know you can win me back and then what?"

"No, you're wrong. I love you!"

Dani laughed but not unkindly. It was born out of pity and relief that his spell over her was finally broken. "No you don't. I don't know if you're meant to be with Victoria but don't make it about us." Dani put her hand on Alex's cheek and smiled at him. "I'll see you next time you're in town." Before Alex could reach out and grab her hand, she was already at the door.

When Dani got outside she quickly walked away, interested in nothing but putting distance between herself and Alex. She called Amanda and managed to catch her just as she was leaving work and cancel their arrangement to meet. She just felt the need to be on her own for a while and Amanda seemed happy to swallow her story that she had to get back to work to sort out a problem. It wouldn't be the first time it had happened.

As she wasn't expected straight home, Dani headed for a bar and taking a table outside, ordered a large glass of wine and simply sat, eyes staring but fixed on nothing, her heart heavy. She felt emotionally drained. When would he give up? When would it all stop? He still needed her. That was the problem but it was for very different reasons now. She believed he really did want to call time on his marriage but he was fundamentally weak so couldn't possibly make the break without someone to move on to. She suddenly wondered what he'd told Victoria. What reason had he given for packing his bags? She shivered at the thought that she was the catalyst; that his romantic dream of them running off into the sunset together was what had finally given him the courage to look Victoria in the eye and tell her that their marriage was over. Well whatever wrongs she was guilty of, that was something she couldn't help him with. His imagined happy ending needed an immediate rewrite. Dani drained her glass. It was time to go home.

As she opened the front door, she was immediately hit by the sound of raucous laughter. She slowly pushed open the lounge door to reveal Sean and Billy, Billy on the sofa, Sean in front of him on the floor. She waited for a moment, looking at the empty beer cans and packets of crisps, most of the contents of which were now scattered over the lovely wooden floors. Finally, Sean saw her. "Hello darling! I thought you were going out?"

Billy's jollity quickly faded. "Aren't you supposed to be with Amanda?" He looked at Sean. "Oh shit, that's me in trouble!"

"I had some trouble at work that needed sorting. And what's so funny?"

Sean did his best to pull himself together. "Oh nothing really. Nothing that would seem funny now anyway. Just unwinding after a hard day's work."

"But you haven't been at work!"

Sean thought for a moment. "Oh no, I haven't have I?" he said with a smile as he got to his feet and began smothering Dani in hugs and kisses. "It's a lovely surprise to have you home early though. Is everything all right?"

"Fine thank you."

Sean kissed her again, muttering to her quietly until they were smiling at each other, lost for a moment in some private place, with a 'Do Not Disturb' notice on the door. Billy stood up. "If you two are going to start gooing all over each other, then I'm off."

Dani pulled away immediately. "No don't go. Stay and have something to eat."

"Do you mind if I call Amanda?"

"Of course not. Tell her to come over."

Dani wandered into the kitchen and opened the fridge. This will put me to the test, she thought, as she looked for inspiration amongst the bizarre assortment of food that looked back at her. She concentrated her mind for a few moments but when no elaborate recipe was forthcoming, she decided on pasta, believing this to be a fairly foolproof option.

"Do you want a hand with anything?"

Dani turned to see Billy come in. "Thanks but I think it's probably best if you don't see what happens in here over the next few minutes. You might lose your appetite."

Billy smiled but made no move to go. "Your problem at work didn't have anything to do with Alex did it?" Billy watched her expression change. "Dani?"

Dani stopped what she was doing to look at him. "He's left his wife."

"No! What did he do that for the stupid bastard?"

Dani shrugged. "It doesn't matter why. I meant it when I said it was over."

Billy took her in his arms and gave her a loud and sloppy kiss on the cheek. "Well done. I knew you could do it."

"Are you moving in on my girlfriend?" Sean smiled at them as they turned around, both hoping he hadn't heard them talking.

"Just filling in time until my own gorgeous wife gets here." Billy moved away and Sean took his place, putting his arm protectively around Dani's shoulder.

Billy smiled as he watched them. "Actually, I was looking for some inside information. Something that would explain why you two are all over each other like a nasty rash all the time. I thought maybe it was something in the cooking."

"Believe me, whatever goes into Dani's cooking is more likely to give you heartburn than heart flutters!"

"Right that's it! Everybody out of the kitchen before I end up pouring this marvellous and unique concoction over someone's head!"

Sean stopped only to retrieve another two cans of beer from the fridge before they both made a hasty retreat.

23

Dani heard through her privileged grapevine that Alex had gone back to Victoria. She had been unable to prevent an incredulous gasp when she'd heard the news. She wondered if he had ever actually told Victoria he was leaving. Or, for that matter, if Victoria had even noticed he was gone. She did actually believe he no longer loved Victoria and genuinely felt sorry for him, pitying him his weakness but pitying Victoria more. She was stuck in a loveless marriage and if she were her friend, she would be telling her loud and clear to get the hell out. But she wasn't her friend. Far from it. At least Alex had accepted Dani was absolutely not interested and for that she was extremely grateful. No one seemed to have noticed the temporary lapse in his supposed marital bliss so it appeared that this time, everyone had come away relatively unscathed.

But, as the days passed, she felt horribly distracted. It started as the tiniest seed of an idea which then grew minute by minute, its branches pushing their way into every corner of her mind and body until she felt totally suffocated. Paralysed. She wasn't sure when she finally felt confident enough to start trimming back the wayward thought but each snip brought with it a growing sense of calm. The final result was a decision made. A decision that she hoped would finally release her from what had been holding her back for far too long now.

Dani looked at her watch, made two phone calls and then left the office.

Billy rushed into the café feeling incredibly tense. The place was packed but it wasn't hard to see Dani, sitting alone at the back of the room. He was oblivious to the people he bumped into on his way to find her. Why was it taking so long to get there?

"Dani! What on earth's the matter?" Dani had called him twenty minutes earlier and calmly urged him to meet her as soon as he possibly could. Billy sat down and his tension immediately turned to nerves as he looked at her.

"I have to tell him Billy."

Billy looked confused. "Tell who what?" And then his heart threatened to pack up and leave him forever as he took in her expression and hoped beyond hope that his assumption was wrong. "No you mustn't! Not now, not after all this time!"

Dani was horribly calm. "But I have to. If I don't, it will slowly destroy us. Alex keeps cropping up. He's always there one way or another and I just can't get past it."

Billy couldn't believe his ears. "But you'll lose him!"

"I'll lose him anyway in time. I'll just have to make him understand."

Billy picked up her drink and in one large gulp, it was gone. He signalled to a waiter for two more and then

287

slowly, he began to shake his head. "No, it's emotional suicide. I can't let you do it, I just can't!"

"It's too late. He's waiting for me now at home and he knows there's something I want to talk to him about."

"Well didn't he ask what?"

Dani took a sip of the fresh drink that had just arrived. "I told him I couldn't discuss it over the phone."

"Jesus, what must he be thinking? If it isn't bad enough that you're going to break his heart, you're drawing the process out like some kind of bloody medieval torture!" Billy downed his drink in one and signalled to the waiter again with a frantic gesture urging him to hurry. And then he thought for a moment. "You're obviously having doubts now though, aren't you? Yes that's it! If you weren't questioning your decision you wouldn't be telling me. Giving me the chance to talk you out of it!" For the first time Billy looked a little less anxious. Finally, he thought he had made some sense of the situation and felt in danger of regaining control.

"No. I just needed to hear myself say it. Just to make sure. I'm more determined than ever."

Billy threw back another drink and then looked at her, his face red with alcohol, his eyes burning with frustration and fear. "You're wrong. This time you've got it so wrong it is incomprehensible! He loves you and you have never looked happier. Why would you want to risk that at the one time when there is absolutely no reason to do so?"

Dani looked at him with such a clear sense of determination and resignation that Billy visibly shivered. "It's because I love him that I have to tell him. Our relationship's built on a lie and I have to change that. I have to be honest. He'll understand. He has to."

Billy sat with his head in his hands as Dani left. He struggled to control his breathing, desperately trying to fight the sudden urge to overturn the table in front of him and to smash his chair against the wall. He rubbed his forehead and squeezed his eyes shut. This time he would need the strongest industrial glue available before he even contemplated the task of picking up the pieces and attempting to put them back together. And he was in no doubt there would be pieces to pick up. And plenty of them.

When Dani got home, Sean was waiting for her in the lounge. He sat quietly, no television on, no music playing. He looked at her as she walked in and she stopped for a moment, unable to read his expression. "So what's this all about?"

Dani slipped out of her coat and knelt in front of him. "I have something I need to tell you."

He attempted a smile. "Sounds ominous!"

Dani tried not to lose her concentration as she continued. "It's not going to be easy but I want you to know that I love you, more than I ever thought possible." Sean said nothing and, taking a deep breath, Dani took the first small step that she hoped would take her towards the end of this nightmare journey forever. "It's about Alex Cambridge." And me, she thought, but couldn't yet bring herself to say it.

"What about him?" Dani was momentarily thrown by his tone as she watched him pull out an envelope from the side of the sofa. She watched, completely frozen in horror, as he started to throw photographs on to the coffee table beside her. "Is it about this? Or this maybe?" Dani gasped as a montage of pictures started to build up, pictures of her with Alex taken on so many different occasions. Pictures of her walking with him, talking with him, kissing him.

"I don't understand. You knew?"

"I've always known."

Dani had never experienced such a feeling. She felt as if she was being strangled so violently that she touched her neck to make sure there was no rope, no strong hands forcing out her final breath. Her heart was so immediately in pieces that broken just wasn't anywhere near adequate to describe its spontaneous disintegration.

"But why didn't you say something?"

"I could ask you the same question." There was such coldness in his voice as he spoke to her and then he was on his feet, needing to find some outlet to vent his building emotion and anger as he paced up and down, up and down. Feelings that had been suppressed for such an incredibly long time they were taking a while to wake up and realise their moment of glory had finally arrived. Sean felt his heart rate quicken as he paced. He had rehearsed this moment so many times but now didn't know quite where to start and then finally, the words just started to spill out. "I always wondered and then I heard it was all over." He shrugged. "We all make mistakes and I thought that was the end of it. And then suddenly it was back on again and I thought, if she would just be honest with me, talk to me, I can forgive her. Jesus Dani! Why do you think I told Billy I thought he was having an affair? I knew he'd tell you and I thought that might finally make you say something." He paused for a moment. "I only wish I'd had the courage to sell pictures of you with him - believe me I came horribly close on more than one occasion." Dani flinched at the idea, unable to look at him as he continued. "But once I'd committed myself through Billy and you still said nothing, I had to go through with it. Not that it wasn't satisfying to see that smug bastard slapped all over the papers." Sean stood still for a moment. "And then I waited again, honestly believing that the exposure would make you admit to a terrible mistake that we could somehow put behind us. Scare you into realising the next time it might just be you on the front pages. Instead I just kept hearing myself apologise for the inconvenience I'd caused you!" He laughed, an almost demonic laugh, so possessed was he with raw bitterness and then he started pacing again, faster this time. "And then we go on holiday and I think, okay, she's making some kind of statement here and you mercilessly made me fall in love with you all over again. And then you see him again! And that, Dani, was just the last straw."

"It didn't start up again because of how I feel about you!"

"It's too late for explanations!" Dani winced as his voice finally started to build on a wave of hurt and anger. "All I wanted was for you to be honest."

Silent tears flooded Dani's eyes, spilling on to her face, forming tracks of watery mascara that quickly stained her flushed cheeks. "I'm being honest now," she cried. "I knew I had to tell you but I was so terrified of losing you. It's over with Alex. It has been for a very long time."

Sean was suddenly on his knees beside her, his face alive with rage. Dani shrank from him as he laughed in her face. "What were you imagining? That after all that's gone on, you could just tell me now, absolve yourself and expect us to just carry on? This isn't for me! This confession, or whatever it is, is for you because the guilt is finally eating away at you and you can't stand it!"

"But I…"

"No, I don't want to hear it! I just want to know why?" Dani hung her head, her body a crumpled heap, so distraught, so desperate and unable to find any words that could even begin to turn this around. Sean looked at her, his breathing loud and uneven. "I loved you and yet you treated me with such contempt that at times I almost made myself believe it wasn't happening." He sighed, desperate in some way to give in to her and tell her what she wanted to hear - that he still loved her and could forgive her. His gut heaved as it over-

292

flowed with hurt and anger. There simply wasn't any room for love or forgiveness. As he turned away, Dani knew she had to say something.

"I do love you Sean."

Slowly he turned back to face her. "This may come as a surprise but I actually do still believe that." He shrugged. "But I just don't love you." And then as he headed for the door, he stopped for a moment and instead walked over to the table and picked up another envelope. Once again, he started to throw pictures in front of her. "It seems only fair to give you the full set." Dani gasped again and again as each time a photograph fell, it was a different pair of eyes that looked up adoringly at Alex. "It seems you were in good company. Some of these actresses are actually quite good." Finally, he let go of the last one. "And isn't that his publicist? Ah yes, the lovely Wendy. She tried it on with me once. I'm glad I turned her down now that I know what appallingly low standards she has."

Dani squeezed her eyes shut as her brain shut down, physically unable to digest any more of this horror. As Sean looked at her, Dani seemed to shrivel before him and every heart-string that connected her to him, tugged so violently that Sean suddenly felt nailed to the floor. He looked on as she struggled to try to say something through the vicious series of sobs that fought to escape from her mouth, spilling out in erratic waves and then biting his lip until he winced with pain, he experienced one final surge of strength that finally released him. "Every time I thought of you with him, I wanted to kill him. And then every time I watched you walk back in here, knowing that you'd had sex with him..." He shook his head, horrified by the memory and unable to find the words to explain how he had felt. "But now that it's all out, the only shame I feel is how I could have let you get away with it for so long. I guess I must have become the fool you took me for." He hung his head, his eyes wide and horribly tired and then he couldn't stand it any longer. Couldn't stand being in the same room as the woman he so loved and yet so despised at the same time.

Dani's reactions were so severely handicapped that by the time she looked up, he was already gone. She had no sensation of time passing as she sat on the floor, unable to cry any more, unable to comprehend how it had all gone so horribly wrong. She was aware only of an incredibly empty feeling inside. No butterflies, no somersaults, no quivering jellies. Nothing.

She knew that midnight had passed because that was when she had called Billy. He had snatched at the phone the minute it had rung, desperate to hear from her and find out what on earth had happened. He had listened to her with an air of inevitability and then, at Dani's request, he had headed off on a mercy mission to try to find Sean while Amanda raced to her friend's side.

Dani hadn't said a single word since Amanda arrived and despite desperately wanting to know what irretrievable words had been exchanged, Amanda didn't force the issue, squashing the immediate question that she

294

really wanted answered which was, why she hadn't been party to any of this? In the scheme of things, she had to accept that really wasn't of any importance. Although she couldn't help wondering if things would have turned out differently if it had been her counsel Dani had sought instead of Billy's. She would have challenged harder that much she was convinced of. What the hell had she been thinking? Was she really trying to fix the relationship or was she intent on simply blowing it to pieces? Because that's what it looked like to Amanda. She was desperate to know how Dani could have imagined a positive outcome after sharing such catastrophic news but all of that paled into insignificance when compared to the equally cataclysmic revelation that Sean already knew. Dani had spoken so briefly with Billy before they had raced over that that simple, mind-blowing fact was all she had. She couldn't get her head around it but what she did know was that it all made her feel very uncomfortable. She sighed. She desperately wanted answers but knew now wasn't the time. So, instead, she just sat with Dani, held her hand and cried with her, unable to stop herself joining in as she witnessed Dani's heart breaking before her very eyes. Until there was nothing at all. No tears left, just a hollow desperate silence.

Billy's choices of possible venues to find Sean were limited due to the late hour and, in a way, he was hoping he wouldn't find him. He was a known conspirator after all. If he had been desperate to find him, if lives had depended on it, Billy knew that the chances were he never would. The fact that he was apprehensive about seeing him naturally meant he found Sean in the first place he looked. A small late-night wine bar they had often been to together.

Picking up a couple more beers at the bar, Billy slowly walked over and sat down opposite him. Sean looked up and sighed and then slowly shaking his head, looked away again. It was obviously down to Billy to do the talking and he quickly gulped down half his drink before starting. He smiled to himself. Between the two of them, they're turning me into a bloody alcoholic, he thought dryly.

"I didn't know you knew."

Sean looked up at him, his eyes tired and sad. "I've been living the lie with her, only without the support that Dani had."

Billy watched him play with the beer bottle in his hands, tearing the label off in tiny little pieces that now littered the table in front of him. "Do you think I should have told you? Is that it?"

Sean thought for a moment. "No. Dani was the only person who could tell me."

"I tried so hard to stop her, I really did."

"None of this is your fault!"

Billy sighed. "I know but I just feel so helpless. I've stood on the sidelines and watched everything spiral out of control and have been powerless all along to stop it." He looked at him for a moment longer. "So what happens now?"

Sean shrugged. "I've been waiting for this moment for so long, I almost believed it would never happen. And things have been so good between us I'd actually started to convince myself it didn't matter anymore, that I could just lock it all away and move on. But now that it's all out, there's no going back."

"She really does love you."

Sean almost laughed. "Oh come on, that's just too easy! She loves me but like what? Like she loves pizza for Christ's sake? Or chocolate fucking ice cream? Not enough to stop herself fucking another guy." Billy looked away. What could he possibly say? He tried to imagine how he would be reacting if he were in Sean's shoes and knew he would be feeling the same. Hurt, betrayed, humiliated. "How could I ever have believed that once it was out in the open we really could face it and deal with it?" There was a pause and for a moment Billy wondered if he was supposed to come up with a response, something truly profound that would make sense of it all. He had nothing to offer so was relieved when Sean continued to rant. "What a complete fucking idiot I am! There isn't even any satisfaction in knowing he was making a fool of her while she was making a fool of me. No satisfaction at all."

"So why didn't you say something? Why tell me you knew Alex was having an affair but not what you knew about Dani? You used me." Sean said nothing. "I don't get it Sean. Why not just tell her you knew?"

Sean continued to sit in silence, his expression giving no visual clue as to what he was thinking. Billy waited as long as he could. "Sean? Why didn't you tell her? This could all have been over months ago."

"I needed her to tell me," he said with a shrug and then struggled for a moment, wondering if that was actually the case or if his reluctance to say more was because he didn't really have the answers. Either way, Billy chose to interpret the extended pause as a sign he didn't want to talk about it.

"So where will you go?" he asked instead.

"No idea."

Billy pushed his keys across the table. "Stay at our place tonight. Amanda's with Dani and we'll probably stay with her tonight. Then you can decide what to do in the morning."

Hesitating for just a moment, Sean took the keys. "Thanks Billy. I'll be gone early and I'll find somewhere tomorrow."

"What about your stuff?"

Sean waved a dismissive hand in the air. "It's only stuff. I'll choose my moment and clear it all out soon enough."

Billy looked at his watch. "This place is closing any minute. Come on. Walk back with me."

In relative silence, they walked together until their different destinations finally meant they had to part. "Let me know where you are."

Sean smiled. "I don't want to put you in any difficult situations."

"You won't. Promise me you'll call."

"Okay, I will."

They stood for a moment and then, with a warm hand shake and something that almost resembled a hug, Sean walked away. Billy sighed as he watched him go, knowing as he turned his back on the frying pan that he had no choice but to head for the fire. Now he had to face Dani.

He walked quietly into the flat and then into the lounge. Two anxious faces looked up at him but it was Amanda who spoke. "Did you find him?" Billy nodded and then as the tears started to flow again, he took Dani in his arms. Her painful sobs said what she couldn't. She knew Sean wasn't coming back.

24

Bernie had come into work early for a special meeting with his partner, Sarah Stacey. There was only one topic on the agenda and that was Dani. She had continued to develop and was fast becoming a formidable force within the entertainment industry. Neither of them was able to think of one single occasion when she had made a bad decision, when she had not been spot on about signing a new artist, however apprehensive either of them may have been, or when she hadn't been able to keep a clear head when trouble hit and needed to be swiftly dealt with. Sometimes nervously, they had taken a step back and given her a free rein. She had never disappointed them.

The result was, they were nervous. Afraid she would either be head-hunted - they were well aware there had been offers - or, worse still, that she would start up on her own. They definitely didn't want to end up in competition with her but it was because they genuinely liked and respected her that they really didn't want to lose her. They had already discussed options and only a brief meeting was needed to finalise their plans.

When Dani arrived at her desk, there was a note waiting for her. She sighed, anticipating a severe bollocking for being such a major pain in the arse recently as she read Bernie had demanded an audience. She knew she had been operating on autopilot, coming into work, doing what had to be done and then heading off on a miserable journey home to an empty flat. All traces of Sean had disappeared within a week. There was no phone call, no note left. She had just come home one night to find his keys beneath the letterbox. The most brutal and conclusive way of letting her know he had no intention of coming back. As she had nervously looked around, it hadn't taken long to realise that everything he owned had gone. The room he had used for work was completely bare and Dani had shut the door, doubting she would ever go back in.

As she had walked into the lounge, her eyes had been immediately drawn to the coffee table and two large envelopes. In it was every photograph he had ever taken of her. That picture from the first night they met, holiday photos and of course, the pictures of her with Alex. Dani had felt as if he was handing back every memory of her, good and bad. Please let him have kept just one, she had thought, as she had tried to hold on to a distant hope that he might just get in touch. But of course he hadn't, leaving Dani to get used to the most profound loneliness, made so much worse by the fact it was so horribly self-induced.

After a few weeks, the pain of coming back through what had been their front door every night became too much. She gave notice on the flat, brought the contract with the agency on her own flat to and end and as soon as was possible, she moved back in.

At work, she had lost her smile, her humour, her spark but at least she could be mildly comforted by the knowledge that none of her artists had suffered as a result. Most of her anger and frustration was being unleashed across the negotiating table and she had subsequently pulled off some cracking deals. She wasn't just ruthless, she became the kamikaze agent, not afraid to push to the absolute limit and scared of no one. There were many times when she had stood up, prepared to walk out of a meeting. It had undoubtedly speeded up the negotiation process and on each occasion, the result had worked hugely in her favour.

She stopped going to the bigger functions knowing that Sean would be there. She didn't want to risk seeing him. What would she say? So instead she hid herself away, just going to work and occasionally seeing Billy and Amanda.

The only times Dani knew she'd gone too far was when she looked at the fear in Caroline's eyes as she snapped unnecessarily or barked an order that could just as easily have been a simple calm request. Or when Sammy or Toby came to her with a problem and she told them in no uncertain terms to get some balls and sort it out themselves. She was making their lives a misery and that was definitely not fair. Aware the potency of her frequent apologies was weakening, she had eventually taken them all out for a drink and given them a carefully crafted summary of what had happened - that she and Sean had split up but with all mention of Alex obviously left out. They of course knew they were only being given a small portion of the story but had enough respect for her to appreciate her attempt at explaining what had changed and now at least understood why she had been so vile.

Dani took a moment to put some make-up on and then went to find Bernie. As she walked into his office, she was surprised to see Sarah sitting there too. So they're ganging up on me are they? she thought as she took Bernie's offer of a seat, her back stiff and ready for a fight. But her tough exterior slowly started to melt as she listened to Bernie praise her, cataloguing a huge list of career highlights and then finally, he got to the point. "You've always worked hard Dani but since we made you a director, your success has been quite unprecedented. So, as a result of everything you've achieved, Sarah and I have had a chat and are both in absolute agreement that we'd like you to become a partner. How does Stacey, Walker & Williams sound to you?"

Boy, had she not seen that coming! Dani was momentarily speechless, knowing as she struggled to look composed that all eyes were on her. "I don't know what to say. I'm completely stunned."

"It would be a big step for you. A big commitment that you should think about very carefully. So are you at least interested?"

Dani smiled. "Of course I am!"

"Good. Then I'll get some paperwork drawn up and you can think about it properly once you know exactly what you're letting yourself in for."

Dani walked back to her desk in a daze. She loved her work and hadn't really thought about her long-term future. Every time she had started to feel she'd done all she could at Stacey Walker, a new challenge would present itself and the moment quickly passed but this was a huge step and, once her ego had deflated slightly, she knew she would need to sit down and consider the offer carefully. Of course she had been approached by other companies on several occasions over the years and sometimes she had gone as far as a meeting when curiosity got the better of her but she had never felt compelled to move on. She knew she worked for the best and now she could actually own part of it. She smiled. If nothing else, it would provide the perfect distraction and give her something amazingly positive to focus on.

When the promised paperwork arrived, Dani took as much advice as she could. Lawyers went through the contract with a fine-tooth comb, accountants poured over the books and financial advisors advised but, whoever she spoke to, the conclusion fortunately seemed to be the same. It was a great opportunity and she would be a fool not to grab it with both hands. So it seemed the decision was made.

Within a matter of weeks, Dani was sitting in an office of her own, the website and stationery all newly amended to include her name and a formal announcement had been made. She had subsequently been flooded with messages of good luck from producers, journalists and, of course, her clients. She did a round of interviews for the trade press and everything that ran was immensely positive. Her office quickly took on the look of an Interflora depot, huge bouquets in abundance. It was a truly great feeling to think so many people were supporting her.

Apart from a few more tedious weekly meetings which she did her best to embrace, on a day-to-day basis nothing much changed, with the exception of one very significant development. Alex was massively important to the agency and was currently back in America working on his second movie. Dani was the first to admit it was Bernie who had the most solid US connections so, after a series of carefully planted comments to pave the way, it had been remarkably easy for her to suggest that Bernie was now best placed to take his career forward. She had chosen her moment perfectly and unable to think of a reason to the contrary, Bernie had happily added Alex to his own roster. It was a massive relief for Dani and hard for Alex to object, knowing that he did now have the absolute best in the business handling his affairs.

As the months slipped by, Dani quickly realised she had indeed made the right decision. The sense of freedom she was now experiencing gave her a completely new lease of life and the results were amazing. Rather than simply expand her team and take on potentially unnecessary costs, she took her time to seek out people who really enjoyed comedy, theatre and television. Whether it was someone booking plays in a small theatre or someone working behind the bar in a comedy club, the only criteria was passion in their field. Over time, she put together a small hit squad of people whose instincts she massively trusted so when a call came from any one of them, it almost always meant she was immediately on the road to a new discovery. In return for a finder's fee, the system was working perfectly and Dani was the first one on the scene when a new comedian started to develop a following or if a young actor landed his first role in a provincial theatre and single-handedly brought the house down.

There was still a constant stream of people knocking on her door, desperate for her to at least talk to them about representation. She had even been approached by the actress who had been photographed with Alex. She had gone from being completely unknown to a minor celebrity in one step, or one shag, depending on which way you looked at it. Needless to say, she had told her with regret that her client list was already full but she wished her luck finding representation elsewhere.

It was Friday and, as the clock stood to attention at six o'clock, the office was quickly emptying, everyone eager to get their weekend started. Dani was in no hurry. Weekends were a solitary experience for her these days and although she had learnt to find some pleasure in the peace and quiet and the Saturdays spent mooching around shops and markets, her Sundays were still particularly tough. For a while, she had kept herself busy unpacking the things she had put into storage, rediscovering her old books and bits and pieces but that was all done now. She woke on Sundays with a heavy heart and only a long stretch of nothingness to look forward to.

At least this Sunday would be different. She had arranged to have brunch with a chap called Will. He owned a great pub and thanks to the mini theatre he'd developed, he had started as one of her scouts and slowly become a friend. Well that's how she saw their relationship. Will was clearly hoping for more and had eventually suggested they go out. Dani didn't want to offend him so Sunday brunch had felt like a fairly innocuous option. In truth, she had wanted to say no but, if for no other reason than to shut Billy and Amanda up who were constantly pushing her to get out and start dating, she had found herself relenting.

When Sunday morning came, Dani was able to walk to their chosen venue. She had dressed casually in jeans, a loose shirt and a jacket, aware that she was hoping it didn't look like she'd made too much of an effort. Oh the beautifully complex psychology of dating, she thought, as she asked herself why she was even going if her only goal was to look like she wasn't trying to either impress or seduce, desperate as she knew she was to leave him wanting nothing more than friendship. It was too late for all that now. Her hand was already on the café door, Will's lovely, smiling face already facing her. He stood as she approached him. "Hi Dani," he said still smiling as he kissed her on the cheek.

Dani sat down. "I'm not late am I?"

"No, I have a horrible habit of always being early." Dani smiled, the irritating voice in her head immediately declaring them totally incompatible. They both ordered various combinations of eggs, bacon and toast and then quickly relaxed into an easy conversation with a quick catch-up on work and what Will had coming up in his small but perfectly-formed theatre. As he mentioned a particular actor, he reached for a copy of a Sunday tabloid in a rack beside their table and positioned it so they could both see it. Quickly flicking through the pages, he explained there was a great review of this young new talent set to appear in his next production that he would love her to see. Will jumped as Dani suddenly slammed her hand down hard to stop his progress, as if she were playing an overzealous game of snap. Hoping she'd made a mistake, she then pulled the paper around so she could properly take in the feature before her, her eyes frantically darting across a series of pictures from a festival the day before, a look of panic slowly taking hold, her mouth falling slightly open.

"Dani? What is it?" Dani didn't answer straight away, simply because she didn't want to believe what she was seeing and now reading. "Dani?"

Dani slumped back in her chair. "I'm so sorry Will, I'm going to have to go." Before she could explain further, their breakfasts arrived. She pushed back her chair and standing up, started to put on her jacket. "One of my clients is in trouble. Can I call you later?"

"Of course," Will replied as he stood up too but despite his swift action, Dani was already rushing for the door. Will sat down with a twang of regret and then his nose was distracted by the wonderful smells floating up from the plates in front of him. He picked up his knife and fork and tucked in, wondering if he'd be able to make room for Dani's dish too.

Dani was already on the phone by the time the door whooshed shut behind her. "What do you know?" she asked the minute Toby answered.

"Drugs, drugs and more drugs. That just about sums it up. Oh, and some fighting and general hurling of colourful expletives."

"And his schedule?"

"He did his first day's filming on Friday and is due on set…." he paused to look at his watch, "…about twenty minutes ago."

Dani stopped, suddenly aware she was marching with great intent but with no idea where she was headed. "So I'll be getting a call any minute from someone wondering where the fuck he is. Find him for me and when you do, get to him as quickly as possible and sit on him till I get there." Before Toby had the chance to answer, Dani's phone beeped. "Shit, that'll be someone from the production team now. Gotta go. Hello, Dani Williams."

"So my instinct was right. Jake was a risk that clearly wasn't worth taking."

Dani's pupils dilated. She hadn't expected the producer. "Simon, it's just a glitch. I'll get him to you as quickly as I can, he'll be brilliant and this will never happen again, you have my word." Dani winced. It was a wild claim to make as they both well knew.

"I love your optimism but I'm sure you've seen the papers too. He won't be with us today and that means I've just pissed tens of thousands of pounds up the wall so I'm cutting my losses. If I do it now, I only have two days to reshoot with someone who's actually committed to the job. Get your lawyers to speak to mine tomorrow but you can tell him from me, if he makes any fuss I'll see to it he never works again."

Dani felt her shoulders drop. She was a woman defeated. "I'm so sorry Simon."

"Not your fault." Dani felt his voice lighten. "And I know you'll kick his arse enough for both of us." Indeed I will, she thought, relieved he had been so professional about it all. It wouldn't have been the first time someone had taken their anger and frustration out on her instead of the true antagonist.

As Dani stood struggling with her own anger and frustration and wondering what to do next, her phone announced an incoming text. It was Toby. Jake was apparently on his way home and Toby wanted to know if he should head over there. Dani's reply was brief and to the point - no, she would be waiting when he strolled back through the door. The text sent, Dani immediately started dialling a number clumsily on her mobile with one hand as she hailed a taxi with the other.

When she arrived at Jake's house, Sadie had the good grace not to look surprised. "He's blown it this time, hasn't he?" she said as she let Dani in. Dani gave her a hug as she continued, clearly wound up and glad to have someone to talk to. "I told him not to go but he wouldn't listen. He never listens to me. And apart from a text to say he's on his way back, his phone's been off all day. Meanwhile mine's been red hot with journalists calling and before you ask, I haven't spoken to anyone and Toby has a list of everyone who's called."

Dani smiled. "If only Jake were more like you."

Sadie was way too preoccupied to acknowledge or process the comment as she put her hand up to her forehead, her eyes watery as she rubbed hard. "I've had a stinking headache all day and Beau's been acting up and he'll just swan back in oblivious to the shit he's in." Sadie paused for a moment and then she looked up. "Cup of tea?"

Dani obediently followed her to the kitchen and they settled at the large table with tea and biscuits. When Dani felt Sadie had suitably calmed, she decided it was time to start putting a plan into play. "Sadie do you trust me?" Sadie nodded, her anger now overtaken by a mixture of angst and self-pity, her quivering chin making it impossible to speak. "Good. Then I want you to go upstairs and pack a bag for Jake. Enough clothes for a week or so, toiletries, maybe a picture of you and Beau, a book to read - anything you think he'd want with him for a brief stay away. Then I want you to leave the bag with me and I want you to take Beau and go out. I'll call you when it's okay to come back."

Sadie hesitated for just a moment but ultimately she did trust Dani and she knew Jake had gone too far this time. Whatever Dani was planning would be fair and, if

311

he didn't like it, it served him bloody well right. Slowly she stood up and headed upstairs.

Dani was forced to wait another hour before she heard a car pull up, followed by the sound of doors opening and shutting and then finally, a key in the door. "Hello!" he shouted without a care in the world. "Sades, I'm home!" Dani took a deep breath, reminding herself she needed to stay calm. Jake walked into the lounge and stopped suddenly as he saw Dani, immediately looking around for Sadie.

"Where's Sadie?"

Dani looked at him, her face fixed, her voice low. "She's gone out."

Jake was starting to panic, no doubt fuelled by a massive comedown from whatever cocktail of drugs he'd taken the day before. And then he clocked the bag. "What's that for?"

"Jake, sit down." Dani waited while he did as he was told. "You do know you were supposed to be on set hours ago?"

Jake leapt up, looking at his watch. "Fuck!" He frantically started checking his pockets for his phone.

"Jake, sit down. It's too late. You're off the film and you'd better brace yourself for a whopping great bill for the money you've cost the production. But worse than that, if you don't do as I suggest, your career's over. I warned you this would happen and surprise, surprise sweetheart, when you get yourself slapped all over the papers as high as a fucking kite when you're supposed to be working, no one else is going to risk getting their

312

fingers burnt in the same way. So your bag's packed, your place in rehab is booked and the car's outside. And if you don't go then we're done too."

Jake looked at her and then he stood up and looked out of the window to see a big black car waiting across the road. His shoulders slumped and for a moment he didn't move. Then, without saying a word, he picked up the bag and walked out.

Dani sat for a moment, her heart thumping, her head pounding. Sometimes her job seriously sucked. She allowed herself a few minutes of self-indulgence and then suddenly remembered she was due at Billy and Amanda's. Shit, she thought as she looked at her watch. She was going to be late, again. Deciding there was no time to go home, she grabbed her bag and made a run for it, calling Sadie as she went to update her and let her know she could now come home.

It was almost an hour later when she stood in front of Billy, a look of extreme apology on her face and a look of 'I expected nothing less' on his. "I'm so sorry. It's been a really challenging day."

"Yeah, yeah, yeah." He smiled at her. "I forgive you but Amanda might not. She's stopped and started dinner at least four times thinking you would at least have called if you were going to be late."

Dani grimaced and taking a deep breath, headed for the kitchen. Slowly, she peeked around the door and was relieved to see that Amanda looked extremely calm as she pottered around. There was no smell of burning and no blackened pans filling the sink.

"Hi Amanda." Dani braced herself.

"Hi!" Amanda swept towards her and threw her arms around Dani's neck. She's going to strangle me, she thought. Squeeze out my last breath with her arms, suffocate me with her ample bosom. "I'm so glad you're here!"

Dani found herself released from the embrace and looked at her friend. "You are? But I'm so late."

Amanda shrugged with a smile. "You're always late."

Billy appeared behind her and Dani's fine-tuned intuition took over. "Okay, what's going on?"

Amanda was unable to wait a second longer to share their news. "I'm pregnant!"

Now it was Dani's turn to take Amanda in her arms. "That's amazing, I'm so pleased for you."

"I didn't realise how badly I wanted a baby until I did the test. I've never been more excited and grateful." Amanda said, her voice breaking as she spontaneously burst into tears as Billy watched on.

"Hormones," he muttered, rolling his eyes.

Dani smiled at him. "Oh stop it. I know you're ecstatic, you can't fool me!" Billy smiled, a big cheesy grin from ear to ear. He looked like a little boy who had just been told he would one day play football for England, or drive a steam train, or go to the moon, or whatever it is that little boys dream about.

"Go and get Dani a drink Billy. I'll be through in a minute."

Dani followed Billy into the lounge where a chilled bottle of champagne was waiting. Before he opened it, she gave him a hug. "I'm so pleased for you. You've got it all so right and that's just brilliant. I can't tell you how happy I am."

Billy looked at her, a concerned look in his eye. "You'll get it right too you know." And then he suddenly remembered Will. "How was your date?"

Dani shook her head. "I had to leave. A work crisis. But I don't think it'll go anywhere."

"Why not? Why don't you just stop scaring people away before you've even given them a chance?"

"I don't know what you mean?"

Billy watched a light go out in her eyes. "Yes you do! You've got to stop punishing yourself. Living like a nun isn't going to change anything that's happened!"

"Oh please, not this lecture again."

"It's not a lecture. If I don't say these things to you, no one else is going to. Let someone in. Take off the armour and have some fun."

"I've tried fun, thank you, it doesn't suit me."

Billy looked at her. He was watching her fade away and felt helpless, a feeling he was fast getting used to where Dani was concerned. He used to have an impact on her life but not anymore. She used to listen to him and welcome his advice. Now she listened with a sense of irritation, her eyes pleading with him to just leave her alone. He sighed. She would snap out of it eventually or she would become a miserable old spinster and, at present, the dusty old shelf seemed to be streaks ahead of the field.

Before Billy could come up with a new approach, the phone rang. Dani smiled, believing she had won a reprieve for the time being at least, as Billy reluctantly answered it. "Hello?" There was a pause and if Dani wasn't mistaken, a slight hesitation. "Oh hi! How are things?……..Good, good……..Yeah great thanks, in fact I have some news. Amanda's pregnant!" Dani listened with interest and her heart was already telling her what her mind was too frightened to even contemplate, as Billy laughed and chatted and then turned to look at her. "We're just about to have dinner actually. Dani's here." And then she knew without a doubt by the way Billy had said her name and the colour in her cheeks started to slip away. Billy's conversation ended fairly quickly at that point and he took his time to replace the handset, aware that Dani's eyes were boring into the back of his head, ready to pierce his eyes as soon as he turned around. When he finally made the move, Dani already had her eyebrows raised, waiting for confirmation.

"It was Sean." Billy was unsure what to say next. He had never made a secret of the fact that he and Sean kept in touch but he knew it was difficult for Dani. She wanted to know every word he said but knew she couldn't ask. Wanted to know if he missed her, if he was seeing someone else, if he was getting any closer to forgiving her but the words always stuck in her throat. It wouldn't be fair to put Billy in such an awkward situation, even though she wanted to hate him for putting himself there in the first place. A feeling she was finding it hard to hide.

"Don't look at me like that." Billy was done trying to justify his friendship with Sean.

"Like what?"

"Like you hate me."

"I don't hate you. I hate myself. I hate the loneliness, the isolation and the label that I carry around every day. A label that will never go away and why should it? I deserve to be reminded what kind of person I am."

Billy shook his head. "Well in that case, you are beyond help. When you decide to start living again, instead of wallowing in the most self-indulgent self-pity and sounding like some dreadful made-for-TV movie, then you let me know. Otherwise, just shut the fuck up!"

Billy left the room, refusing to be softened by the tears in Dani's eyes and returned with dinner and his wife. In her current euphoric state, Amanda was oblivious to any tension and had more than enough conversation for all of them. The perfect antidote, thought Billy, as he forced himself to ignore Dani before she dragged him down with her at a time when he had so much to be happy about.

The next day started with a regular staff meeting of the senior team. After the usual round of good mornings and chitchat about what was new, everyone sat quietly waiting for Bernie. Another man incapable of being on time, thought Dani, then immediately found herself reciting that well-known phrase involving pots, kettles and the colour black. Then suddenly, he literally flew through the door. "You'll never guess what?"

Dani looked at him and sighed. "Go on, surprise us."

"Alex has got another nomination. A Golden Globe this time and the word is he might just pull it off!"

Everyone cheered and Dani managed to smile. "That's great Bernie. Does he know yet?"

"I just called him. He was over the moon but I've told him he has to keep it to himself until it's announced officially. He's home in a couple of weeks so I said we'd throw him a little party."

How simply marvellous, thought Dani. The film for which he'd been nominated had been an enormous success on both sides of the Atlantic. Bernie had managed to get him released from his current film for a few days to do some publicity but it had been a whistle-stop tour to London and he had barely had time to sleep, never mind contact anyone. At least that was what she had told herself when no call came, no message, no note. Although she had no idea why she wanted him to get in touch. She certainly wasn't looking to rekindle anything between them. She just felt horribly abandoned by the two men in her life who had both turned their backs and kept on walking. Served her right.

Dani was relieved to hear that Bernie did indeed mean a small party for Alex with a watertight guest list. He would ensure in the way only he could that it was a genuine private affair and Dani kept everything crossed that Sean wouldn't hear about it. The three of them together in one room was completely inconceivable.

When the night finally arrived, try as she might to fight it, Dani was a complete bag of nerves. She dressed very simply, this time trying to make it look like she had made little effort, while at the same time trying to ensure she looked her absolute best. Arriving fashionably late, almost everyone was there ahead of her making it easy to slip in unnoticed. She had only just collected a drink when she just knew without turning around that Alex was beside her.

"I was beginning to think you weren't coming."

She smiled at him. "Hi Alex, how are you?"

"I'm fine. You look great as always." He looked around for a moment. "Look, do you think we could talk somewhere?" He saw the immediate look of fear in her eyes. "Nothing heavy, I promise."

"What about that alcove over there? That's as private as it gets in here."

"Perfect." And taking her arm, he led her to the secluded table, picking up another glass of champagne on the way.

For a moment they sat looking at each other. "I heard about the partnership. Congratulations, you deserve it." Dani smiled a thank you as Alex raised his glass to her. "I also heard Sean moved out. I'm really sorry about that."

She looked at him, unsure exactly how sorry he was and then decided there was no point in still feeling bitter. "It's nothing less than I deserved under the circumstances. It was foolish to think he didn't know already."

"He knew?" Alex couldn't hide his surprise as he struggled to take this on board.

Dani shrugged. "He lives in the shadows. Of course he knew."

"Then why didn't he say something? Surely he had the chance to take control of the situation but instead he chose to…" Alex stopped, unable to miss Dani's back stiffen. He hesitated and then decided just to leave the thought hanging. The look in Dani's eyes made it clear he had nothing to gain from laying into Sean and he knew he wasn't best placed to take even the smallest step towards the moral high ground. "Oh well," he said instead, "I guess we're all scarred in some way by this insane world we move in."

For a brief moment, Dani suddenly saw herself as part of the inner circle. The circle she had always felt she operated outside of, eyes open, immune to the endless personal indiscretions, fighting for good from the safety of the real world. What an awful moment to be reminded she was just as shallow and weak as the rest of them. Dani gave her head a quick shake to dissolve the hideous thought and looked up at Alex. "And what about you?"

"I barely see Victoria which is probably the only reason we're still together but at least that means I still get to see as much of the kids as possible when I'm not away working. It's hard enough to play a consistent role in their lives without throwing a messy divorce into the mix. But there isn't anyone else. There hasn't been anyone since I lost you for good. I learnt my lesson the hard way too you know. Whatever you think of me, I did love you. It may have taken me too long to realise it but I was prepared to give up everything I had for you." He looked at her for a moment. "And I still would. That hasn't changed."

"No Alex. That moment has well and truly passed."

"Only because I remind you of all the guilt and the deceit - all the bad things. If you would just look past that…."

"No Alex!" I don't have to look past anything, she thought. It's all here in front of me, staring into my eyes and what I see, what I feel, is simply nothing.

"But if there's no one else in your life, isn't it different now?" Dani sighed and watched as his hands were suddenly holding hers. "I still have feelings for you. Doesn't that mean anything?"

"I don't know. You throw a party for someone and they hide in the bloody corner!" Dani immediately pulled her hands away and sat back in her chair as Bernie loomed over them.

"Sorry Bernie. Dani and I were just catching up on old times."

"You can talk to each other any time! Come on Alex, there's some people I want you to meet."

Bernie walked away as Alex stood up. "I'll be right back. Wait there."

Dani watched him go. She had no problem at all reminding herself why she had found him so irresistible and it was strangely reassuring to hear that he did still love her, as if that meant that somehow, it hadn't all been in vain. She sighed, knowing that it really made no difference at all. In fact it felt rather pathetic to acknowledge her need to feel she was special amongst her fellow mistresses when she knew she should be consumed by nothing but shame that she was part of the sorry group at all.

By the time Alex came looking for her, Dani had already slipped out. She hurried away, keen to put as much distance between them as quickly as her heels would allow. She was so focused on achieving her goal there was no chance of her seeing Sean, sitting at a pavement table in a café opposite, a coffee in front of him that had long since gone cold. He wasn't sure why he was there, although he could say it was worth the wait just to see Dani leave alone. As he watched her escape through the lens of his camera, he felt a rush of relief, immediately followed by a hollow disappointment in himself that it still mattered. With the zoom stretched he could see the expression on her face, part fearful, part reflective, a sadness definitely. He slowly lowered his camera as she disappeared out of view, taking a sip of his coffee and then grimacing, its total lack of temperature a reminder of how long he'd been sitting there.

Following Dani had become a habit he was finding hard to break. He had been documenting her deception by collecting evidence against her but the need for such collateral had passed now. Impossible to justify, therefore, why he was still in pursuit. For a fleeting moment he allowed himself to question why it was still so much easier to watch her than it was to face her.

He slowly started to pack away his things, a well-timed distraction to stop the onslaught of self-analysis that he had no intention of indulging. He lived life through the lens. That was just the way it was.

25

"Good morning lovely lady!" Dani turned to see Steve Preston fall into step beside her as she headed towards the office.

"How do you do that?" she said, as she looked around. "Just appear from nowhere?"

Steve smiled. "Years of practice. So what you up to?"

A spark appeared in Dani's eyes. His sense of mischief was infectious, forcing her to admit this annoying bastard did actually bring a little ray of sunshine to her world which, on balance, outweighed the hassle he caused her. Well, almost. No need to get carried away.

"Obviously I'm going to work. What do you want?"

"You promised me lunch months ago. Let's do it today. I have news. I'll see you in Brown's at one."

Dani's instinct was to object but he had already gone before she could say another word.

Steve was already waiting when Dani arrived for lunch a few hours later. He smiled as he saw her approach and stood up to greet her.

"Look at you getting all gentlemanly! You're making me nervous already." The truth was Dani was actually a little apprehensive. Apart from just being a default position where Steve was concerned, there was an unusually relaxed air about him today. What the hell did he know? As they sat down, Steve put the menu under her nose. "Choose something and let's get the ordering out of the way so we can talk."

The job duly done, Dani sat back for a moment and then decided she simply couldn't wait any longer. "Come on then, let's hear it."

"I'm leaving the paper."

Dani looked genuinely surprised and a little relieved that they weren't about to wage war over the usual crap. "Wow, that is news. But it can't be that long since you earned your showbiz editor stripes. What could possibly have tempted you away?"

"I've got a job editing a new men's monthly magazine. But the mag's only a small part really. It was the online and social element that was the real pull. Time to drag myself into the 21st century!"

"Bit grown up for you isn't it?" Dani teased.

He smiled. "I felt it was time." And then he paused for a moment, his face suddenly thoughtful. "Thing is, the only way to do this job is to keep your eye on the goal which in my role means simply being the first to expose a celebrity and the more salacious and outrageous the reason the better. To be successful, there just isn't room to think about the people involved and the impact of what gets printed." He shrugged. "Comes a point where you just don't want to be that person anymore."

Dani was completely taken aback, not least by the emotion in Steve's face. "Well bugger me. The man has a heart after all!" She smiled at him. "I always knew there was a big softie in there fighting to get out."

"Steady on! It's a significant change I'll give you that but let's not completely lose touch with reality."

They were interrupted by the arrival of their lunch and the conversation immediately switched to how amazing the food looked and then on to how it tasted even better, if that were possible. If they had been having a moment, it had duly passed. They chatted about nothing in particular, both enjoying the chance to relax and let down their guards. As coffee arrived, having woven its way through their working world, the conversation turned more personal again.

"So do you have a girlfriend?" Dani wasn't sure why she'd asked and suddenly felt embarrassed that she had.

Steve smiled mischievously. "Are you hitting on me?" Dani raised her eyebrows and he laughed, a definite stalling tactic as he thought about how to answer. "No, no girlfriend." Dani remained silent, a smile encouraging him to open up a little. "And that's been part of the problem. You spend so much time wrapped up in other people's twisted lives you lose track of what's real." He shook his head. "I've made some terrible decisions along the way, used people, hurt people, constantly blurring the line between work and play." And then he stopped for a moment and smiled. "Listen to me getting all philosophical!"

Dani blew gently on her coffee and then took a sip before slowly returning it to the table. "I know what you mean. Surprising isn't it, how easily you can get sucked in, however strong you think you are."

Steve watched her for a moment, her eyes down, suddenly finding something bizarrely captivating in the large white mug of coffee that she had immediately picked up again and was now clutching with both hands. "Dani?"

Can he see through me? she thought, wondering how much he might know about her own messed up relationships. If Sean had known all about her and Alex, then why not Steve? She dared to look up, immediately smiling in reaction to the gentle eyes that met her own.

"What are you thinking about? You were miles away there for a moment."

"Oh just thinking about some of my own poor decisions."

Both retreated into their own thoughts momentarily and then it was time to go back to work. They stepped outside the restaurant and stood awkwardly, both unsure how to bring this rather exceptional meeting to a close. It was Steve who finally broke the silence. "Thanks for being so brilliant to deal with. I know it's sometimes been painful for you but it's been fun too I hope?"

She smiled. "Yes, a veritable barrel of laughs! But we'll still be in touch, won't we? Only now you'll want big in-depth interviews which we both know can be just as troublesome so I doubt it will be long before the gloves are off again."

Steve kissed her warmly on the cheek. "I'll look forward to it."

Billy and Amanda were sitting across their kitchen table from each other, Billy's eyes fixed on his phone that he'd just carefully placed in front of him. He rolled it around in his hand a few times, lost in thought and then forced himself to look up. Amanda was staring at him, waiting. There was no comfort in seeing his own sense of nervous apprehension reflected back at him in her anxious eyes. "Shit." He felt the single word more than adequately summed up the situation.

"Indeed." Amanda had nothing else to add as they both retreated back into the safety of silence. Eventually Billy looked up again.

"What do we do?"

Amanda took in a deep breath and slowly exhaled as she rubbed her growing tummy. "I'll tell her."

"No, I will."

"Why do you get to do it?" Amanda was suddenly angry, sitting up as straight as her aching back would let her.

"Fine. You do it. It's a fucking shit thing to have to do so knock yourself out."

Billy pushed back his chair, aware of Amanda flinching as it scraped loudly along the floor and he left the room. He still found it astonishing that all these months on, the fall-out from Dani's mess just kept on coming and always just after he'd convinced himself life had found a new normality. Then bam! Something else happened, bringing with it a new tsunami of tension. Tension that tended to manifest itself as frustration with Dani as he watched her struggle with her demons and, most of the time, simply give in to them, leaving her wading in self-pity. Then there was the seemingly unavoidable tension between him and Amanda which felt bitterly unfair. As always, it revealed itself in some kind of fight about who knew what first or who should take the lead with Dani. Or, put another way, whose relationship with her was bigger, better, closer. He was happy to admit it was at best ridiculous and at worst, incredibly childish. And then of course there was Amanda's frustration that he had maintained any contact with Sean at all when Dani was clearly their priority but he had stood firm. Sean had been the best man at their wedding and he wasn't prepared to just drop him.

All squabbling aside, whether they liked it or not, they were still in it up to their necks and there was nothing to indicate any of that was about to change. Quite the opposite in fact. Billy sighed, the voice in his head lamenting his new dilemma. So Sean was in a new relationship. Was it really a big deal? He and Amanda had actively encouraged Dani to meet someone new and although they hadn't talked about it, he was pretty sure Sean had been putting himself out there but this was different. Cleary Sean felt it was significant enough news to call and let them know. He had said the last thing he wanted was to put them in a difficult position so wasn't about to start suggesting double dating but he would be taking her to the party they were all due to attend the following week and therefore felt he should warn them in advance. Billy had no idea what he was supposed to do with the information. Was he supposed to tell Dani or protect her from the news? Amanda had clearly assumed one of them would tell her. Did that mean keeping it to themselves was worse?

"How is that helping?" Amanda walked into the lounge to find Billy banging his head against the wall.

"The pain is a surprisingly welcome distraction," he said without stopping.

"So how long's it been going on?" Billy shrugged. "Do you even know her name?"

"Anna I think. Or maybe Emma."

Amanda shook her head. Hopeless didn't even come close. "We have to tell her. She'll find out at some point and then it'll be much worse trying to explain how we knew but didn't say anything. She'll assume it's because we've been cosying up with them and we can't have that."

Billy stopped head-banging. "You're right. It all sounds so simple when you put it like that. I can't get my head round any of it."

She may be able to make sense of it but that didn't mean she was looking forward to actually telling Dani. Instinctively, she had merely wanted to win the right to tell her, without actually stopping to think about the prize. That would teach her. She only hoped Dani wouldn't go down the overly dramatic 'I deserve nothing less' victim routine. She was having enough trouble with chronic indigestion without having to swallow that too.

"I'm surprised it's taken this long. I hope it works out for him."

Dani and Amanda were having coffee, or camomile tea in Amanda's case. It was Saturday afternoon and they were sitting in a café, trying to summon up enough energy to do some browsing, Dani looking for nothing in particular, Amanda weighed down with a list of apparently vital baby-related paraphernalia that she absolutely had to buy if she had any hope at all of being considered a worthy mother. Amanda stopped, her cup halfway to her mouth. That wasn't anywhere close to what she was expecting. Not only the choice of Dani's words but the tone too which was totally absent of any bitterness or self-pity. Dani smiled. "Were you hoping for something more dramatic?"

"No, I'm just relieved you've taken it so well," Amanda replied, replacing her cup slowly and choosing not to mention the sadness in Dani's eyes that she was clearly trying to mask. "I know it's hard."

Dani shrugged. "Life goes on I guess."

"Hey, clichés are my trademark!" she said, forcing a smile. "And in case you're wondering, of course we won't be arranging nights out with them but I'm afraid meeting her is sadly unavoidable."

Dani sighed. "The party. Oh well, at least I know my decision not to go was absolutely the right one."

"I'm sorry Dani."

"It's not your fault!" Dani forced a smile. "It was always going to happen and now it has so let's just move on."

Amanda went to say something and then stopped herself. She hadn't expected to be the one looking to wallow so was surprised to find her instinct had been to keep rolling with the sympathetic eyes, to hold Dani's hand and reflect once again on the hideousness of recent months. But if Dani was going to be strong then it was time for her to move on too. She looked at her watch. "Come on, let's mooch."

Dani immediately started gathering up her things and as they stepped outside, she linked arms with Amanda and steered her towards a shop, its window a veritable marshmallow of fluffiness and all in perfect shades of pink and blue.

26

Finding a dress to wear to the party had been surprisingly easy and Amanda had quickly settled on something loose and floaty. Its perfect empire line skimmed her spherical tummy and, despite her widening girth, she felt feminine and elegant which was frankly unexpected. She had subsequently declared the shopping mission a job well done. It had felt strange shopping for a dress without Dani but it would have been worse to ask for her help. It would have felt like she was rubbing her nose in it which was obviously something Amanda was keen to avoid.

The party was an annual event hosted by a women's glossy magazine and she'd long forgotten why they were even going. No doubt a throwback to when they enjoyed tagging along with Dani and Sean. She had asked Billy why they didn't just drop out. For once, they had the unusual opportunity to actually avoid getting embroiled in this latest development but he had been adamant they should go. She had decided it was yet another misplaced act of defiance. A chance to prove they were just getting on with their lives regardless, despite the fact their lives would undoubtedly only suffer as a result of meeting Anna or Emma, or whatever her name was. Oh well, at least she felt good in her dress so it wasn't all bad.

When the night arrived, Amanda allowed herself to feel just a little excited. She always loved the sense of occasion at these events; the beautiful way the venues were styled and the chance to study the array of dresses on show. It was like research but conducted in the most non-work like setting. It gave her a real buzz to know she would leave with an abundance of fresh ideas for her own designs.

Billy got them both a drink and then his roving eye spotted Sean. He took Amanda by the hand. "Come on, let's get this over with."

Sean smiled as he saw them approach. "You look stunning," he said as he kissed Amanda's cheek. "Hello mate," came next as he laid a hand on Billy's shoulder. There then followed the slightest tinge of awkwardness, all three of them aware of a presence beside them. Amanda braced herself.

"Amanda, Billy, this is Mia."

Billy immediately took her hand. "Hi Mia, good to meet you."

"Yes, good to meet you," Amanda echoed, the words 'it's not her fault, it's not her fault' going round and around in her head.

Mia smiled. "Lovely to meet you both too. And congratulations. You look amazing Amanda."

"Thank you," was all Amanda could manage, her hand instinctively moving to her tummy.

Sean waited for just a moment and when no further words were forthcoming from anyone, he decided it was probably best to cut and run. "Right, well we need to do some work so we'll look out for you later."

"So you're a photographer too are you Mia?"

"No, I work for Belle. We're hosting tonight's party."

"Oh great," Billy said with an enthusiastic smile. "Well done!"

Billy and Amanda watched them go. "Well done?" Amanda looked at him. "What was that? And Mia?"

"So I got her name wrong. I'm finding this all a bit awkward too you know."

Amanda sighed, tempted to remind him she had suggested not coming but decided there was nothing to be gained from more childish point scoring. "Come on, let's just try to enjoy ourselves," she said, pushing him in the direction of the extensive buffet that she had been secretly eyeing up from the minute they had arrived.

When Amanda stumbled across some acquaintances from the fashion world an hour or so later, Billy took the chance to look for Sean again. He was hoping to have a quiet word alone, just to reassure him that this didn't need to be difficult and that, as always, they would find a way of making it work.

After his second circuit of the main room, he changed direction and noticed a small courtyard. As the large glass doors opened, he caught a glimpse of someone sitting on a bench and immediately headed out.

"What are you doing out here?" Billy sat down next to Sean, clocking immediately that he looked distracted, his eyes heavy with sadness. "Sean? What's going on?"

335

"Who was I kidding? Not Mia, that's for sure." He shook his head. "This is all so fucked up."

"What's happened?"

"It's finished with Mia. She didn't think my heart was in it so thought it was better to stop now before she got hurt."

"Oh."

Sean couldn't help but smile. "Nicely put."

Billy thought for a moment and then, before he could stop himself, he had a sudden moment of clarity and the words just started coming. "Do you want to know what I really think?" He didn't stop for an answer. "You're right. This is all totally fucked up. Dani's struggling to come to terms with what she did because she always loved you and she still does. What happened may not make any sense to us but, trust me, it makes no sense to her either. And I know you still love her too but your pride won't let you admit it." Sean went to interrupt but Billy put up his hand and just kept on going, more impassioned now and louder to prevent any further interjection. "She made a mistake! I know it hurt but it was totally out of character. And the worst part now is you're both stuck in some kind of tortured limbo, unable to move on, unable to do anything other than fester in all the bad stuff. You think taking her back would make you look weak but who gives a fuck if you love each other? Swallow your pride and just fucking talk to her!" Billy stopped, his eyes wide with the unexpected rush of adrenaline.

Sean looked at him for a moment and Billy was surprised to see a softness in his face. "You're right, of course you're right. But I can't just forgive and forget."

"No one expects you to! And if you really feel you'll never be able to get past this then fine, go after Mia and convince her to give things another go. But if there's even the smallest part of you that thinks there's a way through all the crap then you need to go after Dani and give her a stab at convincing you that she's the one who deserves a second chance. Or at the very least a chance to explain herself and clear the air. Anything's got to be better than this."

Sean put his arm around his friend and squeezed him tightly. As Billy turned to look at him, Sean's hold on him remained fierce. "If you tell me you love me I will have to punch you, just so you know."

Sean smiled. "I….!" He ducked as Billy swung at him and then stood up. "Come on you big lump, let's go and find Amanda and go home."

27

Dani and Caroline were having an early meeting. A rare opportunity to catch up with what was going on before the phones started ringing. They sat either side of Dani's old desk, her office sitting empty nearby. It hadn't taken long for her to decide sitting in an isolated bubble was not for her. It felt old-fashioned and it was way too quiet. She had ended up wasting far too much time dashing out to find out what was so funny, or why Toby was suddenly up and doing his victory dance, or what could possibly have happened to make Sammy suddenly look so thunderous. The office was useful when quiet chats were required but otherwise, being part of the mayhem was definitely where she wanted to be.

"Has Howard called back yet?"

Caroline shook her head. "He's vanished off the face of the earth."

Dani immediately looked irritated. "How could he? Look, forget everything else this morning and find him. Whatever it takes just don't give up till you have him by the short and curlies."

It was almost three hours and her first grey hair later when Caroline finally found him. She eagerly waited for Dani to finish a call. "I found him. He's five minutes away so said he'll pop in."

Dani raised her hands in the air. "Hallelujah!"

A moment or two later, Caroline disappeared off to reception and returned with Howard Brett. In his late twenties, he was several inches over six feet and very thin which only made him look even taller. His short dark hair was hidden under an oversized woolly hat, despite the uncomfortable heat of the city, and his blue eyes were bursting with life and full of mischief. He was perfectly unshaven, casually but fashionably dressed, a battered leather bag draped across his body. Dani smiled as she saw him approach and then stretched up on her tiptoes to kiss him on the cheek. "Remind me to find you a producer who wants to re-make The Invisible Man. You'd be perfect."

"I've been away for two days! Jesus, what could possibly have happened?" Dani looked at him, eyebrows raised and he suddenly looked scared. "Oh shit, what's happened?"

Dani's face was giving nothing away. "Oh nothing much. Just your first film role!"

Howard whooped with delight. He threw his arms around Dani and hugged her tightly, his height meaning her feet immediately left the ground. "Oh my God I can't believe it! This can't be happening to me!"

"Howard, put me down!" Dani was shouting above Howard's excited rambling. "Put me down!"

Finally pulling himself together, Howard did as he was told. "Sorry, I just can't believe it!"

His enthusiasm was infectious and Dani smiled as she went back to the safety of her desk and sat down. "For goodness sake, sit down like a sensible person so I can tell you about it properly," she said, pointing at the chair opposite her.

Howard did as he was told but as soon as his bottom hit the seat, he was up again. "I can't believe it! I really got the part? I can't believe it!"

Dani had found Howard in a small comedy club and had thought he was brilliant. He wrote and performed sketches with a small group of fellow actors but his talent had so outclassed the others, she had been unable to take her eyes off him throughout the entire performance. Since signing him, he had guested on numerous television shows to help to build his profile but it was all about finding him the right acting role. She had of course risen to the challenge and he had just finished a small part in a six-part drama but with such limited on-screen experience, the film he had recently auditioned for had always been a long shot. Despite that, Dani had been convinced there was a small but key role that Howard would be perfect for. His natural comedy timing and infectious personality were more than ideal and she had used up all sorts of favours to get him seen. He may not have done that much but he already had a substantial following and Dani had generated a fair amount of publicity for him which she hoped would count for something - perhaps with the exception of some unplanned exposure thanks to a fleeting but inevitable on-set dalliance with a co-star. Some things never changed. Five meetings later, the producers finally conceded and the part was now his.

Howard struggled to take it all in as Dani explained he would soon be off to America for around eight weeks of filming. From relative obscurity to the big screen in one giant step. It was just too much. "Tell me over lunch. It's the least I can do."

Lunch was an absolute joy as Howard went into overdrive. His excitement was truly heart-warming and manifested itself in non-stop pure comedy as he babbled away at a hundred miles an hour. Exhausted from laughing, Dani finally convinced him she had to get back to work. As they stepped outside the restaurant the light of the day was already fading, making the sudden barrage of blinding flashes all the more dramatic. Dani immediately froze, her heart racing, her cheeks flushing with colour, her knees weak and trembling as Sean put out a hand to Howard. "Well done mate! I hear you're off to the dizzy heights of Hollywood."

Howard grinned as he took Sean's hand. "Bloody hell, news travels fast!"

Dani watched in silence and then finally Sean turned to look at her. "Hello Dani." She smiled, afraid to open her mouth in case no words were forthcoming, or worse, nothing but a long line of drivelling nonsense spilled out. "How are you?" She smiled again and nodded, aware Howard was watching her, obviously wondering why this formidable woman who always had something to say had unexpectedly lost the power of speech. "Do you have time for a coffee?"

"Look I'll leave you." Howard suddenly felt like the proverbial spare part and decided it was time to go. He kissed Dani on the cheek and gave her a big hug. "Thank you. I love you!" He took Sean's hand again. "Good to meet you." And then he was gone.

"Dani?" She dared to look at him. "Coffee?"

"Yeah, sure." At last, he thought, wondering for a moment if she was ever going to answer. He looked around and choosing the nearest café, took the lead and gestured towards it.

A few moments later, they sat across from each other, two cups of coffee dutifully steaming in front of them but neither touched them. Dani felt like everything about her was suddenly in conflict. She was so pleased to be near him but terrified too. She wanted desperately to appear calm but her heart was racing. She wanted nothing more than to just sit and stare at him, take in every detail of his face but the truth was she couldn't even look at him.

"So how are you?"

Dani looked up, her eyes glistening and attempted a smile. "I'm good."

"I heard about your partnership. You must be thrilled?"

"Yes, I am." Dani looked at her coffee and picking up her spoon, started to play with the inch of foam that sat on top of it. Sean took a moment to study her. She had lost weight. That had been his first observation but she still looked as beautiful as she ever had. Her hair was slightly longer and, as usual, she was wearing practically no make-up, her skin pale and flawless, her brown eyes providing all the colour needed to bring warmth to her face. And then the silence was just too much for him and Dani jumped as he snatched away her spoon, causing a wave of coffee to spill on to the table. "Dani. For God's sake!"

She looked up at him. "Well what do you want me to say? I don't know what to say to you. Is that so hard to understand? Do you want to hear how sorry I am again? How much I hate myself? How I can barely look at myself in the mirror without being overwhelmed by shame?"

With his elbows on the table, Sean rubbed his eyes and wondered for a moment what was worse. Knowing that she did still have some kind of hypnotic hold on him or the sudden realisation that, despite that, it actually wasn't about second chances after all but simply about finding resolution.

As Dani shifted uncomfortably in his presence, she too was struggling with her own reaction to finally be sitting opposite him. Her love for him had never been in doubt but the guilt and shame that were now so firmly embedded, had been distorting what she thought she wanted. But now she knew. She simply needed to know that Sean could forgive her. Or, if that was too much to expect, that he could at least release her from the overwhelming sense of disgrace she had been wearing like some kind of unbearably heavy coat.

Suddenly they were looking at each other, faces clear of expression, eyes wide and unblinking. Then Sean took a deep breath. "You cheated on me."

"You spied on me."

Sean flinched ever so slightly. "We weren't honest with each other."

Dani held his eye. "We didn't trust each other." There was a pause as they continued to sit completely motionless, a silent standoff, on the cusp of something but not really sure what. With a sudden sense of focus, Dani then decided it was time to finally put this whole angst-ridden, tortured chapter to rest. "I did love you." Her face softened. "I do love you. But for whatever reason I couldn't, couldn't…" She stumbled for a moment, so determined was she to get this right. "I couldn't just throw myself in at the deep end and give into it. Something kept me in the familiar comfort of shallowness. Blame it on my childhood experiences, blame it on the world we operate in." She looked at him and smiled. "Or you could just blame it on me. Blame me for simply being an idiot, for being incapable of conducting a grown-up relationship, for being a total fuckwit." And then she felt her eyes sting slightly with a lone tear. "I'm so sorry I messed things up so spectacularly."

Sean smiled back at her, his chest swelling with a heady concoction of love and regret. He reached across the table and took hold of her hands. "No, don't. I played my part too. I've done my own fair share of soul-searching and, if I'm honest, some of my decisions might be seen as a little questionable."

"You mean like choosing to tail me rather than confront me when you found out?"

Sean sat back in his chair and his expression darkened. "Yeah, there is that."

Dani looked at him. "You're uncomfortable with me saying that?" Sean's demeanour had definitely changed. "But that's what you did. You have to admit that was a little fucked up too? Loving and committed to my face but bitter and angry and skulking around after me behind my back?" There go those blurred lines again, thought Dani, wondering if he was prepared to accept that if he had made questionable decisions, that had to be right up there at the top of the list.

Sean shrugged, unsure what to say. That was what he did, wasn't it? "You want some of this to be my fault do you?"

Dani looked bemused. "Of course not."

"Because if I'd confronted you, it would still have been because you cheated. Whichever way you cut it, that part still looks the same."

Dani looked away for a moment, aware that Sean was slowly becoming very defensive, angry almost. However tempting it was to retaliate, she desperately didn't want this to turn into some kind of bizarre competition about who was the more despicable of the two. All that really mattered was that she knew she had behaved despicably and that was what she needed to accept and deal with - and that was something she could do alone. At which point she realised with the most wondrous sense of clarity that she didn't actually need his forgiveness. She had thought it was the only way she could be exonerated but it was truly liberating to finally work out that she simply needed to forgive herself. Not in a self-help manual, showy, self-congratulatory, 'I've seen the light' kind of way. Just to face up to what she'd done, learn something from it and make the decision to let it go and move on. Sean could fight his demons or choose not to, it really made no difference to her at all. She was in no doubt he would bounce back. He was made of sterner stuff than most after all.

She took a few sips of coffee and then she smiled with a genuine warmth. "I'm not trying to blame you for anything. I wish I could explain better what happened but I can't." She shrugged. "I messed up. But I'm going to choose to remember that for a time, I loved what we had and I really hope you can do that too."

Dani watched as Sean relaxed in front of her, his jaw and his shoulders, which for a moment had tightened in preparation for a fight, now visibly loosened and he smiled. "Works for me."

"Sorry, I'm confused."

Dani had arrived at Billy and Amanda's with a large Chinese takeaway, a bottle of wine for her and Billy and a bottle of elderflower pressé for Amanda, along with her favourite box of assorted doughnuts. If cravings were all part of the deal, Amanda had decided early on that she certainly wasn't going to waste her time on pickled eggs or raw chillies.

Dani had recounted her meeting with Sean and was now hungrily tucking into her dinner, feeling more alive, more liberated and more hungry than she had for months. She washed down a mouthful of delicious crispy beef and noodles with a large swig of red wine as Billy struggled to take it all in.

"I thought you were going to put it all behind you and start again?"

"That's what I'd been desperately hoping for but then, in that moment, when he was there in front of me, it just didn't feel right. And I know he felt the same. Do you want that last prawn toast?"

Billy shook his head and watched Dani practically inhale it, immediately searching cartons for something else to pile on her plate. Amanda meanwhile sat quietly, happily passing on the main course and delving straight into the doughnuts, her mouth now coated in sugar which she licked intermittently with pure joy. With only a month left to go, she was huge and uncomfortable and such moments of extreme pleasure were to be savoured. She subsequently only contributed to the conversation in the odd polite pause between finishing one doughnut and moving on to the next.

"Well you look very relaxed and happy which is great. She looks happy doesn't she Billy?" She nodded at Billy eagerly as she sunk her teeth into something perfectly filled with light, vanilla custard.

Billy shook his head again. "You don't think this is a tiny bit unexpected?" Amanda, mid-doughnut, could only shrug. Truth was, she had started to think that Dani and Sean getting back together would have been far more of a surprise. Having an affair was massive for Dani. Messing up someone's family, doing what had been done to her to someone else's children - inconceivable. And yet it had happened. Her relationship with Sean was therefore forever damaged. Amanda felt that, for Dani, wanting to get back together was motivated by nothing more than a desire to somehow put things right, make up for all the wrongs and somehow lessen her guilt, which would only have meant further catastrophe at some point. An opinion she would have happily now shared if her mouth wasn't so full.

Billy was still unsure, frantically running the many soul-searching conversations he'd had with Dani through his head, and the chats with Sean too. He had been convinced them getting back together was inevitable and right. Hadn't he just encouraged Sean to give her a second chance? He sighed, feeling like a bit of a chump. And then he looked at Dani. Really looked at her. Her eyes were bright, her cheeks full of colour, although that could be down to the wine. She was laughing and smiling, she was animated and beautifully comfortable in her own skin. He had almost forgotten what her laugh sounded like, that rich, deep chuckle that was always so infectious. And then it slowly dawned on him. A tiny realisation that grew and grew until he had no choice but to stop rerunning old conversations that were now irrelevant and acknowledge the reality of what had actually happened.

He smiled. Finally, it was all over.

28

"She's here she's beautiful Amanda was amazing I'm so full of love I could burst!" The words came out in one great lump of emotionally-charged excitement. And then there was a pause. "Dani?"

Dani's eyes were immediately blurred with tears. "Sorry," she stuttered. "I'm speechless. Congratulations! I'm so happy for you. Name?"

"Anna."

"Beautiful. When can I meet her?"

"We're hoping to be home this afternoon so come over tonight. The sooner the better. You have to see her. She's so small but so beautiful, I'm in total awe."

"See you later then. Text me a list if you need me to pick up anything."

She sat back in her chair and enjoyed the wave of pure joy that immediately swept over her. Anna may indeed be perfect but she was already a terrible time-keeper. She was an agonising two weeks late which meant Dani had been jumping every time Billy or Amanda called her, waiting, waiting, waiting. And now she was finally here and everyone was fine. Big beautiful sigh of relief all round.

Dani snapped herself back to the moment, suddenly aware of Sammy and Toby staring at her, waiting expectantly. They had been halfway through a catch-up when Dani had snatched at her mobile the minute she saw Billy's name. "Amanda and Billy have finally had their baby."

"Yay!" Toby cheered.

"That's great," chipped in Sammy.

"Yes it is." Dani straightened her back and did her best to focus. "Now where were we?"

"We were talking about Imogen," said Sammy.

"Oh yes, Imogen. So everything really is going well?"

"Yes. TV series done. Interviews done. Tantrums nil." Sammy smiled.

"Unbelievable." Dani shook her head, her surprise genuine. "Is everything ready for her book launch?"

"Yes, details all checked a million times. Guest list bulging with a few celeb friends to brighten the place up." Sammy had a wonderful air of confidence about her, a veritable glow of contentment as she relished in the fact that everything was going so well.

"Maybe writing it all down has done the trick," Dani pondered. "Who's she seeing?"

"No idea."

Dani sighed. "That'll be the next bombshell then. Oh God, I wonder who it is?" She thought for a moment and then shrugged. "It'll come out soon enough so let's just enjoy the moment! Well done Sammy."

Dani and Toby raised imaginary glasses as Sammy grinned then Dani scanned her notes one last time. "So just to be clear, we have no crises to discuss? No problems at all? Can that really be right?"

"Would this be a good time to discuss pay rises?" said Toby, his words accompanied by his most cheeky of smiles.

"Nice try, but no. Okay, off with you. Back to work!"

Duly dismissed, Sammy and Toby headed back to their desks and then Sammy stopped. "Oh, there was just one other thing."

"I knew it," said Dani, bracing herself for the worst.

"Nothing bad. I just forgot to mention Steve Preston wants to do a cover feature on Jake. A celebration of the reformed man."

"Great. Let me know when. I might pop in and say hello."

"He said something similar," she said as she left Dani to it.

Dani sat back for a moment and smiled. The last few weeks had been a breeze. With a renewed lightness of touch and her head held high for the first time in a while, everything seemed to be going really well. The team was completely on it and even her clients were behaving. Reward, she decided, for finally drawing a line under the whole sorry mess with Sean and Alex. She felt like herself again and for that alone, she was extremely grateful.

While she tried to decide what to give her attention to first, her phone started to ring. "Hello?"

"Well hello to my most favourite agent of all time ever!"

A warm smile immediately spread across Dani's face. "Well hello back to my most annoying ex-tabloid hack of all time ever!"

"I'm interviewing Jake next week."

"I just heard."

"You coming?"

"I thought I might pop in at some point."

"Make it towards the end and then I thought we could grab a drink and catch-up?" In the ensuing pause Steve felt his confidence waver. "If you want to, that is?"

"Yes, sounds good. Now go away, I'm busy." Dani hung up, the broadest of smiles still firmly in place and then grabbing her bag, she decided she had done enough good work for one day. She had far more important things to concern herself with, like finding suitable gifts for Billy, Amanda and Anna.

Several hours later and overloaded with an assortment of bags, Dani was standing outside Billy and Amanda's door full of nervous excitement. When it finally opened, there was Billy with the tiniest little bundle held with one large hand high up on his shoulder. The smallest of heads with a shock of red hair was just visible above a soft blanket, nuzzling into his neck. Dani gasped. "Let me see," she whispered, carefully dropping her bags as Billy turned around. She gently lowered the blanket and there was Anna, her delicate little features suddenly visible. Dani took a moment to study the cute nose, the rosebud mouth, the long eyelashes fanning out from her closed eyes, a little hand settled on her smooth cheek. Her heart skipped a beat. "You were right. She is absolutely perfect."

"At least let her in first Billy!"

Amanda appeared beside them and Dani immediately hugged her and then pulled back to take a proper look at her friend. "You look amazing."

Amanda was literally glowing, her hair shiny and her skin smooth and fresh-looking. She shrugged with a smile. "That's adrenaline for you."

Dani gathered up her bags and followed them into the lounge, now full of endless baby stuff that was spread across the floor. She carefully stepped over a car seat, bouncy chair, unopened presents and several bags of who knew what. "'Scuse the mess," Amanda said, waving her arm across the sea of disorder.

Dani sat down and immediately rummaged in her bags for a perfectly chilled bottle of champagne. She handed it to Billy who passed it straight on to Amanda. Obediently, she stood up and went in search of glasses as Dani turned to Billy with a bemused look. His answer was simply to raise his eyebrows and gently rub the back of his tiny daughter.

"Go on, give us a cuddle." Dani held her arms out.

"Maybe in a while. She's settled where she is."

"Good luck with that," Amanda said as she reappeared and handed Dani a glass of champagne. "He's hardly put her down since she was born. Even I can barely get a look in."

Dani smiled. Hard to object when waves of pure joy were literally radiating from his every pore. She unpacked more goodies. First lots of lovely snacks that were high in fuel - a vain but nevertheless much appreciated attempt to boost Amanda's energy levels, plus doughnuts, obviously. Then there was a selection of beautiful outfits for Anna, relaxing bath products and all manner of soothing body oils for Amanda and a big fat chocolate cigar for Billy. Billy and Amanda then recounted every detail of the previous twenty-four hours, some of which Dani could happily have lived without knowing, until Anna finally stirred, letting out the tiniest of cries.

"She needs feeding," Amanda announced, her voice suddenly empty of all previous enthusiasm.

"How's that going?"

"She's chewing the life out of my nipples but we're getting there."

Dani winced. "Right, I'll leave you to it. Try to get some rest and I'll pop back tomorrow night to put some washing on, make you some dinner, whatever you need."

Dani saw herself out and shut the door behind her with a contented sigh, wondering for a moment with a wry smile what kind of night her beloved friends were in for.

"To Billy and Amanda!"

"To Anna!"

Dani and Sean clinked their glasses and took a celebratory sip. It was a week later at the exclusive event to launch Imogen's biography. No doubt the first volume of many, given her tender years.

"Have you seen her yet?"

"Yes, I popped round briefly at the weekend. They couldn't say enough times what a great help you've been."

Dani smiled. "Well when people are actually pleased to eat my cooking you know they're really in trouble!"

Dani and Sean had slipped easily into a comfortable new way of existing together. Work ensured their paths had crossed a number of times already and they had always found a quiet corner for a quick drink and a catch-up. They had helped each other out on a few occasions, provided it suited their own needs obviously. They looked out for one another as friends should but there were boundaries now. An acceptance of the fact that any friendship would always be coated with a thin layer of fakeness, put there by their respective jobs and yet bizarrely, it was the most honest their relationship had ever been. There had been times when she had watched him from a safe distance with a slight tinge of sadness but it never lasted long. What was done was done and, all things considered, the outcome felt pretty good. Onwards and upwards.

"So how's tricks?" Before Dani could answer, a polite but still very audible gasp swept around the room. Dani and Sean's heads whipped around simultaneously to see Imogen making her entrance. There on her arm was Benjy Blue, a member of the latest red-hot boyband currently setting the world on fire. He was more than ten years younger than her, assuming she was only lying about her age by just a few years which was debatable. Whatever the number, he was barely more than a child.

"Oh, my, God." The words came out slowly and deliberately, the weight of them leaving Dani's jaw suitably lowered, her mouth unattractively open. Sean pushed his chair back and picked up his camera.

"Excuse me a moment," he offered with a smile.

"Knock yourself out," Dani replied flatly, waving him away without taking her eyes off Imogen and her new beau. She only hoped Sammy was already sitting down and then at the thought of her poor protégé, she jumped up, knowing Sammy would need some help with this one, her own left eye already starting to twitch in perfect harmony with the sound of Sean's clicking camera.

Needless to say, Imogen's book was somewhat overlooked in the ensuing coverage with pretty much every news outlet opting to run pictures of her wrapped around Benjy. Proof if it were needed that however hard you try to make plans, the outcome is always impossible to predict when you're dealing with people whose sense of reality is at best warped and, at worst, completely off the scale. Something Dani tried hard to impress upon Sammy as she sat slightly deflated at her desk the next day.

"It's only annoying because of the total lack of thinking. Why sabotage your own launch? There was no need to bring Benjy and all she did was detract from the reason we were all there. And who stands to lose out as a result? She does!" Sammy banged her hand against her head, unable to grasp what she saw as nothing more than stupidity on Imogen's part. She was angry too at the effort she had invested in the launch which now all felt wasted. Then, as always, she pulled herself up and moved on. "Right," she said as she started to gather up her things. "I'm off to Jake's shoot. What could possibly go wrong with that one?"

Dani smiled. "He'll be fine. He's enjoying being hailed as the 'turnaround kid' so for now I think you're safe. I'll see you there later." Sammy raised a hand in acknowledgement as she quickly disappeared through the office.

As Dani walked into the studio several hours later, a slight flutter of nervous anticipation in the pit of her stomach could not be ignored, hard as she tried. As she slipped in, it was Jake who spotted her first. "Uh oh, the boss is here! I must be in trouble!"

Dani kissed him warmly and a broad smile swept across her face at the heartwarming sight of him, his eyes alive and clear. She was immediately hit by his overwhelming sense of health and well-being and she allowed herself a highly self-indulgent moment of self-congratulation. Here was one she had most definitely saved. "How's it going?"

"Nearly done," said Sammy, appearing from behind him. "Interview in the bag and photos almost finished. Just one last change." She looked at Jake who, taking his cue, went in search of his final outfit. Waiting till he was out of earshot, Dani turned to Sammy, eyebrows

357

raised in a silent question. "It's all been fine, really," Sammy insisted with a relieved smile. "The interview was actually great. Steve did a really good job."

"You talking about me?" Steve approached them and the temporarily forgotten anxious flutter immediately awoke and whispered through Dani's body, making her feel slightly hot.

"Look at you!" she smiled. "Looking very dapper today, Mr Preston."

Steve's eyes brightened. "Well you know how it is. One has to live up to the expectations of the job. Come on, I'll get you a coffee."

Dani watched him as he disappeared. He looked very different. The clothes were the obvious starting point. The uniform white shirt and blue suit had been swapped for black jeans, a more casual shirt and a jacket but it was his demeanour, the way he held himself, that marked the most significant change. He looked so relaxed, surrounded by a lovely air of calm confidence. His hair was a little longer too, which only served to soften him further.

"Dani?" Dani turned around to see Sammy, a curious look on her face.

"Sorry, miles away." And she quickly followed after him before her highly intuitive side-kick started to ask questions she had absolutely no desire to answer.

A series of poses later, the shoot was declared a wrap with a celebratory cheer and a polite round of applause. As the small gathering - photographer, stylist, make-up artist and a couple of girls from the magazine - started to pack stuff away, Dani watched Steve shake Jake's hand warmly before Jake hurried off with a wave.

"You must be really proud of him," he said as he wandered over to her.

Dani's smile said it all. "Yes, I am. I don't mind admitting it was touch and go for a while. Things could have turned out very differently so yes, proud is exactly what I am."

"I hope he knows how lucky he was to have you on his side? He couldn't have turned it around without you." Dani felt herself blush slightly, feeling typically awkward when faced with a compliment, however much it was deserved. A pause followed and then Steve jumped in before it got uncomfortable. "So," he said, "how about that drink?"

Dani looked at him and smiled. "Sure."

"Great. I'll just grab my stuff and say my good-byes."

Dani watched him as he thanked everyone in the room individually for their efforts before stopping for a brief chat with the photographer. It was like she was seeing him for the first time, seeing qualities she never knew he possessed or, more truthfully, had never stopped to consider he might have. She had been so preoccupied with just winning, with beating him into submission and fighting off that ruthless determination which was all he had ever presented to her. Until their last meeting of course, when he had opened up to her ever so slightly and given her a glimpse of what lay underneath. A warm, self-aware and, dare she say it, sensitive soul.

"Right, come on then." Dani snapped herself away from her thoughts and happily followed him out of the building and across the road to a bar. She found them a table while Steve got the drinks, joining her moments later with a bottle of wine, a couple of glasses and a selection of crisps and nuts.

"Perfect," she said, immediately diving into the nuts as Steve poured them both a drink. "So I'm guessing it's all going really well?"

Steve handed her a glass and then beamed. "Yes, I never expected it to be this good so quickly but I'm loving it. And, more importantly, missing nothing. That's what's really amazing."

"Well it suits you. I've never seen you so relaxed."

"I feel relaxed. Not that there isn't still pressure. There are still deadlines and targets to worry about but that constant need to expose, to sensationalise is gone." He shrugged. "Like I said to you before, my time was done and I was ready to move on." He stopped, suddenly unsure how to explain it further, not actually convinced that it really needed any further dissection and then he smiled. "Time to let some other little fucker take up the mantle! Talking of which, have you met my successor? I hear he's a bright young thing!"

"A rude, annoying, arrogant little oik is more like it. But then I've only met him once so that may be a little harsh." Steve laughed, happy to concede she would have had his character nailed after thirty seconds or less. "Anyway, I'm leaving him to Sammy. I'm trying not to get involved in so much of the daily scraps anymore and to be honest, it's not the…" and then she stopped mid-flow, suddenly aware of what she was in danger of admitting and an all-too-familiar barrier shot up to gag her. But Steve wasn't about to let it go.

"Not the what? Not the same without me? I'm touched," he said, clutching at his heart, that famous electrifying twinkle in his eyes. Dani quickly looked away. "I always knew you fancied me."

"Then you're deluded," she cried, her eyes immediately back on him, her confidence returned with a vengeance.

"You can deny it all you like but it changes nothing. You fancied me rotten and you know it."

Dani threw a nut at him and laughed. "God you're so annoying!"

"But irresistible it would seem?"

Steve looked at her and felt his chest swell with an unfamiliar but welcome sense of warmth. He was of course teasing her, knowing that he was the one who had harboured feelings. Feelings he had never dared to act on while he worked at the paper. But changing jobs had brought with it a glimmer of hope. That, with a different working relationship, he might just get the chance to show his hand. He felt his heart flutter slightly as he realised that moment may have arrived.

"Shall we argue about it over dinner?"

Steve held his breath and then smiled as Dani reached for her coat.

Acknowledgements

I'm incredibly grateful to so many people for their help with this book. To my team of readers - Mary Collins, Tammy Kempinski, Emma Carboni, Nicky Briggs and Alison Blood - your time and feedback were a massive help to me. Your enthusiasm even more so.

Big thanks too go to Simon Urwin. The final draft would not have been the same without your pain-staking edit. (That incorrect hyphen is especially for you!) Then the incredible eye of proofreader, Alison Parkin, took the book to a whole new level. And the magical moment when it all started to feel real definitely goes to Anita Mangan for the amazing cover.

No thank yous would be complete without expressing my heartfelt appreciation for the love and support of my husband, Steve. Your belief in me as a writer has kept me going and been a constant source of inspiration. And how wonderful that I can now prove to our beautiful boys that I do, on occasion, actually do something useful with my days!

About the Author

Elaine spent twenty-five years working in marketing and publicity in the media and entertainment industries. This included seven years marketing national newspapers and a variety of senior executive roles in TV, radio and film. I Can't Tell You Why is her first novel.

Elaine lives in North London with her husband and their two sons.

Printed in Great Britain
by Amazon

87302335R00207